Possession

Possession

DEVYN QUINN

APHRODISIA

KENSINGTON BOOKS

http://www.kensingtonbooks.com

APHRODISIA BOOKS are published by

Kensington Publishing Corp.
119 West 40th St.
New York, NY 10018

All Kensington Titles, Imprints, and Distributed Lines are available at special quantity discounts for bulk purchases for sales promotions, premiums, fund-raising, and educational or institutional use.

Special book excerpts or customized printings can also be created to fit specific needs. For details, write or phone the office of the Kensington Special Sales Manager: Kensington Publishing Corp., 119 West 40th St., New York, NY 10018, attn: Special Sales Department, Phone: 1-800-221-2647.

Aphrodisia and the A logo Reg. U.S. Pat & TM Off.

ISBN-13: 978-0-7582-2852-9
ISBN-10: 0-7582-2852-X

First Kensington Trade Paperback Printing: September 2009

10 9 8 7 6 5 4 3 2 1

Printed in the United States of America

Possession

The manuscript is old ... very old. Its title is simple, deceptive.

Delomelanicon.

Penned by Satan, the text in its various forms has disappeared and reappeared through the ages. Lost for centuries, the writings coveted by scholars of demonology have again reemerged to infest mankind.

Those daring to possess the book will be taken on a sinister journey guaranteed to change their perception of body, mind and spirit. . . .

1

In a library crammed wall to floor with a collection of books unmatched by any public collection in the world, a specially constructed steel lectern stood by itself. A leather-bound book rested beneath an enclosure of glass. Adorned with a discolored pentagram that might once have been etched in a rich carmine shade, a faded title printed in Latin was barely discernable: DELO MELAS.

To summon darkness. . . .

Looking at the book, Kendra Carter felt a chill form at the nape of her neck. "Don't tell me you've found it."

Gerald Carter smiled. "Indeed I have. The book you are looking at now is one of the few surviving copies of the *Servants of the Realm of Darkness.*"

The icy sensation crawled down Kendra's spine, sending a splatter of goose bumps across her skin. "I thought there were no surviving copies to be found."

"One came onto the market just a few weeks ago," he explained. "The owner was very eager to sell."

Kendra gave him a sharp look. "And you no doubt stepped right up to buy it," she commented dryly.

He maneuvered around her disapproval with ease. "You're damn right I did. Do you know why this book is so coveted by collectors of demonology?"

Kendra shook her head. "No, I don't." She'd never cared for Gerald's interest in the supernatural. Her stepbrother's collection of demonic- and witchcraft-themed items unsettled her. Other pieces of cultic paraphernalia enhanced his collection, including an impressive array of ceremonial daggers from all over the world. Like the book, they were displayed behind glass, never to be touched. Altogether the entire assortment was priceless.

"This book is a rarity because it's presumed to be based upon a composition written by the Devil himself after Christ resisted his temptations in the Gardens of Gethsemane," Gerald explained. "The original text of the *Delomelanicon* is reputed to have been in the possession of the papacy since the arrival of Saint Peter in Rome. What you are looking at now is one of the few surviving copies of a book privately commissioned by Pope Alexander the Sixth in 1495, supposedly transcribed from the firsthand version."

Kendra's brows rose in surprise. The not-so-familiar name jarred a memory. "The Borgia pope?" she asked, recalling a college class she'd attended on religion and culture.

Gerald's frown turned to a smile of approval. "Yes, correct. The relic you see here is five hundred and fourteen years old. That is a rarity within itself and well worth the investment."

"I'm not a complete moron," Kendra huffed. The crucial root of their conversation had yet to arise, namely how much he'd paid for his newest purchase.

"I never said you were." Gerald reached toward his prize, hands clenching into fists a few inches above the glass protecting its delicate pages. "But this is a prize—indeed, the *un*holy bible. Of the thirteen copies Pope Alexander commissioned for his private collection, only half a dozen have been located after the Holy Inquisition."

Kendra sighed. He'd obviously done his research. "You seem to know its history well."

Amusement lit Gerald's gaze. "It's taken me over a decade to track the history and verify the authenticity of this book," he said. "Of the six surviving volumes, four have disappeared into the hands of private collectors who aren't inclined to part with their copies."

The math was simple enough. "That leaves two copies."

Gerald nodded gravely. "More fascinating still is that the fifth copy is believed to have fallen into Hitler's hands in 1933. His interest in the occult and attempts to use it to manipulate his rise to power are well known. Though it's unconfirmed, that book is supposedly held under lock and key in Germany's war archives, never again to be viewed by human eyes."

And that left one. "And I suppose yours is the sixth and final surviving volume?"

"Yes." Gerald gloated with no small satisfaction. "Thanks to the persuasion of two million dollars, the *Delomelanicon* now belongs to the Carter estate."

Jaw dropping, Kendra gasped. Though she'd suspected he'd spent lavishly to acquire his prize, she'd had no idea he'd squander such an outrageous sum. She bristled. "You don't have that much free cash in your personal account, Gerald. How did you get the money?"

He shot her an infuriatingly bland look. "I drew it out of our trust." In an attempt to mollify her, he added, "It's an investment for the estate and certainly worth the cost to obtain it."

Patience thinning, Kendra folded her arms across her chest. Because Gerald tended to be so damn frivolous, she had to be the tightfisted one. Money was the one thing they argued about, bitterly and constantly. "And you didn't bother to discuss it with me?"

Gerald's eyes narrowed, his gaze glinting in subtle challenge. "Considering you were incapacitated at the time, I was well within my right as cotrustee to authorize the withdrawal and transfer of the funds for this purchase." He sighed with long-suffering patience. "I've been holding things together the best I could since your nervous breakdown."

Insides clenching with trepidation, Kendra shivered at the implication behind his words. *Nervous breakdown*—society's polite way of saying she'd gone temporarily bonkers. Her alleged suicide attempt was little more than a blur, her senses addled by grief, too many glasses of wine and a handful of sedatives.

She didn't remember swallowing the pills. Perhaps it had been in the back of her mind when she'd opened the wine, downing one bottle and then another. The pain had to stop. The memories had to stop. Since her father's death, her mind had pushed REWIND and PLAY, relentlessly plying her with the terrible images of glass and metal grinding around her from all sides.

Horror started low in her belly, bubbling upward, expanding and growing until it threatened to choke her. *The accident.*

Swaying on her feet, Kendra thinned her lips. Eleven months had passed, but time had failed to dull the ache of tragedy. As the only survivor, she wore the scars.

And carried the guilt.

Nathaniel Carter had been angry, driving recklessly. She'd begged him to slow down. He'd ignored her, punching the accelerator in his rush to get home—to get away from the daughter he'd just threatened to disown. Ignoring the hazards of the rain, he'd been driving too damn fast for the narrow exit lane, rounding the curve in a deadly arc. . . .

Clenching her fists and taking a deep breath, Kendra mentally willed the ugly visions away. *It wasn't my fault, damnit.* Despite her efforts, remorse continued to linger. She should have been the one who'd died, a worthless and weak fool. Not a man in his prime and at the top of a prominent legal career.

She would have to work on her depression—but without the aid of alcohol and pills to help her cope. That lethal combination had almost managed to squelch her guilt.

Permanently.

A strong hand closed around her arm. "Are you all right?" Gerald's question interrupted her turbulent thoughts.

Kendra opened her eyes, blinking a few times to regain her sense of place. "I'm fine," she murmured. "Just a little dizzy."

Gerald's grip tightened. "I shouldn't have said that to you," he said by way of an apology. He started to lead her away from the lectern. "If you need to rest—"

Shaking her head, Kendra dug in her heels. She tugged her arm out of his grip. "I'm fine. Stop treating me like a halfwit and invalid." It was time to take responsibility, get a better grip on her emotions. She was twenty-three, for God's sake, not twelve.

His hand immediately dropped, and he took a step back. "Of course."

Murky thoughts washed through her mind, the black tide rising. "I—I didn't try to kill myself, Gerald. It wasn't a deliberate overdose. I just had too much wine and forgot how many pills I took."

Mouth tightening into a thin line, Gerald tossed off a shrug. "You don't have to try to make excuses, Kendra." He sighed. "It's been a bad year. First the wreck; then Michael breaking off your engagement." He reached out and gave her hand a quick squeeze. "Anyone would fall apart. I should have been there for you, paid more attention..." His words trailed off. His mother had committed suicide over a decade ago, and the topic was one he preferred to avoid.

The rise of depression receded a little. Despite their differences as non–blood-bonded siblings, she and Gerald had always managed to overcome their differences and live in reasonable peace. "Let's just not talk about it, okay?" She offered a little smile. "It won't happen again. The past is over and done with."

He gave her a little chuck under the chin, the way he'd used to when they were children and he was trying to cheer her up. "Promise?"

She took a deep breath and nodded. "I promise."

"Then that's the last we'll say about the whole matter."

Facing an awkward silence, Kendra blinked, trying to refocus on her reason for being in the library to begin with. "I still don't understand why you feel you had to spend two million. Daddy is rolling over in his grave now, I'm sure. Why is it so important you have *this* book?"

Tossing back tawny locks, Gerald graced her with a slow, intimate look that slammed into her gut like a well-aimed fist. Her stepbrother was a master at putting on the charm, a persuasive tactic he often used to get his way.

"Let the old man roll. Aside from its absolute rarity on the collectors' market, I believe the writings to be absolutely authentic."

Kendra stepped back, looking up at him keenly. "You believe the Devil actually wrote a primer on demons?"

He arched a single brow against her sarcasm. "Think about it a minute. There must be some kernel of truth rooted in the legend for the church to have taken such pains to preserve the writings—and to suppress them."

The unbidden chill returned, whisking across Kendra's skin. Though not overly religious, she'd always believed there was a battle between two opposing forces—equally strong, but precariously unbalanced by the passions and emotions of mankind. "Why would anyone want private copies?"

Another seductive grin flickered effortlessly across Gerald's unblemished face. "Beneath the robes of the papacy, Rodrigo Borgia was a human who succumbed to the temptations of the ultimate thing forbidden to him as a man of God: summoning demons to serve him. It is historically accurate to say that during his reign as pope, the church was brought to its lowest levels of degradation."

She shot the lectern a narrow look and scowled. "Those were his own vices at work, not the intrigue of demons. The same with Hitler and his attempt to twist the world to fit his megalomaniacal visions. They were men who reaped the consequences of leading evil lives."

"Are you so sure?" Gerald spread his hands reverently toward the precious treasure it guarded. "These writings are reputed to be the Devil's gift to mankind. The power of all hell's demons are said to be contained within these pages. Summon them, and they will answer. It's no wonder the book is so coveted."

A laugh of disbelief escaped her. "Do you seriously think that book is the key force behind Borgia's and Hitler's rise to power?"

Gerald leveled a laser-beam stare at her, one that cut right through to the bone. "I am saying nothing of the sort. I merely put forth my own speculations as a collector and observer of human nature, though I would urge you to remember the grimoire's purpose: any desire a living soul seeks will be granted."

Contemplating the unthinkable, Kendra licked dry lips. "You're not going to try to use this thing, are you?"

Gerald laughed, breaking the tension. "Don't be ridiculous. I'm a collector. Owning the book is one thing. Calling up the Devil is another—a fool's errand. I'm knowledgeable enough to know the occult is nothing to be trifled with. It is only to the man who attempts to use this knowledge unwisely that misfortune will fall."

Relieved that her brother wasn't a total nut, Kendra nodded. "I'm glad you don't take such nonsense seriously."

Even as the words left her mouth, the strangely magnetic force of half-repulsed fascination drew her attention back to the ragged tome. Its austere leather cover was no more attractive than her own face, and yet the glass that surrounded it was another reminder how her life had changed since the accident.

She mentally flinched at the sight of her pale features reflected in the transparent glass. She felt a surge in the pit of her stomach. The coppery tinge of self-revulsion welled up in her mouth. No one with eyes found her worth looking at nowadays. Not with the scars.

If it were possible to have my greatest desires fulfilled, what would I ask for?

With just a flicker of consciousness, she realized the light reflecting across the glass gave the volume a soft, luminous glow. Awareness of a force, awake and sentient, slithered into her mind.

Kendra sensed the space around her shifting, the pressure on her lungs robbing her of breath. Her senses coalesced, coming together in a single, coherent moment of understanding. A cool rush of air brushed her scarred cheek like a lover's caress. The fine hairs at the nape of her neck prickled. The whisper of a voice unknown crept into her ears.

Seek me.

The book was speaking.

To her.

It was a ludicrous idea, but she couldn't avoid the rush of impressions suddenly invading her mind.

The invisible pressure stroked the line of her jaw and then down her neck. *Open. Explore.*

She trembled, a tiny flare of forbidden heat flickering inside her core. The featherlight sensation moved to the hollow of her throat, stopping only a second before traveling lower, tracing the curves of her breasts. Her nipples hardened. Heat pooled between her thighs, dampening her panties. *My God. It's seducing me, making love to me.*

"No," she murmured softly. "Please . . ."

Unaware of her distress, Gerald glanced her way. "Did you say something?"

Kendra's pulse pounded, driving up her blood pressure. She closed her eyes, swallowing against the raw need rocketing through her. A chilling sweat drenched her, giving rise to a strange odor. *Brimstone.*

Her stomach cramped. Arousal drizzled away. "I—I don't know. Something's happening. . . ." The ability to verbalize suddenly deserted her. As her tongue morphed into lead, her words ended, unfinished. She stood, muted by the bizarre manipulations.

Gerald reached out to steady her. "If you're having one of your spells, I should call the doctor."

Kendra barely heard him. As his hand made contact with her skin, the seething energy surrounding her turned unpredictably violent, lashing out with ferocious intent. A barrage of sharp needles tipped with white-hot fire pierced her skull, penetrating her brain.

She lifted a hand, pressing ice-tipped fingers against the vein thudding in her temple. Her breath came faster. The oxygen filling her lungs felt like sharp-edged points, ripping her open from the inside out.

Impossible! Sinister impressions smothered her mind, cloaked her thoughts. *This can't be happening.*

From out of nowhere, a veil of shadows closed in around her, trapping her in an airless void. She screamed within the boundaries of her skull as glacial claws she couldn't see penetrated every part of her skin, reaching inside to clutch at her guts and rip them out. Horrendous, ear-shattering wails swirled around her with the force of a tornado.

As quickly as it had arrived, the force emanating from the grimoire suddenly let go.

Losing all coordination, Kendra crumbled, striking the ceramic-tiled floor with bruising force. Her struggle to cling to consciousness failed. A wave of darkness crashed in, sweeping her away with hurricane force.

Then everything went black.

2

Swimming past the thick murk of oblivion sloshing around in her skull, Kendra slowly regained consciousness. Her lids cracked open, giving her a somewhat tilted view of the library. A veritable ocean of books surrounded her on all sides. Softly dappled lights hovering overhead lent the library a sense of tranquility. A soft surface cushioned her body. The pungent smell of old leather and rich, dark tobacco tickled her nostrils.

Head thudding, Kendra struggled to make sense of her surroundings. Her vision was blurry, fuzzy. Everything seemed out of proportion, oddly sized and placed. She heard nothing. Only silence all around.

The answer finally floated to the forefront of her mind—no easy task. *Daddy's favorite reading longue.* Gerald must have scooped her off the floor before going to summon help. Surely he'd be back any minute.

Nerves sparking and mind awry, Kendra decided to stay put. Swallowing hard, she fought off a wave of nausea. Closing her eyes, she pressed a hand to her lids and rubbed hard. Her skin felt clammy under her touch, absolutely icy cold. She heard her heart beating in her ears, felt the reverberating thud in her chest.

God, how she'd love a glass of water. Her mouth was dry, her throat as parched as the desert in high summer. It felt as if she'd been dead to the world for ages.

The one good thing about her headaches was that they never lasted long, most times less than thirty minutes. The bad thing was that she could sometimes go through several cycles of pain that lasted an entire day. She'd found herself relying more and more on painkillers and wine, her self-prescribed treatment. A trauma from the accident, the damage would probably last for the rest of her life.

This was the scariest episode she'd ever suffered. She'd never before fallen into a dead faint. One moment she'd been speaking with Gerald, the next . . . nothing.

Except . . .

Awareness began seeping back into her brain. The dream of Gerald's grimoire trying to seduce her had faded, but the memory of invisible hands caressing her skin lingered.

Kendra's hand immediately came down from her eyes. Her gaze flicked around, her mind in its usual chaos, like a volcano about to blow. Though outwardly calm, her thoughts were raging like tigers locked in a steel cage.

Her gaze sought and found the strange book. It still rested on the lectern. The showpiece of the library, it could be seen and viewed from every angle. But only for show, not for touch. Its pages were well protected under the thick glass shielding its fragile pages.

Kendra's mouth turned down in a frown. The damn thing— or something coming from it—had practically assaulted her.

A shiver pressed up her spine. She shook off the tremble with determination. The damn thing looked so innocuous, so . . . harmless. "I just imagined it," she whispered. "Nothing happened."

She was wrong.

Kendra didn't recall becoming aware of the presence. It was suddenly there. At first, she didn't see anything. Rather, she felt it. First came the scent, deep and musky, the way a man would smell after a hard workout. The presence was not in any one spot in the library but was something that was gradually surrounding her, like the air she breathed. It wasn't frightening or menacing. She had the uncanny feeling someone was watching her.

Hearing a sound, she cocked her head, body stiffening, going absolutely still so she could listen. A voice was definitely speaking to her, the muffled composition peculiarly intriguing, barely decipherable.

Kendra . . . A man's voice whispered out of nowhere. *Can you hear me?*

Not really comprehending the call, Kendra nodded. Despite the fact that she couldn't see anything, she inexplicably knew she wasn't alone in the library.

A delicious sensation of anticipation filled her. Her pain receded a little. An eon had passed since she'd been so excited. She listened. Was she imagining it? No. Surely not. She felt it as clearly as she heard it. Some *thing* was present.

Something that desired her.

Though her perception was saddled with pain, it all made perfect sense. "Yes." The word exited her mouth as an almost inaudible hiss. Her voice was hoarse, almost unrecognizable to her own ears. "I do hear you."

The voice spoke again, clearer and more persistent. *Seek me.*

Slipping off the longue, Kendra walked toward the lectern. She wasn't even sure what she was expecting to find when she arrived. Maybe it was because she felt so goddamned helpless she wanted something to happen.

Without thinking, she put out her hand, letting it hover above the glass. Heat emanated from its surface, barely shielding her from an incredible force just waiting to detonate. A series of tiny cracks formed on the surface of the glass. The fragile panes began to crack and split. The tiny hairline fractures grew larger.

Kendra should have been afraid. But she wasn't fearful. She was mesmerized. "I know you're there," she whispered. "I felt you touch me."

A reply arrived in the form of a light breeze winnowing across her skin. Though no windows were open, she felt air displacing around her.

The cracks multiplied, branching out in a spiderweb, snaking with unnerving speed through the glass panes. A demon stirred, fighting its bonds, growing and whirling as it emerged from enforced captivity. No more gentleness.

Harder. Harder. Harder.

Sensing the explosion to come, Kendra stumbled away from the lectern. Seconds later, the panes surrounding the grimoire shattered.

Kendra screamed, expecting razor-edged shards to slice through vulnerable skin. Her hands flew toward her face, a delayed attempt to lessen the inevitable damage.

Nothing happened.

No sting. Not a cut on her.

The library was as silent as a tomb.

Kendra dared a peek through her fingers. The glass had vanished, down to the last piece. Gone without a trace.

A crimson-shaded mist streamed around the grimoire, unfettered by any force. With a great, shuddering heave, the cover slowly opened. Several pages followed, turned by an invisible hand. The book faded away as the mist took on substance, thickening and taking distinct shape. Wafting closer, it settled in front of her. Thicker and denser, the scent of hot musk grew more intense. The glimmer of an actual figure evolved, assuming a new solidity. A six-foot hunk of demon materialized.

Too stunned to move, Kendra simply stared. Looking at

him, she felt anything but sane at the moment. What she was looking at couldn't be real. Like stepping into a fun house full of mirrors, it was surreal, bordering on bizarre. Between waking up and getting up, she'd somehow slipped over the edge of reality, stepping into the realm of wild hallucination.

Not that she minded this hallucination one bit.

She tilted her head back and found herself staring into eyes the color of a stormy evening sky. Her breath caught in a hitch, and heavy awareness pulsed through her veins. She wondered how many women had stood with their mouths hanging open at the sight of such a striking being. Long blond hair with touches of fiery red and shimmering gold hung past his broad shoulders. A straight nose, fine mouth and strong jaw completed his face.

All sinew and muscle, he stood almost completely naked. Except for some sort of loincloth fashioned around his narrow hips, he wore nothing else. Almost wholly exposed, a series of ebony tattoos was etched over his skin. More a series of ancient symbols than any coherent design, the markings ran from the back of his hands all the way up his arms and over his shoulders and upper body. The effect was eerie but totally breathtaking. His presence lent the library a strange, spellbinding appeal.

Gulping, Kendra tried to swallow past the lump forming in her throat. The world shook a little beneath her feet at the sight of him. She closed her eyes. When she opened them again, the specter still hovered. A glow of unearthly radiance emanated all around him, as though he generated his own light source.

"What are you?" she asked, words tumbling stupidly from her mouth. "Why are you here?"

The gorgeous apparition reached out, stroking the tips of his fingers lightly across her forehead. There was a quick bunching of muscles in his biceps when he moved his arm. Her heart skipped a beat. His touch, though cool, was not unpleasant.

A slow smiled pulled at his full mouth. Between his parted

lips she could hear wisps of breath. "Your pain calls me, and I have answered."

Though he spoke perfect English, his words were shaded with an accent of indefinable origin. His voice was clear enough, but it was tinged with . . . what? Layers of *eternity?* It was a ridiculous notion, but she couldn't shake off the impressions bombarding her mind: emptiness and longing, melancholy companions, one devouring the other.

Never satisfied, never fulfilled.

Kendra trembled, feeling a strange pressure emanating outward, pressing at the edges of her mind. Her migraine receded, inexplicably pushed back by the gentle waves generated by his intimate stroke across her skin. For the first time since the accident, she felt normal. Whole.

She released a sigh of relief. "Thank you," she murmured.

His hand moved to her cheek and then her chin, mimicking the caresses she'd felt before passing out. "You are not whole," he said softly. "You haven't been for a long time."

His prescient words struck a strange chord deep inside her. "It's like I've lost pieces of myself," she confessed. "Pieces I fear I'll never find again."

An unearthly twinkle of certainty lit his beautiful eyes. "You will find them," he predicted. The touch of his gaze was nearly as tangible as the touch of his hand.

All knowing. All seeing. All powerful. The words echoed through her mind. She shivered with a sharp, sexual thrill. "How?"

He answered, low and silky. "I am Remi, bringer of revelation. You seek answers to many things. I can help you find them."

Entranced by this beautiful creature and his promise of clarity, Kendra nodded. "I would like that," she whispered.

Through the last months she'd been driven by confusion and uncertainty, unable to remember the simplest thing. Like a person wrapped in thick cotton bunting, she'd ceased to feel, ceased to function, wishing only to slip into the ground the way her father's coffin had at his funeral.

He traced the line of her jaw. "I know."

Kendra's lower lip trembled. The rise of tears stung her eyes, blurred her vision. "I've been so confused. It's like I can't think for myself anymore."

Remi smiled again, lightly stroking her mouth with the tip of a single finger and generating some sort of energy as a subtle vibration emanated from the tip. "I can help you find your way," he promised.

Kendra felt tiny fingers of luminous warmth move throughout her body. Mesmerizing waves of radiant heat easily penetrated bone to enter her core. Like a cleansing fire, the sensations shimmered through her all the way to her toes. Tension drained away.

"There is one condition," he drawled, flashing a lazy smile. Watching his gorgeous lips move made her guts clench with need.

"What do you want?" Somewhere in the back of her mind it vaguely occurred to her that making deals with demons might not be a wise thing to do. She didn't care. If he demanded her life, or her soul, she would probably sign away both in a heartbeat.

He appeared enormously pleased she'd grasped the scenario so quickly. His smile grew wider. "Completely surrender to my every carnal desire."

She gulped, licking dry lips. "Carnal desire?" She spoke slowly, working her way through what he'd said. From the way he spoke, he intended to devour her in a single bite. "As in, sexual submission?"

Stepping closer in a subtle power play, he grinned at the hesitation in her question. His move shifted the loincloth around his hips, leaving no doubt that he was blond all over.

Remi's eyes glinted with lusty delight. "Absolute and total compliance," he said.

Sensation and imagination took over, sending Kendra's thoughts into overdrive. An image of Remi lying naked across her white silk sheets flashed onto her mind's screen. Out of the blue she wanted to taste him, touch him, lay beside him and experience what it would be like to meld her flesh to his.

Her cheeks heated at the thought of his strong hands caressing her naked skin. Her scarred skin. In another place, at another time, she would have been eager to take him up on the sexually charged temptation.

But not now. Not after the accident.

Feeling desperate, scared and more than a little bit out of control, Kendra jerked back, breathing hard. "No. I—I can't." She looked up, expecting to see a sneer of derision cross his handsome face. What she saw was yearning, raw and eager.

Remi's gaze narrowed, probing into hers with an intensity that stole her breath away. "You think you are ugly to my eyes because you are scarred?"

No answer would cross her lips. She couldn't even nod.

With no warning Remi circled around, coming to a stop behind her. Big palms spread over her shoulders, holding her in place. His grip was strong, firm. An electrical connection again sizzled between them, his touch immediately warming her skin and causing her heart to skip a beat. A delicious throbbing came to life between her legs. There was no doubt that he couldn't put those hands to work, fulfilling every fantasy a woman could ever imagine.

"Every woman is beautiful, Kendra. So many humans are so busy looking at the outside they fail to see the real beauty inside."

The fine hairs at the nape of Kendra's neck rose. Just thinking about his hands sliding over her bare skin made her senses hum with a venereal awareness she couldn't mistake. She had the feeling he'd be a good lover—very good.

And resisting him would be like trying to scale a mountain without gear. Almost impossible.

Yet Kendra did resist, shaking her head to clear it. "Nice, even if it sounds clichéd," she deadpanned with deliberate disinterest. "I'd think a demon as good-looking as you wouldn't waste your time on a woman like me."

A hard sting tinged her words. After Michael had walked out, she'd ceased to believe she was still a desirable woman. It was easy to fall into the habit of thinking herself a physical ogre because of a few surgery scars.

"The accident may have changed the map of your body," Remi continued, clearly able to discern her thoughts, "but the damage didn't change who you are inside, who you are as a human being."

Hearing his words, Kendra wavered. She hadn't had sex since the accident—eleven long months of physical deprivation.

Remi's hands skimmed lower, his touch seeming to burn through her clothing before his hands settled on her hips. He bent close to her ear. "You've shunned becoming intimate with any man. All for what? To sleep alone at night? That is stupid. In the dark how you look doesn't matter to a man. It is how you feel, how you respond to your lover's caresses."

Kendra closed her eyes, reluctant to acknowledge she could be so easily seduced by the first man—no, the first demon— who tried to bed her. Desire mingled with desperation, fusing into something explosive and wholly unstable. Fear and craving and a thousand other emotions surged through her with each heavy thud of her heart. Deep down inside she was terrified she was going to acquiesce. What made it even worse was that she wanted to!

Completely and without reservation.

"It's crazy," she murmured, shaking her head. "This can't be real."

Remi's grip tightened. "It is real. I am real." Warm breath scorched. "I answer the call of those who need me, Kendra. You have many desires yet to be fulfilled." He lowered his head, nibbling lightly at the soft flesh between neck and shoulder.

A soft moan of pleasure slipped over Kendra's lips. She hadn't meant for things to get out of hand so quickly, but the tempest of desire twisting inside refused to be easily harnessed.

Despite herself, she leaned back into him, desperate to feel her heat merge with his. His cock pressed against the cleft of her ass like an iron bar. He had to be at least eight inches, maybe more. If she'd believed him to be nothing more than a figment of her fevered imagination, the feel of his body against hers left no doubts.

He was a real, solid and all aroused male.

And an evil spirit, her mind filled in.

A remnant of long-abandoned religious training floated to the forefront of Kendra's mind. Since becoming an adult, she hadn't set foot in a church, but that didn't mean she'd forgotten her Sunday school studies. Surely Remi had to be teasing her, toying with her. That's what demons were supposed to do. Mislead. Deceive. Betray.

Oh, God. What was she thinking?

She broke out of his grasp. This whole thing was just too crazy to be real. The accident must have done more damage than her doctors were aware of.

Whirling around, her hands clenched at her sides. "I think you should stop."

He grinned, a piranha's hungry smile, all toothy and raven-ous. "Why?"

Racking her brains, Kendra blurted out the first words that came to mind. "Because you're a demon, and I'm a human." She spoke with forced calm through the creeping panic wrapping its fist around her heart and beginning to squeeze. Flirting with a demon was one thing. Agreeing to fuck one was quite another.

Morphing from light gray to gunmetal, Remi's eyes brewed displeasure. His gaze settled on his face, intense and focused. "I scare you." Not a question. The implication behind his words sent a hot tremor through her.

Panic tightened its grip, dangerously painful. Her lungs hung in her chest like two-ton anvils, incapable of drawing a fulfilling breath to clear her addled mind. "More than you could imagine."

His eyes narrowed, lending him a distinctly feral look. He spat a derisive laugh. "You think I'm out to get your soul?"

Her jaw tightened. "Isn't that what demons do? Deceive humans?"

Remi cleared his throat. "It is the human mind—and the human heart—that deceive themselves. If a demon takes advantage of that fact, we can hardly be blamed."

Lifting a skeptical brow, she regarded him with suspicion. "Is that what you're doing? Taking advantage of me?"

Forcing a wry shrug, he flashed a bandit's grin. "I am as I told you," he purred seductively. "A bringer of revelation." He spread his hands in supplication. "Nothing more. Nothing less."

Drawing herself up straighter, Kendra eyed him from head to foot as a shudder of pure desire passed through her. Despite her misgivings, temptation beckoned. "And if I give in to your proposal, you'll show me things I want to know?"

A laugh broke from his throat. "Oh, no. I do not show you things about other people." His brows went up innocently. "I reveal things to you about yourself. Things you refuse to look at within your own soul."

Thinking about it, Kendra's mouth quirked down. "And you show me with sex, I suppose?"

Remi's head angled down slightly. He eyed her mouth with

sensual speculation. "You would be surprised what unlocking your inhibitions can reveal." He grinned again, and her heart skipped a beat at the flash of perfect white teeth.

A vision of their bodies entwined in passionate lovemaking flashed through Kendra's mind. To her utter shock, she angled her head up as though to accept the kiss hovering between them.

But though it was torture to resist his perfectly formed mouth, she didn't kiss him. "God knows I'm tempted. I'll admit that because it's true." She shivered. "But I know enough about demonic things to know you're something I'm not ready for."

Narrowing his eyes, Remi absorbed her declaration. "Oh, you're ready." He caught her in his arms, pulling her against his concrete-hard body. Their breaths mingled, sultry warmth caressing her lips. "And I intend to show you why. Over and over again. . . ."

Without giving her a chance to answer, he brought his mouth down on hers.

3

Kendra melted against Remi, suddenly desperate to take everything he was willing to give. Their tongues waltzed and tangled in erotic play, each determined to devour before the other bit first.

Her hands lifting to his shoulders, Kendra's fingers dug into his skin. She couldn't get enough of his rich, honey-dark taste, a nectar she'd willingly drink until glutted. In turn, Remi's tongue probed deep, sending stimulating shocks racing through her veins.

Kendra tightened her arms around his neck, pulling him deeper, closer, disappearing completely into the sensual void descending on her senses.

Breaking their kiss, Remi's hands slipped to her breasts, cupping them. His thumbs brushed her erect nipples, so prominent through her blouse. "Very responsive. I like that."

Drawing a startled breath, Kendra arched into him. "It's almost impossible not to be," she breathed. Her hands quickly found the line of his loincloth. Shooting him a look, she traced the line of his straining erection. He moaned as her fingers explored his entire length.

She looked at him and smiled. Her need for him was running on high. She knew he felt her vibrations. Pure, unfettered lust. The wanting, the needing could no longer be denied. Still, she felt there was something she should confess. "I haven't been with anyone—intimately—in quite a while."

Pupils dilated, Remi's nostrils flared. "Do not try to tell me *no* right now," he grated. Need glinted, hot and bright in his eyes. "It has been more than five hundred years since I have taken my pleasure with a woman."

Holy shit. Five hundred years was a long time to wait for sex. She'd thought *she* was on edge from lack of physical fulfillment. Eleven months without an intimate touch was a drop in the bucket compared to his wait—close to an eternity in her mind. No wonder he was as eager as a Satyr turned loose on a temple full of virgins.

Heart raging against her ribs, she swallowed the lump forming in her throat. "I'm not." Her voice was shaky, hesitant. "I'm just asking you . . ." She licked her kiss-bruised lips. "Please don't hurt me."

Sensing her panic, his gaze gentled. "I am here to serve your needs," he said in a most persuasive way. His hands moving to her hips, he pulled her against his forbidding frame. Compared to her, he was huge. Her chin barely reached his shoulder. If he wanted to, he could snap her in half with little or no effort.

The hard ridge of him pressed against her belly, reigniting senses she'd believed had burned out. "I don't know what my needs are," she wavered. "I don't think I ever have."

Holding her tight, Remi lowered his head. "I do," he said and recaptured her mouth.

His kiss consumed her like a lightning bolt stabbing through her head and running the length of her entire body. Long-denied emotions coiled inside her, snapping and crackling like burning fuses leading to dangerous sticks of dynamite.

Kendra desperately tried to deny the entity smoothly dousing her intellect, but she was totally swamped, lost. To reason. To sanity. To everything but his delicious touch. Nature demanded her body remember the touch of a man, the feel of hard muscle against her soft curves. The promise of more coupled with the anticipation of getting it was too irresistible to deny.

Remi's mouth wove seductive magic, an effortless combination of gentle coupled with fierce longing barely leashed. Kendra's legs trembled under the assault. Her mind warned her away from him even as need tempted her to throw all warnings to the wind.

Her senses flickered. Caution was tossed, common sense fluttering away like a hummingbird caught in the grip of a cyclone. She was vaguely aware of Remi lifting her, carrying her toward the old chaise. She'd forgotten how wonderful it was to be swept away in a man's strong arms; the excitement of it fractured all control.

Feeling the chaise's cushions beneath her back, Kendra released a breathy giggle. "I've always wanted to fuck on this chair." She stretched out across its generous length. Another naughty giggle escaped. "When I was a teenager, I used to come in here and read all the racy books Daddy had."

Remi stretched out beside her, grinning. "I know." He waggled a lascivious brow and reached for the buttons of her blouse, expertly undoing them. "And you would masturbate until you climaxed."

Heat suffused her cheeks. Oh, goodness! Did he know everything before she confessed it? Biting her lower lip, she nodded. "Yes."

Remi tugged her blouse open, revealing breasts cupped in a

plain white bra. "I intend to make you come just the way you used to."

Kendra automatically stiffened. All of a sudden, she didn't feel so brave or sexy. "Don't." She reached for her blouse, tugging it back into place. Since the wreck, she'd never let anyone but medical personnel see her unclothed. That night, she hadn't been wearing a seatbelt. Too busy arguing, she gotten into the car and slammed the door—determined to continue the fight her father had declared finished.

Remi caught her hand, moving it out of his way. "Let me," he insisted gently.

Her fingers tightened into a fist. "It's not pretty."

"Beauty is in the eye of the beholder." He tugged her blouse open again.

She winced, unwilling to look down at the damage. A series of jagged hairline scars traveled over her chest and abdomen, looking as if someone had stamped her flesh with a strange, abstract pattern. She grimaced. "See? I told you it's not beautiful."

His gaze tracing every inch, he smiled. "To my eyes, they are."

She closed her eyes, relieved that he wasn't repulsed. "You say that like you believe it."

A single finger settled at the curve of her collarbone, tracking a path toward the peak of her left breast. "I do."

Kendra gasped at the sensation of touch on her damaged skin. Arousal mingled with urgency flooded through her. Her blood boiled as thick and hot as lava bubbling up from the mouth of a volcano. Beneath her bra, the tips of her nipples came to pebble-hard attention. She would have never guessed her scarred flesh would be so sensitive to another's touch.

Goose bumps rose. "That feels so good," she murmured.

Remi unsnapped the clasp between her breasts. She smothered a cry when he bared one rosy peak, giving it a light squeeze. "It's about to feel better." His head dipped, and his tongue swirled around the darkened areola.

Going damp between the legs, Kendra's vision blurred when he began to suckle. She ran her hands through his thick hair, guiding him, wanting every ounce of pleasure he gave. Desire hammered her core, tiny waves cresting through her. Pressed against her, his cock branded her thigh, steel encased in velvety skin.

A lusty moan broke from her lips. "Don't stop," she gasped. "That feels so good."

Kissing the valley between her breasts, the demon's mouth quickly moved to the other nipple. He suckled it slowly, letting his tongue explore the soft ridge. His fingers caressed her scars, moving slowly down her abdomen.

Reaching her skirt, he expertly inched up over her thighs, and his hand disappeared beneath, fingers making contact with the crotch of sensible cotton panties. The material was soaked through.

His fingers stroked her damp softness. "You are so wet."

"I can hardly help it." Kendra spread her legs wider, allowing him all access. She shivered as his fingers settled on her clit, making slow circles over the sensitized tip. The small organ pulsed deliciously, crying out with need. "I've needed this," she confessed in a breathless rush. His touch possessed her, molding her desire as he wished.

His lips brushed a nipple. "Mmmm . . . so have I."

Threading her fingers through his gloriously long hair, Kendra guided his head back down. His mouth opened, suckling. Her senses tilted when Remi slipped his fingers inside her panties. She burned and ached and felt if she didn't come soon she'd shatter.

"Then take me," she moaned. "Do anything you want."

"I intend to." Fingers slipping farther into her panties, Remi delved through her folds.

Kendra's breath drizzled out of her lungs. The intimacy of skin-to-skin contact shattered her senses. A burst of brilliant light exploded inside her skull, as violent and shocking as a sledgehammer striking concrete.

Hovering on the edge of an unexpected orgasm, she cried out, inner muscles clenching as he invaded her with two fingers. He began to stroke her, knowing precisely how far and how much pressure to apply.

Heat rose inside her, a relentless rush of pleasure spilling through her veins. Clinging to the sensations, Kendra rode the waves of gratification, letting the power of orgasm tumble her head over heels.

"I'm going to come," she warned, delighted.

Remi slowed the action. "Not yet," he grated. Hooking his fingers in her panties, he pulled down, tugging them over her thighs. "I want to taste your arousal."

Sliding down, he knelt beside the longue and repositioned himself between her legs. Hands parting her thighs, he pressed his mouth to her slit. His tongue snaked through the petals of her labia, making electric contact with her clit.

Kendra's legs started to shake as he pleasured her with his mouth. Her fingers dug deep into the edges of the longue. Greed twisted brutally inside her, more painful than any wound she'd ever suffered. She marveled at the feel of his tongue against her most sensitive center, the brush of torment each slow lick delivered. The rush of pure bliss made her dizzy, took her breath away.

"I need you," she whimpered. "I want your cock inside me." It was probably a mistake to rush the moment, but urgency was more powerful than restraint.

He lapped, long and slow. "Are you sure?"

Suppressing a moan, she nodded. "Of course."

Another slow nip followed, and then he grinned up at her. "I should warn you."

Curiosity niggled. "About what?"

"I am quite large," he answered matter-of-factly.

Again delighted, she returned his grin. "Bring it on, demon boy."

Remi climbed to his feet. One big hand whisked away his loincloth. It vanished without a trace.

Kendra gaped at the sheer, naked magnificence of his body. Broad shoulders, a lean abdomen and narrow hips were supported by legs as sturdy as tree trunks. While God was reputed to have created mankind in his image, she had to admit the Devil hadn't done too bad a job creating demons. Remi was perfect in every way.

Lifting his arms, he sifted his fingers through his long hair, letting it cascade around his shoulders and down his back. The multihued highlights glinted and sparked. Much longer than the eight or so inches she'd initially guessed, his erection arced up toward his cobbled abdomen. Thick and laced with bulging veins, his cock was a magnificent beast.

His perfection and beauty impacted her with a solid blow, humbling her. "You're so beautiful," she said. Her breath shallow and fast, a hot rush of blood burned through her.

Remi smiled. "You flatter me with your worship, but I am not worthy."

Kendra's mouth watered. "I would beg to differ."

One big hand circled his shaft. Touching himself with sinuous grace, he slid his palm down its pulsing length and then back up again. A single droplet of pre-cum glimmered at the tip. His grin widened. "Oh, you will beg," he promised. "Turn around."

Kendra's brows went up. "Excuse me?"

"Turn around," he repeated. "And present yourself. I wish to penetrate you from behind."

A violent shiver ran down the length of her. "But . . ."

Another long stroke. "You will submit," he rumbled, repeating his earlier command. "Completely and totally."

Kendra knew she was going to do exactly what she shouldn't.

She obeyed, positioning herself on her hands and knees. The extra height afforded by the longue perfectly aligned her rear with his hips. Her nerves zinged with anticipation.

From behind, Remi rumbled his approval. "Perfect."

She tossed a glance over her shoulder. "I wish it were."

Pushing up her skirt, he bared her ass. Big hands descended, cupping and squeezing her firm flesh. "Oh, it is. Trust me. I know a fine piece of ass when I see it."

His touch was hot enough to burn her alive. She trembled, anticipating the intimate, sensual act of complete penetration. "You're just flattering me."

He gave one cheek a little slap. "No, I'm not," he assured her. "I'm fornicating with you."

A cry escaped Kendra when he spread her cheeks, pressing his cock into the cleft. The silky tip pressed against her anus, testing the resistance.

Clenching tight, she gasped out her protest. "Surely you aren't—" she spluttered, cheeks going red hot at the image of his cock impaling her like a red-hot poker. Anal sex was something that lingered among the realm of sexual taboos, a dark and forbidden thing.

Kind of like submitting to a demon's desires, her mind filled in.

Remi pressed just enough to send a hot rush of desire through her body. "Not today," he warned. "But soon."

His cock moved lower, brushing her slit in promise. Instead of entering her quickly, he swiped the broad crown against her eager sex before stabbing her clit.

Kendra closed her eyes, relishing the feel. Her clit was flushed with heat, her labia swollen, throbbing with need. Every minute he waited set her on fire, tested her control. She'd never experienced such an unabashed display of male sexuality, one that made her eager to submit to his control. Far from feeling dominated, she felt free to enjoy herself, finally liberated enough to embrace her own repressed sexual urges.

She whimpered, pushing back against his body, trying to entice him to enter her.

"I'm taking my time," he whispered. One hand slid around to fondle her breast. Trapping her nipple, he tugged it gently, enjoying the way she squirmed. "I want this to last."

"Oh, God," Kendra gasped, tossing back her head. "I can't wait. . . ."

Lifting her so that her weight was supported on her knees, his other hand slid across her abdomen. A shiver went through her when he slid his hand over her mound to cup her. Her body reacted instinctively. Her clit was engorged, poking from between her nether lips. She heard a moan slip past her lips as he slipped his fingers between her thighs, stroking her creamy slit.

His touch was as electric as it was spellbinding. "God has nothing to do with this."

Kendra had never been so entranced. For the first time in her life, she needed to be fucked. Needed Remi, his commanding touch. She needed all those things as much as she needed air to breathe.

Even as his thick fingers rubbed her slit and mauled her breast, she ached for him to impale her, force her to take every last inch of his splendid cock.

Kendra guided a hand behind her, latching her nails into his skin. Her fingernails dug deep as she grasped a handful of his flesh, making her frustration painfully apparent. "Damnit," she growled, digging deep. "Fuck me now."

A low chuckle of delight broke over her shoulder. "I intend to," he said. "Repeatedly." The lean flex of rock-hard hips drove his cock inside her dewy sex. A single hard thrust sheathed him to the hilt.

Taken without warning, Kendra felt her body go rigid. He pulled back and then stroked back in. Once, then twice. She melted, contracting around him as her inner muscles relaxed to accept his length.

"Feel good?" he purred, fingers giving her nipple a nice little tug for good measure.

Kendra felt her sex contract around his length, so hard and filling. "Better than good," she breathed. "Mind-blowing."

Remi pulled back, taking a deep breath to control his own desires. " 'Mind-blowing' doesn't begin to describe this delight," he marveled. "I have never taken a female so delightfully tight. It is like having a virgin."

Kendra felt heat again suffuse her cheeks. "Almost," she gasped. "I've had only one lover."

Remi's hips struck her buttocks. "A cunt like this should be enjoyed by many men."

Jarred to the bone, Kendra clenched her teeth. "That's a compliment, I hope," she grated. She wanted to say more, but she couldn't draw enough oxygen into her lungs. Each spearing of his lethal erection penetrated to the center of her core, hitting the bull's-eye every time.

All of a sudden there were too many sensations for her brain to process at once. Raw and exposed, her senses overloaded, shorting out.

Remi never stopped pummeling her. Never stopped his hips for a second. It was as if he wanted to brand himself on her insides. There was nothing left except the blistering conflagration of lust streaking through her like a red-hot meteorite smashing into the earth.

A sound started down in her throat, working its way up as he pounded her, loosening a cry that said she was ablaze with passion.

Remi hammered into her harder, his own needs hurtling him toward a glorious climax. "Come hard!" His cock surged, a jet of hot semen spilling inside her womb.

Feeling his release trampling hard on her heels, Kendra arched back against his solid frame. "Oh, hell, *yesss* . . ."

She closed her eyes against the flood of physical sensation, enjoying the power that melded into a single and profound ache deep in her core. Unbidden tears burned behind her lids even as her body cried out, reveling in a release that couldn't be contained a second longer.

She fought the current and lost, totally swept away by the crush of a skull-shattering climax. . . .

4

A male voice, and a hand shaking her shoulder, succeeded in blowing apart Kendra's rapturous daydream.

She opened her eyes, assailed from all sides by a veritable ocean of ceramic tile. The pungent smell of the cleaner used to shine the floors invaded her nostrils—a vague lavender scent. It felt almost as though she was lying on a cold, hard floor.

Moaning softly, Kendra closed her eyes, willing herself away from this terrible reality and back into her carnal encounter with the delicious demon she'd somehow conjured.

The hand shook her a second time.

She ignored it. She didn't want to wake up. Nothing about this moment made sense. "No," she moaned, reluctant to open her eyes. If she did, the pain would come back.

The voice returned, cutting through her confusion. "My God, Kendra. Are you all right?"

Images of the beautiful demon faded, draining out of her mind as consciousness crept back in to take over.

Kendra reluctantly opened her eyes, casting the intruder a startled look. Recognition of the face hovering over her gradually seeped through her muddled wits. "What did you say?" she croaked, neck and shoulders stiff from her awkward position.

Gerald stared back, his eyes huge and filled with concern. His lips stretched slightly, an indication of relief. "I asked if you are all right," he repeated slowly. He might have been speaking to a small, dim child, for all the emotion he put behind his words. Tight lines bracketed his mouth—the ones that said he found her little more than a nuisance.

She blinked. "Well, no," she gasped, terribly aware that she was sprawled out on the floor in the library. "If ever *not* applied to *all right*, now is that time." She struggled to sit up, but her limbs wouldn't seem to obey her commands.

Sliding a hand behind her back, Gerald helped lift her. Being physically lifted and settled into place reminded her of her recent hospitalization. She'd been barely able to lift a hand then, having to rely on other people to help her perform the simplest tasks.

Clenching her teeth against the rise of nausea, she ungratefully swatted his hand away. She wasn't helpless. "I'm quite all right," she insisted.

Gerald frowned, his gaze searching hers as though he were trying to look straight inside her skull. "You didn't look it to me," he said tightly. "My God, for a minute I thought you were having a convulsion."

Heart slamming like a jackhammer, Kendra's blood chilled. "Why would you think that?"

Gerald answered with a straight face. "Because you started writhing around on the floor like a woman in the throes of an orgasm."

A snippet of memory popped into her head. Of Remi. Naked and aroused.

Her gaze turned toward the lectern. Nothing about it had changed a bit. The glass surrounding Gerald's old grimoire was perfectly in place, unblemished and untouched. And her brother was definitely not a six-foot-tall, tattooed demon.

She shivered and instinctively rubbed her hands over her arms to still the rising goose bumps on her skin. The library was cold, an icy breeze echoing the wintry decor of white walls and white marble tile. But that was not the cause of her chill. It was a strong impression of being watched.

She glimpsed a shadowy movement, dark and stealthy, from the corner of her right eye. Stiffening, she turned her head but saw nothing to warrant her burgeoning sense of unease.

Had the movement been a trick of the light?

No. Kendra was sure she could feel something else in the room. But the grimoire lay untouched and untouchable under glass. Only Gerald was present, and he didn't appear to be aware of anything unusual. But as she turned her head to look at him, she thought she saw the air around him shift and then shimmer like heat waves rising from desert sands.

She blinked to clear her vision. It didn't help. She was dizzied and felt faint when a distinct whiff of sulfur burned her nostrils, bringing her upright with the sudden awareness of its presence.

"Kendra?"

Kendra placed the back of a hand to her clammy brow. A headache was building behind her eyes, the pain suddenly sharp. "What?" she snapped. She looked up to find Gerald standing directly in front of her, concern warring with curiosity in his expression.

"Are you not feeling well?"

"I'm fine. Just tired, I guess."

"You went very pale."

She lowered her hand. It wouldn't do to tell him she had hallucinated. "Just tired," she repeated, managing a small smile.

Seeds questioning her sanity took root in her mind. Surely she hadn't dreamed the whole strange encounter. She felt as if she'd just awakened from an out-of-body experience, a very erotic astral leap that had left her not only shaken but completely wrung out. Such travel had propelled her into a place far beyond imagination, perhaps even another realm.

Heat rose to her cheeks. "How long was I out?" she mumbled, embarrassed that Gerald should have witnessed such a display.

"Five, maybe ten minutes," he said slowly. His forehead wrinkled in consternation. "I'm not sure. It seemed like—" He looked into her eyes as though searching for something inside her mind.

She looked at him sharply. "What?"

He frowned. "For a few minutes it looked like there was something else controlling you."

The significance of what he'd said slammed into her. Another abrupt image came to her of Remi's cock punishing her with long, jarring strokes. Her heart tripped at the thought of his masculine flesh conquering her sex.

Kendra swallowed, sour bile slipping down her throat. Good grief! That could not have been real! It all had to be a figment of her imagination run amok. She shivered. "Nothing happened," she said quietly more to herself than to Gerald. "It was just one of my headaches."

His grim reply hit her ears. "I should get you back to the hospital."

Hospital. That dreaded place where physicians poked and prodded, invading her privacy on every damn level.

Resisting the slow rise of panic, Kendra's hand dropped. "No. Absolutely not."

Gerald fished out his cell, a sleek, expensive little number. "You're clearly not okay," he countered, flicking his phone open. "It was a mistake to release you from rehab so soon. I am calling your physician at once to have you readmitted to the hospital." His short, brutal intention to take immediate charge cut right through her. Leave it to Gerald not to mince words or actions.

She reached for the phone, attempting to bat it away. "I'm fine," she insisted. "I don't need to go back into the hospital. Put that thing away."

Flipping his phone shut, Gerald sighed heavily. "We can't have this starting over again, Kendra. The lying, the drinking, locking yourself away in your room. . . ." An eerie shadow of resentment passed over his features and then vanished. "And if something else is wrong, it needs to be dealt with before your health deteriorates."

She cut him off. "I've been home barely a day, Gerald. Of course I haven't had time to break into the liquor cabinet. And the only pills I'm taking are those the doctor prescribed."

His grip tightened around his cell phone, and he scowled at her. "I am not even sure the shrink you've been seeing is any help."

The last of her energy drained away. "I don't know that anything's helping me," she confessed quietly. "All I do know is my life can't go on the way it has." She looked up at him, a silent plea for sympathy. "I want my life to be good again. Like it was when Michael and I were together."

Tucking his phone away, Gerald shook his head sadly. "You just don't get how bad Michael was for you, Kendra. Dad was right to do whatever he could to keep him away from you."

His final observation arrived like a physical punch. She stared in disbelief. "Having Michael picked up and thrown into jail wasn't the way to convince me," she snapped.

Gerald's eyes grew stormy, darkening with anger. "Michael had a warrant on his head for unpaid parking tickets—and several ounces of marijuana in the trunk of his car when he was finally arrested."

Kendra shook her head, refusing to countenance a single a word he said. His accusation shouldn't have surprised her.

She'd known Gerald would eventually begin throwing Michael's transgressions in her face. "He was holding it for a friend."

Staring at her as though she'd shed all common sense, Gerald snorted. "Yeah, right. For all his bad-boy, rock-star appeal, he's still a druggie and a loser. If he was any sort of a man, why did he dump you after Dad died?"

Startled by what amounted to a verbal slap in the face, Kendra just glared at her brother. Though Michael Roberts hadn't said so in so many words, she knew exactly why he'd dumped her.

Because looks were important in his business.

A man like Michael couldn't afford to be seen with an ogre. Not a hotshot indie rocker with a record company interested in signing his band.

Raw pain simmered as her guts twisted when she remembered all the excuses he'd given her. Then, her face and upper body had still been swathed in white cotton bandages. Had she auditioned for the lead in a mummy movie, she probably would have gotten the part. Without much success, Michael had tried to explain he'd be on the road, that the grind of touring would be too much for her to handle. It was better to break it off clean; that way she wouldn't hang on, waiting.

Hang on. Like she'd been clinging to him with hooks.

Lost in the haze of pain and medication, Kendra had barely managed to comprehend that he was calling off their engagement, walking out on her at the time she needed him to be at her side.

His abandonment had cut a deep track. In her mind she was nothing, damaged goods no man would ever want. She wondered which was worse, the wreck that had scarred her flesh or the indelible tears Michael had inflicted on her soul.

A shattered psyche and a broken heart. Throw in the guilt that the last words she'd spoken to her father had been angry ones, and you had a certain recipe for complete disaster.

The thought stuck, the track repeating over and over in her mind. *Complete disaster. Complete disaster.*

Yep. That pretty much summed up her present state.

Suddenly self-conscious, she touched the scar arcing down her cheek and tried to remember that her physical injuries hadn't been fatal.

Anger and jealousy over Gerald's unblemished face suddenly melded inside her, twisting into a snarling beast. She wanted to lash out at him, drag her nails over his perfect face. Rip him open, subjecting him to the same pain she'd experienced. Until then, he wouldn't understand. Could never understand.

She stared at her brother through narrowed eyes. "He dumped me because I don't look like a supermodel," she snapped, the anger she'd suppressed until now boiling to the surface.

Scrambling inelegantly to her feet, Kendra stumbled away from her brother. Her jaw ached from clenching so long and so tightly. She wanted out of this hateful, terrible place. Away from the hateful, terrible book that mocked her with words of deception.

Moving too fast, a blank black wall passed in front of Kendra's eyes. She wavered, her legs close to giving way all over again. Her reflexes were inexplicably sluggish. She grappled for control, but her limbs refused to respond. Anger dribbled away, replaced by something far more terrible and tangible.

Coming up beside her, Gerald managed to catch her before she took a second spill. Steadying her, he guided her toward her father's old chaise. "That was stupid," he fussed. He bent, lifting her onto the longue.

Her hands slipping around his neck, Kendra held on to him tightly, trying to hold all her fear inside but knowing there was too damn much. She barely stifled a sob before it broke from her lips. Her homecoming wasn't going as well as she'd imagined. Home barely a day, and she was already falling into a heap on the floor.

Gerald lowered her into place. "You're clearly not well," he said, watching her closely. "My God, you've got all the strength of a newborn kitten."

A shiver went though her when her body made contact with the familiar leather cushions. Remi immediately popped into her head, his intimate touch warming her skin in a way that took her breath away. In her mind, he'd never stopped kissing her, never stopped touching her.

But her demon lover wasn't real, nothing more than a figment of a demented brain.

Wrenched from somewhere deep inside her, the cry at last escaped.

Gerald froze, going rigid. "Kendra?"

Embarrassed because she'd made a total fool of herself, Kendra didn't want to answer. She looked away, attempting to gather her frazzled nerves along with the fractured pieces of her composure. In other words, she needed to get her shit together and bag it.

"Nothing," she mumbled. "It's nothing."

Gerald knelt, hand cupping her chin, forcing her gaze to his. "What is the matter?"

Blinking back tears she didn't dare unleash, Kendra shook her head. She reached up, pulling his hand away. "I'm afraid I'm losing my freaking mind." She choked out a laugh. "Does that make any sense?"

One side of his mouth rose—not a smirk, but not quite a smile. "Of course it does. You've had a hard time."

Tension spiked all over again. "Isn't that the truth?"

He held up a hand to silence her. "But that doesn't mean it has to keep going on and on. You're home now. It's time to work on getting well, getting your life back on track."

Suddenly cold, Kendra drew her knees up to her chest. "God, I wonder if that's even possible," she mumbled. A thousand emotions tangled inside her; she tripped on every one, sure they were rigged to explode.

"It's possible only if you believe in yourself," Gerald said.

She wrapped her arms around her knees, the way she used to as a child after her father punished her for some transgression. Her daddy had always been the deliverer of corporal punishment, wielding a nasty belt with the buckle still attached. A tough man, he brooked no nonsense from silly little girls.

Kendra had to smile. "Is this where we join hands and sing hallelujah?" She glanced up to see a shadow of unease cross his features. As quickly as it had come, though, it vanished, and a slight if somewhat strained smile curled up the corners of his mouth. He didn't quite laugh. "That isn't funny. You know I'm a lapsed Catholic."

Kendra lowered her head to stare into her lap. A short burst of air escaped her nostrils as the last of her energy drained away. "And I'm just lapsed," she muttered, more for her benefit than his. She closed her eyes, expecting soothing darkness. No such luck. Her memories came flickering back, bright and luminous as Technicolor motion pictures. Her blood heated as a carnal slide show of sexual images flashed across her mind's screen.

Her breath caught. A vague sense of unease rippled through her. How was it possible she remembered the solid length of Remi's body pressed against hers? Or the brush of his hands over her needy skin? What about the nudge of his velvet-tipped penis against her puckered anus? Every nuance came not only with a sight but a sensation.

The memory shook her. For a moment she couldn't breathe.

Finally, a long, shuddery breath escaped her.

I imagined it all.

5

Kendra looked into the oval mirror hanging over the vanity. Thanks to her dive into the floor, there was a nice bruise on top of the painful lump.

She winced. Damn. Just what she needed. Yet another something to make her even uglier than she already was.

Leaning closer, she studied her reflection. Her jet black hair was razored off in short, shagged layers framing her face. Her bangs had been arranged and sprayed to remain absolutely in place across her forehead. Her eyes were lined and shaded to brighten the green irises. The bronze blush on her cheeks added a hue that helped offset the unhealthy pallor of her skin. Though skillfully applied, her cosmetics did not completely conceal the long scars on her face, one stretching from the corner of her eye to her jaw line. She was lucky. Going through the windshield could have cost her the eye.

These are a part of me now. They're who I am.

There was no way to reverse the damage or wind back time to before the accident had occurred. On the night of October 12, 2008, she'd made a choice that had forever changed her life.

She had been trying to reason with an angry man, a man whose respect she'd desired—even more than his love. A man who would brook no argument, nor accept any reasonable compromise.

"What a stupid thing to do," she muttered, thinking back.

Kendra had had no business getting in the car in the first place, and she knew it. Her father's mind had been made up, and nothing she could say or do would ever have changed his views. Nathaniel Carter disapproved of Michael Roberts, to the point of raw hate. And there was no way in hell he'd ever sanction their marriage. The fact they were planning to move in together had sent him into fits of rage.

Nathaniel Carter was speeding toward the exit that would take them into the sedate Philadelphia suburbs—a turn designed to be taken at no more than thirty-five miles an hour. It shouldn't have taken them long to reach home from Michael's downtown loft. Twenty minutes, perhaps. Maybe longer. The rain-soaked highway was a black stretch of asphalt beneath a cloud-infested sky rolling with thunder and tossing down bolts of lightning.

Her father had just begun to make the turn when the car had hit a slick patch, hydroplaning over the water. Simultaneously, he overcorrected, jerking the steering wheel hard to the left, forcing the speeding car into the guardrail. The car had flipped into the air, pitching them into oncoming traffic. The harsh grating sound of metal rolling on asphalt had deafened Kendra to all else as the vehicle had impacted with another.

The collision had happened so quickly she barely remembered the details. She'd heard the shattering of glass a split second before she flew through the windshield. Glass shards had slashed deep, the claws of a thousand angry tigers tearing at her skin.

Kendra recalled no pain, just a curious sense of numbness. In addition to being sliced into ribbons, she'd also suffered severe blunt-force trauma. Amazingly, she hadn't broken a single bone. The police had said she would have been almost completely spared had she been wearing a seatbelt and been cushioned by the airbag; while arguing with her father, she'd neglected to snap the seatbelt into place.

Kendra sighed. Since childhood, her father had possessed a lead foot and a bad temper. He'd never failed to break the speed limit wherever he drove; he'd only retained his driver's license because he was an important figure in local law. And while high blood pressure and too much cholesterol might have been killing Nathaniel Carter slowly, it was speed that brought his life to an abrupt end. Thrown clear of the wreck, Kendra had barely escaped being crushed to death by oncoming traffic.

She frowned. Her eyes opened, and she rubbed them to clear the blur floating in front of her vision. "Everything would be different if only I'd gone with Michael," she said for the benefit of no ears, save her own.

Her whole life had changed in an instant simply because she'd chosen her father over her boyfriend. The road not taken, the turn not made had kept her in turmoil for months on end. The *should haves,* the *could haves,* the *would haves* had all piled on top of her like concrete slabs.

Enough, she thought. *I can't keep going over it.* If she kept thinking about things, she'd surely be reaching for the wine in an attempt to quell her unquiet mind.

She now automatically avoided even seeing the scars the wreck had etched into her face, a process she was perfecting each time she looked at a mirror. If she didn't dwell on them, she could pretend they were not there.

God, I should be dead. She turned away from the mirror. *What grace has allowed me to live?*

Shuddering, she bent over to put the stopper in the claw-foot tub and turn on the hot water. Since getting out of the hospital, she was cold all the time, even on the hottest of days. To make the atmosphere a little more enticing, she'd dimmed the lights and lit several fragrant candles. The scent of cinnamon and sandalwood mingled nicely.

Adding a few capfuls of scented body oil, she sat on the edge of the tub, adjusting the water temperature as it filled to the desired depth. Once she turned off the taps, she pulled off her clothes, dropping them onto the floor.

Stepping into the warmth of the bath, she sank down into the water. Ah, this was just what she needed. A little privacy and a long, hot bath to wash away her stress.

The moment she closed her eyes, she couldn't help but think of the man who'd once consumed her life. Michael's image reared up in her mind. He'd been everything she thought she'd wanted in a lover. Good-looking. Puppy-brown eyes under a mop of shaggy brown hair that perfectly complemented his tanned physique. Onstage, he never failed to send his female fans into wild screams of rapture. Talented enough to write his own songs and music, he was a star on the rise.

One of his favorite haunts had been the Gwynedd-Mercy campus, playing gigs with his band. Not only could he usually entice a few coeds to grace his arm, he also bought enough pot and beer to guarantee he remained the center of attention at any party. Her college roommate had introduced her to Michael, just a few years her senior and already making his mark as a singer to watch.

Why had Michael chosen her over the countless other girls clamoring for his attention?

She was everything he shouldn't have wanted. Bookish. Nerdish. A straight-A honor student studying criminal justice, just like her daddy wanted. She was also a virgin, owner of a body explored by few men, conquered by none.

In contrast, Michael Roberts was a dropout, a slacker, living on dreams of making a living with his guitar. Perhaps he'd chosen her because she was everything a boy from the wrong side of the tracks shouldn't be able to attain: the daughter of a prominent judge, a man poised to take his career up the ladder into the realm of national politics.

She anad Michael should have mixed like oil and water.
Quite the opposite.

They came together like a flame to a stick of dynamite. The
first time they'd made love, Kendra had shaken for hours over
the first orgasm she'd ever had without the help of a battery-
operated boyfriend. Losing her virginity had also been a relief.
Carrying that stigma around in college life had been like wearing a sign that said LOSER.

The water was cooling, so Kendra lifted a foot out of the
water and flicked on the tap. A gush of hot water shimmered
over her body. Mmmm. It would be much nicer to have a pair
of nice, strong hands stroking her skin. Given that there were
no hands around offering to caress her, she supposed she'd have
to make do with the hot bath.

Flipping off the flow, she wished Michael were here, eager
and available to scratch the sexual itch she'd recently developed.
Since hallucinating her encounter with the dreamy demon, all
she could think about was sex in every way, shape and form.
While she and Michael had had a pretty nice sex life, the things
she'd imagined doing with Remi defied physical limitations.

She'd always tried to please Michael, eager to do anything he
asked. It was only natural. For her daddy she'd worked to be
the perfect daughter. A high achiever, she was more than eager
to please. But the two most important men in her life had clashed,
and in the space of less than six months, everything good had
gone terribly awry.

Taking a deep breath, Kendra slid down into the water,
briefly disappearing underneath. As her father was a rigid and
unbending personality, conservative in every way, it was only
natural that Nathaniel Carter would explode like an atom bomb
when she'd introduced him to Michael. A struggling, unedu-
cated musician was the last thing the judge envisioned for his
only daughter. In the back of her mind, Kendra couldn't help
but wonder if she'd chosen Michael to set her father off, shake

up the staid and stolid life he seemed to want to inflict on her and Gerald. He'd tried to do it to Abigail, his second wife and Gerald's mother, with tragic results.

Abigail and Nathaniel had met when Kendra was born. Kendra had never known her mother, aware of her existence only through several faded photographs. She had not a single memory of the woman who'd died delivering her. The name Renee Jessup Carter meant nothing to her. As though betrayed by his first wife's untimely death, Nathaniel Carter had never spoken her name aloud. Not once in Kendra's lifetime.

Her father had definitely been a stiff-upper-lip man.

She grimaced. *Or a crotchety old bastard.* Though respected for his principles and integrity, the late judge had not been a popular man.

Until the age of ten, Kendra had known only Abigail as her mother—and Gerald as her brother, five years her senior. Gerald's own father had passed away the day Kendra's mother had died, a heart attack at the age of thirty-one. And so it was that two recently bereaved people—each with a young child—had come together in grief. Somehow it only made sense they should fall in love and get married.

The marriage was not a success.

Browbeaten, berated and bullied through a decade of marriage that had revealed Abigail to be a less-than-perfect spouse, Abigail had committed suicide when Kendra was ten years old. At fifteen years of age, Gerald had been devastated to lose his mother. She had been his sole ally against the old man who'd adopted him but never really treated him as a son.

Kendra, on the other hand, had been the apple of her father's eye. Which was probably what had prompted the old man to make sure most of the assets from the living trust he'd set up for his estate were under her control.

Suddenly losing her breath, Kendra bolted to the surface of the water. Mouth open, water dripping from her skin, she took in great heaving gulps of air. A tortured sound scraped past her lips. Her head hurt, and an inexplicable ache gripped her heart.

She pressed a hand to her forehead, mentally willing the twinge not to turn into an oncoming freight train. She couldn't stand any more headaches. Or the demons they unleashed.

Don't think about those things anymore, she warned herself. The past was gone, as dead and cold as her father and stepmother in their graves. Digging up their bodies and examining their corpses wasn't only painful, it was wholly unnecessary. Abigail had been a harmless, pretty little ditz who couldn't organize her checkbook or sew a seam on a little girl's skirt. All bubbles and giggles, Abigail had been light and fun until the realities of an unsuitable marriage had set in. An addiction to alcohol and too many sedatives had followed in the wake of disillusionment and disappointment. Divorce was forbidden to Catholics. Therefore she'd chosen what she perceived to be the lesser, more honorable sin.

Suicide.

As much as Kendra had loved her father, she knew his faults exactly. Her father, all perfection and public performance, had been a tyrant behind closed doors. Even in death he'd tried to maintain total control by giving his daughter his estate. Nathaniel Carter had never liked his stepson, nor trusted that Gerald would grow up into a responsible man. Since Abigail's death, the two had clashed to the point where it seemed one man would surely murder the other.

Kendra's insides tightened. A Mercedes driven too fast on a rainy night had accomplished what Gerald never had the nerve to do.

Brow wrinkling, Kendra looked around. After Abigail's death her father had shut down this suite of rooms in the east wing, preferring to close it down rather than face the terrible truth that his second wife had chosen to take her own life inside these walls.

Staring at the ceiling without really seeing it, a vague memory, long tucked away, emerged.

Abigail died here.

Smacking her hand against her forehead, Kendra instantly groaned. Barely ten at the time of her stepparent's death, she hadn't really understood the circumstances of her passing. She'd viewed opening up the old suite and taking it over as her own as a move of independence after her father's passing. The ramifications of her choice now had made a belated appearance.

Kendra's heart rose up into her throat, and she blinked against the tears stinging her eyes.

Gerald had found her unconscious in this very place, the apparent victim of an overdose.

Just like his mother.

The pain in her head unexpectedly doubled, crushing her brain and pushing against its confines. All warmth drained away. She was suddenly as cold as an ice cube and of the opinion she would never feel warm again.

A groan escaped her as nausea rolled through her stomach. No wonder Gerald was treating her like some fragile object, walking around on eggshells, hardly having anything to do with her. Why had she never put two and two together? Five years older than her, he would clearly remember his mother and her tragic demise. Having to repeat the experience with a sister—even if they weren't connected by blood—must have been devastating for him.

Kendra took several deep breaths in a desperate attempt to quell the razorlike cramps slashing at the lining of her stomach. Instead a bitter wad of phlegm rose in her throat. She gagged and then gulped it back down. Her serene getaway presently held all the appeal of a cemetery at midnight.

She sniffed to clear her throat, to breathe.

Before moving into the wing, she'd had it gutted, completely redecorated. Plaster and paint, new carpeting and furniture, every effort had been made to wipe away all traces of the old. In having everything razed and redone, she'd unwittingly rolled over every memory Gerald must have held dear about his mother. At the time she'd seen it as an attempt to renew and rebuild her own life. She had so desperately wanted to take control of that life. So desperately wanted to embrace happiness.

She closed her eyes and rubbed her lids with the heels of her hands. *What an insensitive clod I've been.*

Clambering out of the chilly water, Kendra reached for her robe. She was aware of her hollow, raspy breathing, of her skin blanketed with goose bumps. If only her blood didn't feel so hot and her skin as cold as ice.

Shaky hands fumbled with silky material, a stupid piece of lingerie to own. Her heart thumped wildly, and a painful sensation nipped at the bridge of her nose. The back of her throat felt terribly parched. She could use a drink. A nice glass of pinot grigio chilled on ice would be nice.

Too damn bad she couldn't have any.

After a thirty-day stint in rehab, she was completely dry and no longer needed alcohol. She'd even managed to convince herself that her daily wine consumption had never actually been an addiction but a way to numb her feelings once in a while. She enjoyed her wine. It should have been no big deal.

Except the *"no big deal"* had left her passed out cold on her bedroom floor on more than one occasion.

With the headache pounding at the door of her mind, all she wanted to do was run away, hide in a dark hole from which she would never have to emerge. She knew there was no such dark corner, though. No easy way to free herself from the past or the mistakes she'd made.

She pressed her lips into a thin line. There was only tomorrow. And the hope it would be better.

6

Kendra had a hellacious headache now, the intensity of which told her she would soon be in the throes of a full migraine attack.

Determined to head the damn thing off before it got any worse, she popped an over-the-counter sedative into her mouth, swallowing it with a gulp of water from the tap. She needed to relax, clear her mind and body of stress.

Her private suite was decorated with a touch of the tropics, something that reminded of her light, air and sunshine. Beneath her feet, plush carpeting in a rich shade of beige stretched out like the sandy beach of a Caribbean island. Thick wallpaper bearing a delicate, pale wash of a tropical scene lent a sense of tranquility. Linen draperies matching the carpeting hung over the windows, tied aside to let the sun and air stream through. When the draperies were let down, the room turned dim and deliciously cool, even on the hottest of days.

In keeping with the light, tropical theme, the furnishings were fashioned from wicker. The design was simple but elegant. The treasure of the suite was the huge canopied bed guarded by matching bed tables boasting antique oil-burning lamps.

A fireplace with a wintry marble mantel provided heat during colder weather and also a romantic place for lovers to cuddle—not that she remembered much about that bit of foreplay.

Her shoulders slumped, and her head dipped forward. Desire painfully burned in her blood. *How long has it been?* Heading toward her bed, she sighed. Too long.

Both lamps were presently lit, their wicks sucking up the oil inside their fat bellies. The last couple of days had been a blur. It had rained or drizzled without cessation, the dampness and grayness felt by all. The steady drumming of hard rain filled her ears, punctuated here and there with rumblings of thunder. With the electricity out and the phone lines downed by the storm, the house was a place truly cut off from the outside world.

Her bedroom was foggy with the thick smoke emanating from the silver incense burner. Acquired from a new-age shop that specialized in healing through nature—not narcotics—sandalwood, musk and cinnamon had been carefully blended with herbs to produce a restful sleep when the smoke was repeatedly inhaled.

Clad only in her robe, Kendra sat down on the bed. She ran her palms over the handsewn quilt she sat upon, feeling its pattern beneath her fingers. This was the sole relic from her mother, a woman who'd sat and sewn every stitch by hand as she'd awaited her daughter's birth. The workmanship was expert, the mattress beneath it invitingly soft.

Determined to beat the migraine at its own game, she sighed and lay back with her arms winged out. She was tired but not with the degree of exhaustion she had come to expect since the accident.

She took a deep breath and then another, filling her lungs before slowly exhaling the air. That helped relax her. Closing her eyes, she concentrated on centering her thoughts, forming a mental picture in her mind. Of herself. Heaving the pain away like garbage.

Here she was safe. Here she was calm.

Her headache receded. Not a lot. But enough to be bearable.

Home. If nothing else, her late father's estate offered her absolute privacy and isolation from the outside world. If she didn't wish to see anyone, she didn't have to. She'd dropped out of college after his death, saying she would go back—but not really intending to. Her studies had bored her to tears, as criminal justice definitely hadn't been her choice to pursue. Given the chance, she would have continued her career as a pianist and studied music. Perhaps that was why she'd been so drawn to Michael Roberts. He had the passion and the gumption to pursue his dream, and damn all naysayers.

How different her own life might have been if only she'd had the nerve to stand up to her father. Insist upon following her own path, rather than the one he'd plotted for her. But the judge had been determined to have his way and had levered verbal intimidation and financial manipulation against her with the greatest of skill.

It was Michael who'd encouraged her to break out of her father's grip, daring her to begin thinking about her own wants and needs—not those her father doled out in so many commands. The old man would have been pleased, though, to know that she and Michael were no longer together. In the end, he'd gotten his way.

Kendra's mouth quirked down. *Chalk up the final win for Daddy.*

Shaking her head, Kendra drew in another deep breath of the scented air. Although the migraine was slowly fading, her head still ached. Once again she was digging into mental graves best left undisturbed.

The grandfather clock in the foyer outside her room intoned the hour. Eleven chimes temporarily drowned out the harsh staccato of the rain pelting the exterior walls. In an hour, it would be midnight.

Her reverie interrupted, Kendra focused her hearing to detect another sound in the mansion. Nothing. The house was a tomb. Hollow. As still as death.

The flames of the oil-burning lamps unexpectedly dipped drastically to the left, as if brushed by a strong breeze. But there was none, and, apprehensively, she turned and tried to see within the lurking shadows.

Nothing.

Kendra closed her eyes for a moment and then opened and rubbed them. The house was huge and old. Drafts weren't unusual.

She settled back down, listening to the rain pattering against the roof. Her eyelids lowered again. With such a night howling outside, it wasn't surprising her thoughts had strayed to the strange episode she'd suffered in the library. During these fitful times, her mind had drifted back to the demon who had seduced her.

Remi. Bringer of revelation.

He had seemed so real. Felt so real.

Slowly, she lifted a hand to her mouth and traced her lips with her fingertips. The memory of the demon's kisses were vivid enough she'd almost swear that Remi had, in fact, appeared.

Although her logical mind told her it had been a hallucination, her body swore it hadn't. It vaguely occurred to her there might be a reason she'd dreamed such an erotic encounter. The event was disturbing, almost too vivid.

I haven't had sex since Michael dumped me. Her dance card was empty; no potential suitors were knocking on her door. She'd given up sex, and not because she wanted to. After her fiancé had unceremoniously kicked her to the curb, she'd crawled off to lick her wounds, subconsciously suppressing her sexuality. She'd decided she didn't want sex, nor did she need it.

Wrong.

Lately she'd been hornier than ever and dying to scratch the itch. The sole things holding her back were her own inhibitions.

On impulse, Kendra reached for one of her pillows. She lay on her side, holding the pillow against her for a time, more than a bit embarrassed by the intention creeping into her head.

Right now, all she had were her own hands—and a sexual ache that was about to drive her insane. She wanted all her senses to feel alive and to experience making love again.

Tucking the pillow under her head, Kendra closed her eyes. Using one hand, she pushed her robe away from one breast, baring it. Her nipple poked up, rosy and hard. She circled the tip with a finger, slowly tracing the sensitive areola. Liquid warmth immediately spread through her veins, pooling between her thighs. Aching need quivered through her.

Lifting and bending her legs, she spread them and slipped her fingertips between her silky labia. Tremors of pleasure coursed through her as her fingers massaged her clit. Adding to the fantasy, she imagined her demon lover awakening her sexuality, his mouth suckling at her breasts and his scent coming directly from his naked skin.

Her orgasm came swiftly and fiercely, and she gasped from the heated depths of its throes.

Drained emotionally and physically, she opened her eyes to peer into the semidarkness of her room. Air shifted against her face like a frigid, moist caress. The sound of her heart thumping against her chest seemed inordinately loud, and her breath came in raspy, reedy spurts.

"Remi," she murmured, her voice hollow with unintended longing. "I'm waiting for you."

Aching with loneliness, she felt an irrational need to cry and laugh at the same time. Perhaps she would have if a deep, amused voice hadn't shocked her senseless.

"Shame on you," he tsked. "Looks like you have started without me."

Jolted out of her dreamy reverie, Kendra scrambled to close her legs, clutch her robe around her breasts. Her vision momentarily blurred, and her head reeled when she tried to sit up. Where had the voice come from?

She blinked hard to clear her vision and swung her gaze back to the room around her. At first she wasn't sure what was charging toward her. A shadowy blur shot out of one far corner, rapidly shifting shape and brightening as it closed the distance. She could no longer see her bedroom or even the glow of the lamps at her bedside.

In an instant she recognized the familiar figure materializing in the heart of the luminance. The oxygen slowly drizzled out of her lungs.

It can't be, she thought wildly.

It was.

Remi stood at the side of the bed, grinning at her. Once again, he was almost naked, and the well-muscled breadth of his shoulders seemed magnified in the lantern's glow. His loincloth hugged his slender hips, on which his clenched hands were positioned.

Mortification threatened to incinerate her. How long had he been standing there? Had he seen—

Kendra gulped, embarrassment heating her face. She could hardly believe her eyes. "Oh, God, you're back." She didn't remember falling asleep, but it didn't matter. Whether wide awake or lost in slumber, one thing remained the same.

The demon had come back.

Remi's stare was penetrating beneath half-lidded eyes, almost intimate in their appraisal. He didn't conceal the fact he was pleased by what he saw. A smile turned up one corner of his mouth, and one eyebrow arched appreciatively. "I'm not God, but thanks for the compliment."

Stepping forward, he placed a knee on the bed and took hold of her right wrist. He lifted her toward him, pulling her into a sitting position.

Through a daze, Kendra peered up to see him inhaling the telltale scent on her fingertips. His eyes were pools of sheer ecstasy.

She yanked, attempting to free her hand. "What are you doing?" she snapped, confused by his unexpected reappearance. Her heart raced. Without doubt there was something about him that made her blood stir.

Remi held on tight, dragging her hand back to his nose for another long sniff. "I love the smell of hot pussy." His chest rose and fell with each labored breath.

Close to losing all composure, Kendra wrenched her wrist out of his grip. "This can't be happening." She shivered, sick to her stomach. "You can't be real." The words left her mouth before she'd even considered how ridiculous they sounded. He certainly had a lot of strength, manhandling her as easily as a mother would her small child.

If anything, this trip back into the sinister regions of her mind was even more vivid than the first, like being lost in a sadistically twisted fun house with no way out.

Her assailant sighed at the implicit rejection. "I assure you I am quite real."

Kendra shook her head in denial. Just when she'd thought she was getting her mind back on track, this had to happen. Fear that she might indeed be losing her mind wrapped icy tentacles around her heart. *Once a demon latches on, it never lets you go.*

The manifestation dominated her vision. "No," she insisted, lifting her hands as if trying to conjure some sort of protective talisman. "You are not real. You can't be real."

He frowned. "Why not?"

She tossed out the first thing that came to mind. "Because I—I didn't s—summon you."

Remi's gaze danced. "Oh, but you did." He eyed her nearly naked form. Her thin robe might as well have melted away, for all the cover it afforded. "Or don't you recall our little bargain?"

Kendra shook her head. "I made no bargain with you," she said, shaking her head in denial. "I couldn't have struck any pact with you. You're not even real."

As if to prove her wrong, Remi reached out and again snatched her wrist. He yanked her toward him again, pulling her onto her knees this time and then nearly off the mattress. The contact between them was pure electricity. At the mattress's edge, Kendra found herself roughly forced to stand.

"I am very real," he rumbled.

Kendra wrenched free and staggered back a step, her eyes wide, her breathing labored. She stared dumbly at him. Her skin tingled as if ants were running beneath it. Her blood heated. Emotions she once believed dead came flooding back, and she didn't have the strength to deny them.

Her heart rose into her throat, and she blinked against the dryness in her eyes. "How can this be?"

Stepping closer to her, Remi placed his lips inches from her ear. Her body stiffened at his intimidating proximity. "It's what you've wanted, what you've dreamed about." His voice reached inside her chest and clutched her heart. She couldn't control the quivering in her core ignited by the touch of his warm breath on her chilly skin. "I can grant you that—and so much more. All you have to do is believe in me. Submit to me. Completely."

Tiny flares of forbidden heat sprang to life. A shiver passed through Kendra. His very nearness stirred wild sensations behind her breast, his presence expertly strumming her sexual awareness. Her bones were becoming jelly. Heat suffused her.

Confused and bewildered, she released a shuddering sigh. "I can't. . . ."

His hard gaze softened. A gentle smile parted his finely shaped mouth. "Why not?"

A fierce, gut-wrenching tremor shook through her. A choked sound came from her before she whispered achingly, "I'm afraid."

A sardonic smile twitched on his lips. "So don't be," he countered. His answer was too quick, to glib to satisfy her.

"How the fuck can I not be?" Kendra closed her eyes, mentally willing him to be gone. Far away. But when she lifted her lids, he hadn't budged an inch. Blinking to clear her mind of the turmoil, she tried to speak. "Why are you tormenting me like this?" Her voice emerged as a harsh croak.

"Because I cannot resist your call," he said in a low tone, staring into her troubled eyes.

A burning ache to cry built up in her chest. But she wouldn't. Not in front of him. She gulped a second time, forcing frozen vocal cords to function. "I've been wishing you were here," she dragged in a breath, "with me."

As if compelled by some greater force, he framed her face with his hands. He stared at her for a long moment and then brushed his one thumb tentatively across her lips. "Your wish has freed me from the pit of hell itself." After a second's hesitation, he finished softly, "For that, I am eternally grateful. To visit this earth, to walk free. To make love to a beautiful woman. It is all a gift I cannot begin to describe."

His confession stunned her. Heat surfaced again in her cheeks, but she refused to break her visual lock with him. "You think I—I'm beautiful?" she stammered.

The demon nodded. "The most beautiful woman I have ever seen." His voice was warm. Tender. Hardly the voice of a demon in command. More like a humble lover, supplicant and grateful.

7

Like a curtain swept aside to reveal the stage, it suddenly occurred to Kendra exactly which one of them held the power. At first, she'd believed Remi was the one playing with all the winning cards, toying with and manipulating her at his leisure.

Wrong. All wrong. His own words had, in fact, tipped his hand.

A demon was summoned.

To serve the will of its conjurer.

Kendra heaved a breath to calm her racing pulse, and she stepped closer to him. Closing the distance, she wrapped her arms around his neck and leaned into him. His muscles bunched beneath her touch. Tension crackled between them. She was conscious of the heat in his body. Of the heart thudding in his chest. But she was especially aware of the hardness pressing against the front of his loincloth.

She had to admit Remi fascinated her for all the wrong reasons. A sane woman would have fled, ran screaming from the room. Was her determination to have him again a product of her newfound belief in herself, or a destructive remnant of the old Kendra Carter? "I think," she murmured, "that I've got you figured out."

Remi's attention settled on her parted lips. He drew in a deep breath and released it slowly. A poorly suppressed shudder worked through him before his hands lifted to rest on her hips. "You believe so?"

She nodded. "Oh, yes. I've listened to my brother ramble on a time or two about the occult. I'm aware that the conjurer must take caution when dealing with demons. Your bunch is a sneaking lot, I know, and a demon who isn't controlled can easily get out of hand."

Realizing things had taken a turn, his eyebrows drew down in a show of stormy resentment. He tightened his grip on her hips. "And you think you 'control' me?"

His words and tone indicated displeasure, but Kendra held her ground, refusing to be bullied. "I think I do."

Remi brought up his right hand to caress her cheek. "Perhaps we control each other because we each have needs the other can fulfill." He chuckled softly and then brushed his lips across hers in a feathery kiss.

"Careful," she said, her voice low and husky. Sexual awareness spread through her like wildfire. All of a sudden, he was a giant, all muscle and heated flesh and more masculine than any man she had ever encountered.

Remi's turbulent gaze centered on her parted lips. "I can't help myself," he confessed. "All I want is to touch you all over, please you in every way imaginable."

Kendra's heart raced at the prospect of another round of lovemaking—this time when she was wide awake and very aware. "Then do it," she said. "Take me. Any way you want." Expectation trilled through her as she rested a hand on his chest, not to stop him but to encourage him to take what he wanted.

What she wanted.

What they both needed.

Slowly, Remi leaned toward her, his head tilting to one side. Kendra expected the kiss to be slow, sensual. Instead he pulled her body against his, kissing her so passionately her fear, her doubt, her hesitations all slipped away into nothingness. He tasted of darkness and power, and his commanding embrace sent out sparks of heat.

An erotic pulse of sheer bliss hummed through Kendra. Her migraine was gone now, completely forgotten. She was rapidly becoming lost to the experience, a woman on the verge of infinite rapture, a woman desperate to feel emotional warmth again.

She told herself she was a fool to succumb to lust. A fool to succumb to fleeting pleasure. A fool to lower her protective barriers, her defenses against the torments of needing the companionship of a demonic lover.

"I want you," he whispered as their lips parted. "Here and now." He nibbled at her left earlobe while his right hand cupped and kneaded one of her breasts.

Arms still locked around his neck, Kendra grinned up at him. "And you think you're just going to throw me on the bed and fuck me senseless?"

Eyes dancing, he nodded. "That's exactly what I intend to do."

"Not so fast." Kendra wiggled out of his arms, away from the bed. "This time, you're going to earn it." She whirled away from his reach.

Remi made a grab for her, but she eluded him. "Teasing a demon is not appropriate," he warned, flexing his fingers. "Once I get my hands on you—"

Kendra seductively ran her hands over her pert breasts, her flat belly, her hips. Her own excitement was evident. Her chest was heaving, breasts rising and falling. Her nipples were hard, swollen. "You'll what?"

This time he did not try to grab her. "I will pound you until you scream my name," he rumbled, his frustration growing apparent. His voice had a strangled tone to it, the suffocated sound of a man in lust. His erection surged beneath his thin loincloth.

Outside in the foyer, the clock struck midnight. Twelve long chimes rang out, each strike thrumming through Kendra's body like a fevered pulse. It was the witching hour, and a demon desired her.

She looked at him, delighted to discover his gaze fixed intently on her bare body. Her robe had come open.

Realizing what he wanted, she slid the robe off her shoulders, letting it pool around her feet. She stood, naked and proud, showing him every flaw, every blemish. "Do you like what you see?"

Remi visually explored every curve of her bare skin. He seemed mesmerized by every inch of her. He nodded. "Yes. Very much."

Kendra looked back at him, remembering the first time he'd taken off his loincloth to reveal himself. Magnificent.

Her gaze caressed the outline of his penis, his arousal more than obvious beneath the thin material. Her tongue delicately moistened her mouth in a slow and sensual way, an unconscious desire to do the same to his lovely cock.

"You can touch me," she invited. "All over my body."

This time, he caught her, pulling her into his embrace. "Why has it taken you so long to summon me?"

Kendra could smell the scent of him, feel the heat of his body pressing against her. He was solid, real, living flesh. "I didn't know how," she said.

"Any time you wish me to come, just say my name," he instructed.

"Remi," she murmured, liking the way his name sounded on her lips.

He slid his fingers through her damp hair, ruffling the short layers. His head dipping, his lips grazed hers. "Never hesitate to call me."

Kendra smiled and shook her head. "Never."

To put them both out of their misery, his lips claimed hers with another hot, deep kiss. Lips and tongues met, mating eagerly.

At the same time, Remi's hands explored her skin, reveling in her nudity. He kept pulling her closer, rubbing, touching, tasting, clearly eager to explore.

A soft moan escaped Kendra's lips when he ran his hands up her rib cage. He cupped her firm breasts with both hands, relished the feel of them in his hands. His fingers found and began to tease the pebbled nipples.

"That feels so good," Kendra gasped, feeling the tips harden even more under his touch. She ached for him to suck them. She shivered and lifted one leg toward his hips when he began to gently roll and squeeze one sensitive tip.

Clearly sensing her need, Remi slipped one strong arm around her waist. "It's about to feel better."

Breath raspy in her throat, Kendra closed her eyes and leaned back, giving him all access. Her pulse was racing. She shivered, welcoming the anticipation rushing through her veins. Her thoughts were starting to spin out of control. She didn't think to question how he had come to be there, holding her. She just knew she wanted him, would do anything to have him.

Remi slowly slid one hand along the plane of her flat abdomen, tracing the path of one particularly wicked scar traveling up between her breasts. The raw power of his touch encased her, holding her immobile. Her scar felt alive under his hand, wriggling with an unearthly life all its own. The sensation mesmerized. And enticed.

Kendra bit back a moan. "I've never felt that before," she gasped. "It's like the scars are alive."

He traced another finger over the curve of her left breast. "Such damages give the skin an entirely new way to enjoy sensation."

She shivered, responding with a deep, sultry, "I never thought they'd add anything to my sex life."

Remi arched a wicked brow. "They're about to add a whole lot." Bending, he licked one nipple, letting his breath warm the bud.

Kendra gasped and writhed against him. "Oh, my," she groaned. Her voice held a sultry lilt, letting him know she was definitely in the mood for a frantic, hot, mindless fucking.

Remi, however, wasn't in any hurry to grant her wish. With a little moan of eagerness, he slowly drew one cherry-tinged nipple into his mouth.

Still suckling, he slid his free hand down to her mound. Finding her damp heat, he slipped his hand between her parted thighs. His fingers traced silken lips dripping with her juices. He rubbed his fingers over her clit—softly at first and then applying more pressure when a soft whimper broke from her lips.

"Is this what you want?"

Bucking against his hand, Kendra moaned. "Mmmm . . . yes, I do. . . ." Her clit ached. Her core boiled, desperate for the sweetest release.

In answer, Remi slid his fingers deep into her. He began to stroke in and out, slowly at first and then building the momentum. "First my fingers," he grated in promise. "Then my cock."

Kendra shuddered all over. Her body shook as her vaginal walls clenched tightly around his fingers. Remi held her tightly around the waist, supporting her so she would not fall as she gave herself to his pleasurable touch.

He pressed his fingers deeper inside her. "Come for me."

Propelled by his sexy command, Kendra started to tremble.

Need was a blistering fire, eating her up inside. Her hips bucked against his hand; her vagina. Her heart flipped over, its beat driven by the power of his words. "I—I . . ." she stuttered and then lost all ability to speak.

Remi held her tighter as climax began to overtake her. To help her along, he pushed his fingers deeper, withdrawing, and then pushing inside again. Moving inside her, in and out, he was driving her crazy with the friction. "Let me see your release."

Kendra obeyed. She could barely wait.

She was going to lose it. Now.

Remi's fingers thrust up into her again, lifted her with a fast, hard jolt. A hot rush of pure heat followed, roaring through her like a train without brakes.

Kendra felt soft wetness close around his fingers even as her entire body began to quiver. A sharp, cracking thunderclap filled her ears, mingling with the moan slipping past her lips. Her hips gyrated, her clit screaming out with delight as a searing bolt of pleasure struck all at once.

Coming apart at the seams, she shattered into a million tiny pieces. Her cries of pleasure echoed throughout the room. She'd never climaxed without direct stimulation, and Remi clearly knew which buttons needed to be pushed to take her over the edge.

And he'd pushed all the right ones in all the right ways.

When she stopped moaning and her body relaxed, Remi slowly let his fingers slide out. "That was beautiful," he murmured, lifting her up and kissing her damp brow.

Utterly exhausted, Kendra sagged against him, fighting to catch her breath. Wisps of damp hair fell haphazardly across her face. A light sheen of perspiration glazed her skin, testament to the intensity of her climax.

She wiped the damp strands out of her eyes. "Glad you think so," she gasped.

Remi grasped her hips, pulling her against his length, rubbing their bodies gently together. His cock was rock hard, aching for its own release. He teased one erect nipple. "What makes it nice is that you enjoyed the pleasure," he said. He gave the little nub a gentle pull, sending tiny shock waves all the way down to her clit.

Gasping, Kendra still tried to catch her breath. Renewed desire rushed through her like wildfire. "Every time you touch me, I want to come," she confessed.

Quirking a brow, his mouth widened into a wicked smile. "Oh, I am not finished." Briefly breaking their bodies apart, he bent. Sweeping her up in his arms, he carried her toward the bed. "By no means is this night over."

8

As Remi laid Kendra on the bed, a delighted grin spread across her face. The want, the compulsion, the desire to give herself to him completely and without hesitation pulsed through her body.

For a breathless instant everything seemed to stop as he hovered over her. There was a humming in the air generated not by the thunder and lightning dashed down from the storm but by something else. Almost as if their own two bodies were giving off some sort of electric force. Though Remi stood inches away, Kendra clearly felt the heat from his body.

She opened her arms. "It's bad manners to keep a lady waiting."

Remi's gaze explored every inch of her, visually tracing every curve. "You're so beautiful," he said in a hushed voice. "I just want to look and to worship." His statement sounded absolutely sincere.

Stuck by his quiet, serious tone, she sat up on the bed. "You say that as if you mean it."

He nodded slowly. "I do." Looking over her nude form

again, heat burned through his eyes until Kendra could have sworn she felt him inside her.

She shivered. "Then this is a dream, I'm sure."

Climbing onto the bed, he stretched out beside her. When he next touched her, it was to press his warm lips on her forehead. "It is no dream."

She looked up at him. "You keep playing that record, and I might begin to believe it."

He leaned in, nibbling on her lips. "Believe it always."

"I want to," she whispered, sliding one hand up his muscular arm, leaning in to taste his lips again. "But somehow I think when the sun rises, you'll be gone again."

Remi's lips were warm, skimming over her chin and then down the curve of her neck. "Then we must make love before the sun rises," he breathed against her skin.

Kendra caught her breath and shifted, giving him a silent invitation to do as he wished. "I would love to." She definitely wanted him inside her again, thick, hot and pulsing. Just the thought of him taking her, claiming her, made her clit simmer with anticipation. How she wanted to rip off that loincloth he wore, spread her legs and guide him into her, feeling his hard—

"Mmmm." She licked her lips. "The sooner, the better."

Remi laughed softly. "How about the slower, the better?" The swell of his erection pressed against one of her thighs like a branding iron.

And then he slipped lower, his lips caressing the curve of her breasts, even as his fingers began teasing one nipple until the tip was hard and round. Her nipples were both flushed a deep, rosy shade.

Kendra jolted as the delight of his touch traveled straight down to her core. She suppressed her enjoyment when he attacked her other breast. His head dipped, tongue flicking out to taste a tender bud. The gentle pressure made her whole body jerk. She moaned, tangling her fingers in his thick hair, drawing him closer. Lust swamped her, dragging her away to an exotic place she'd never before dared to imagine. All she could do was lay there and feel the moist slide of his mouth on her skin.

With a merciless drag of his tongue over the tip, Remi continued his exquisite torment. He began to suckle harder, teasing each nipple in turn, giving each long, slow licks as if tasting a delicious nectar.

When he nipped one gently with his teeth as he twisted the other with his fingers, Kendra nearly hit the ceiling. With each pull on her sensitive nipples he drove her closer to release. Adrenaline surged through her veins, mixing with excitement and pure euphoria.

Struggling to squelch the sounds threatening to rise up over her lips, she arched back against the mattress. The ache between her thighs burned like a thousand suns ablaze. Her clit pulsed furiously, fiercely. Nothing could extinguish the need blazing through her except that delicious cock of his.

"That feels so damned good," she finally gasped.

Remi grinned up at her. He kissed his way down her abdomen, stopping a moment to dip his moist tongue into the dip of her navel, finding nerve endings she'd never before known existed.

He dipped again, giving the little cleft a lingering lick. Her core surged, reaching for the orgasm just out of reach. Before she could make full contact, it slipped through her fingers. Hovering. Just waiting for the right second. Then its full power would detonate.

Kendra growled. "Damnit, I was so close." If he didn't touch her between the legs soon, she would explode into a billion shards of frustration. Though she'd already had one delicious orgasm, she was greedy and wanted more. Many more.

"Patience," Remi counseled, finding the nest of soft curls covering her mons.

Catching her breath, Kendra wriggled her hips against his hand. "That's what I want," she breathed. The words were a hiss from her lips, dry now from the eager rasp of her breath. "And your mouth." Not a very subtle hint, but hopefully an effective one. To make sure he got the message, she lifted her legs, bending them at the knee. And opened. Wide.

Rolling over on his stomach, Remi positioned himself between her spread thighs. "I've been intending to revisit this delight," he said, his voice husky with strain. He dove in for the feast.

Kendra gave a primitive cry as he parted her silky labia and splashed a quick lick against her protruding clit.

Remi briefly glanced up, eyeing her shuddering body. "You taste delicious," he informed her with a grin. Diving down again, his tongue circled the small hooded organ until she began to squirm with pleasure.

Reacting to the sensual assault, Kendra felt a small, warm shiver press its way up her spine. "Glad you approve," she gasped.

Without answering, Remi began to suckle the little nub, his tongue beginning a waltz that set her hips into motion.

Kendra closed her eyes to better concentrate on the sensations—like a thousand little bottle rockets taking off at once, speeding toward the horizon. Her body seemed to escape her control, moving with a wildness of its own.

The sensations were so fantastically intense she wanted to shout and scream at the same time. His oral skills were wonderful, hitting all the right spots with the perfect pressure to deliver exquisite satisfaction.

Climax built, threatening to erupt. She drew in a sharp breath, wanting those wonderful vibrations of arousal to last forever. She was quivering, need stringing her tighter than a guitar string.

Michael Roberts had been the only other man to ever go

down on her, but his technique had never come close to what Remi was doing. Though Michael had turned her on (or at least she thought he had), nothing he'd done had ever come close to the searing hot, relentless assault Remi's touch delivered.

Just when Remi had taken her to the edge, he would draw back, letting her cool down a moment before sending her temperature rising into the red zone again. She shuddered under each slick caress of his tongue, her hips grinding at every touch until every nerve in her body was wound tighter than a yo-yo.

At the vital moment, Remi's fingers joined his tongue. Fastening his lips around her clit, he pushed two fingers into her buttery slit.

Rapture slammed into her gut like a fist. It dragged a cry from her, made her body jolt with shock. Her hips bucked against his mouth as molten lava poured through her veins. Her climax was fierce, setting her whole body trembling. It seemed to go on endlessly, lifting her to a plateau she'd never reached with any other man.

She came back to Earth reluctantly, gasping for air, her heart pounding fiercely against her rib cage. She felt like clay that had been shaped and reshaped until the perfect form had been attained.

Preening like a tomcat, Remi gave her a lazy smile and shifted his body, tugging his loincloth away from his narrow hips. His cock arched up against an abdomen as hard as concrete. The massive red crown strained, ruling over a vein-covered length.

Remi's eyes glittered with fierce desire as he stretched out over her dazed, perspiration-soaked form. "I've been aching to feel that tight cunt of yours again," he breathed.

Through half-lidded eyes, Kendra watched him settle his hips between her spread thighs. Her pulse began to race as he guided the tip of his erection toward her waiting sex. She lifted her head to stare down between their bodies, riveted by the sight of his penis poised to enter her.

She lifted a leg, winding it around his waist until the heel of her foot was propped comfortably on his perfect ass. Giving him a little prod, she playfully licked her lips in anticipation. "Come on," she murmured. "Take me now. I've been aching to feel that big cock of yours."

Using just the engorged tip, Remi slowly rubbed up and down her slit but didn't enter. "I have thought about nothing else," he said in a low, rumbling groan. "Your sweet sex has bewitched my thoughts."

A groan of tension slipped past her lips. "And my sweet sex is begging for your big cock to come on inside." Arousal made her bold enough to ask for what she wanted. What she craved.

Remi's eyes were luminous with craving. Hips flexing, he pushed in, sliding the head of his penis between her labia. He stopped himself when just an inch had made penetration.

Kendra opened willingly, whimpering a little in delight. The heat and promise staggered her. Need was immediate. Every neuron in her body went on instant alert. "That's not enough," she grated between clenched teeth. For a moment she was still, savoring the sensations. "I want more." Anticipation threatened to smother her.

Breath hitching in his throat, Remi granted her another searing inch. The struggle for command drew his handsome features taut. "Is it me you want?" he asked, brushing a spicy kiss against her lips. "Or my beautiful cock?" The beast strained for release, but he controlled it masterfully. He trembled with the effort of holding himself back.

Intrigued by the taste of her feminine juices, Kendra eagerly suckled at his mouth. "Both," she whispered against his lips. A wave of anticipation swept over her, and her body convulsed, desiring more contact.

It was all he needed to hear.

Like a diver cutting cleanly through the water, Remi plunged deep, sliding into the heated depths of her sex.

The abrupt sensation of fullness made Kendra cry out softly. She wrapped her other leg around his waist, locking her ankles together to keep him planted. His shaft felt wonderful, filling her to the last inch—and more.

Sliding his arms under hers, Remi pillowed her head in his huge palms, tilting her head back so his mouth could plunder her mouth the way his cock conquered her sex. His kisses were intense and greedy.

Pressed beneath his weight, Kendra plastered her palms to his bare back, reveling in the pulse of hot muscle beneath her hands. All gentleness was lost between them as need turned into something desperate, something hungry, something devouring.

Remi's hips ground against hers, forcing his cock deeper than she'd ever thought possible. She greeted each pummeling blow with joy, loving the sweet ache until waves of liquid heat began to shimmer through her from head to toe.

The air around them was redolent with the scent of sandalwood, cinnamon and the sweat generated between two bodies swept away by furious, unremitting sexual passion.

A violent climax nearly ripped through Kendra's body. Biting into his shoulder, she pressed her fingernails deeply into his flesh, digging slashes of crimson down his back. Desperation snapped at her heels. "Harder!" she urged. "I want to come with you inside me."

Obeying her command, Remi slammed hard a final time, his thrust triggering the magic needed to carry her over the edge into the abyss of complete bliss. In the blink of an eye, everything changed.

She cried out raggedly as Remi's cock surged inside her, setting off a multitude of ripples, a widening circle of liquid sensation that filled her core to overflowing. At the same time, Remi's body stiffened. His shudders were violent, as if the experience were excruciatingly painful for him. A low moan spilled from his lips. Warm semen jetted, sending a burst of red-hot sensation rushing through her, driven by an intensity that threatened to split her apart at the seams.

Shaking and quivering under his weight, Kendra silently nudged him to roll onto his side.

Remi did so without hesitation.

Naked and uncovered, they lay facing each other, entwined in the afterglow of sensations—most of which, for Kendra, was a gentle throb between her thighs.

He stroked a warm palm down her face. "I felt your climax."

Kendra smiled shyly. Her body still trembled from the force of her release. "I did come." She snuggled into his body, amazed at how wonderfully their bodies fit together. It was as though they had been made for each other.

Remi's strong arms enveloped her, drawing her farther into a cocoon of warmth. "When you have had a little rest, I will make you come again." He flicked a kiss onto her lips. "And again."

Exhaustion fled in the wake of his promise.

Slipping a hand between their bodies, Kendra cupped his warm penis, impressive even when flaccid. She grinned. "Who the hell needs sleep?"

9
_____

Sunlight was flooding her bedroom when Kendra forced herself to wake up. The clock at her bedside read nine. Exactly. She yawned and stretched. Her muscles ached, and the temptation to succumb to two or three additional hours of sleep was difficult to resist—until Remi crept into her mind.

She sat up, half expecting to find him sleeping beside her.

But her mysterious lover had again vanished, leaving her in an empty bed with empty arms. Aching.

A low groan escaped her as she surveyed the empty room around her, the incense burned down to ashes, the oil lamps at her bedside sucked dry.

An image flashed through her mind of Remi naked upon her bed, his cock hard and surging with anticipation. It was so vivid, she shuddered.

But she'd only had a dream.

A very erotic dream.

With the demon. Making love. To her.

Kendra hugged herself as a strange chill coursed through

her. The prospect of having a demon haunting her in her sleep—even if he was pleasuring her—was more frightening than anything she'd encountered. Conjuring an imaginary lover went beyond the boundaries of a sane mind. She was in a vulnerable position, needing sympathy and reassurance to rebuild her life.

Kendra frowned at the unbidden images of Remi kissing her. Touching her. Penetrating her.

Remembering his every sensual caress, her heart slammed against her chest wall and then seemed to rise and lodge in her throat. Her blood turned to ice while her skin felt afire. Her lips still tingled from his consuming kisses.

In a bid to override the memory of the demon taking her, she tried to recall what she had been doing to trigger his appearance.

Nothing.

A great gap of nothingness met her mental query. Past the thunder and the lightning of the storm outside, all she remembered about the previous night was the sex.

Pure, wild, reckless sex.

A cold, biting breeze passed through her, as if mocking her memories. Her naked skin was clammy, cool and moist to the touch. It occurred to her that she never went to bed naked; she always slept in clothes—panties and a nightshirt.

Memory niggled.

Despite her initial grogginess, she sensed something in the room, something out of the norm. She had the distinct, sickening feeling some*thing* had been in her room as she'd slept. Cool, incense-laced air stirred to her left, as though someone had passed through the space.

Kendra's gaze drifted to the center of the room. Lightheadedness swept through her like a gale. Darkness closed in at the periphery of her vision, tunneling her view of the discarded piece of clothing on the floor. Her robe lay in a pile in the middle of her bedroom. In the very place she recalled slipping it off as she'd bared her body for an unholy touch. . . .

A gasp of shock and disbelief escaped. "Oh, no."

What she'd experienced last night had been no dream. She would never have just dropped her robe and gone to bed nude. It wasn't in her nature to be so cavalier, even when alone.

Turning onto her side, Kendra shut her eyes against the morning light seeping through the drawn curtains. She clutched at her midriff and drew her knees to her chest.

I've been fucked by a demon.

In her heart she felt the idea to be not only true but frighteningly real. Too real.

Something vastly more threatening, suffocating, had crept into her life. Something that, no matter how many times she satisfied her needs with it, would never be enough. An inexplicable gut feeling that the demon had somehow latched on to her—and had visited her last night—set to tormenting her, eating away at her denial like a ravenous beast determined to have its insatiable fill.

The room was chilly and quiet.

Kendra gulped several times to keep her stomach's contents from rising into her throat and blinked hard against the painful dryness of her eyes. She took several deep breaths in a desperate attempt to quell the brutal cramps slashing at the lining of her stomach.

Her hands and feet were cold, as if her circulation had come to a stop. Vivid-colored images of the fragmented remnants of Remi's lovemaking traipsed across her mind.

An omnipresent whisper burst into the room, echoing all around her. Remi's disembodied voice. *You enjoyed my touch.*

Her pulse jackhammering inside her throat, Kendra bolted up. Her hands flew up, clutching her head. Memories of his touch suddenly made her feel vulgar, filthy.

"Get out of my mind," she gasped. Her mind was awhirl with contemplations of a thing too terrible to comprehend; tears pressed for release. She was afraid if she undammed those tears, she'd surely lose what remained of her self-control.

Sick to her stomach, Kendra struggled to push herself off the bed. Half standing, half bent over, she lurched toward the bathroom, using every piece of available furniture to keep herself upright. Inside she stumbled to the tile floor, barely making it to the edge of the toilet. She vomited the contents of her stomach and then endured several minutes of dry heaves.

Pushing herself away from the porcelain bowl, she flushed away the remnants of her stomach. Lifting her listless body, she closed the toilet lid and sat on it. She was dizzied by the sudden move and bent over to cradle her head in her hands. The cramps had lessened some. In the silence, she could hear the rush of blood through her veins, feel the pressure of it against her skin.

Surely I'm not . . . she grimaced . . . *pregnant.*

The thought would have been stupid enough to make her laugh if a sharp pain hadn't immediately shot through her middle, causing her to grimace.

"Kendra?" her sister-in-law, Jocelyn, called from the bedroom door.

"I'm in here. Just a minute, okay?" Kendra turned just in time to see Jocelyn peering into the bathroom.

Concern shaded her sister-in-law's eyes. "I heard you throwing up. Are you all right?" Gerald's wife of five years, she was a plump woman in her early thirties, dressed in navy slacks and a blazer designed to conceal her bulges. She wore sensible heels, and her brown hair was fashioned in a sleek, short style. Her features were pleasant, light makeup used only to hide the puffiness under her eyes and the uneven tones of her skin. Her eyes were a lovely shade of cornflower blue, and she had an easy laugh.

Kendra slowly shook her head. "A migraine caught up with

me again, I'm afraid." She reached for a towel to cover her nudity.

Jocelyn frowned. "I'm sorry, Kendra. Is there anything I can do?"

"I'm fine now." Kendra scrunched up her face. Feeling normal again, she almost managed to convince herself the demon's visitation had been the result of the pain—a subconscious attempt to replace something unpleasant with something more palatable. Sex was certainly preferable to pain.

Dreams were such curious manifestations. And it was little wonder she was having convoluted imaginings of demons lurking: Gerald had filled her head with tales about his damned book and, for some strange reason, her subconscious had latched onto it.

"I hope so," Jocelyn said, her eyes dim with worry. "You know you can call me or Gerald anytime."

"Really, I'm fine. It was just a little headache, that's all." She sniffed. "All this damn rain has clogged my sinuses, making me absolutely miserable."

Jocelyn's eyes narrowed with sympathy. "Oh, my. Little wonder you feel so terrible then." She reached out and patted Kendra's hand. "It's supposed to rain all day. Perhaps you'd better cancel your appointment to see Dr. Somerville. Have it rescheduled when you feel better."

Since leaving rehab, Kendra had been ordered to follow up with her doctor once a week. This would be her first time seeing Dr. Somerville out of rehab.

Rescheduling was the last thing Kendra wanted to do. In fact, he was just the person she felt she needed to see.

As soon as possible.

Coldness formed in the pit of her stomach. Fighting to keep from being ill again, she swallowed hard. The last thing she needed was to be on the edge of a second nervous breakdown.

Jocelyn interrupted her thoughts. "I suppose this means

you're not up for a real breakfast. I'll tell Gabrielle to send up some toast and coffee."

The previous night's visitation fled as Kendra's stomach rumbled. "I *am* hungry," she admitted.

"That's my girl," Jocelyn exclaimed.

Kendra offered a small smile. Going downstairs and having breakfast would give her a chance to talk to her brother—pick his brain. Since laying eyes on the gem of his collection, she'd had nothing but trouble. "Tell Gerald I'll be joining you for breakfast."

Jocelyn smiled. "Excellent. I'll have Gabrielle set a place for you at the table." Bustling off, she left the bathroom.

Alone, Kendra turned on the tap to the bathtub. She added a capful of bubble bath. Carried by the steam, an aromatic scent of vanilla embraced her as she lowered herself into the water.

"I don't know what you've brought into the house, Gerald," she said for the benefit of no other ears but her own, "but if something came with that book, it's got to go."

10

Twenty minutes later, Kendra went downstairs for breakfast. There, she found Gerald and his wife in the dining room, along with Gabrielle, the housekeeper.

"You look better," Gerald commented, lowering his morning newspaper. He glanced toward his wife. "Jocelyn said you've had another migraine."

Kendra shrugged, unwilling to tell him more than she had to. "They're not as bad as they used to be."

Gerald lifted his coffee cup. "I think you should talk to a physician if they're still plaguing you. I've read that problems from head trauma can sometimes take months to appear."

"I would only agree," Jocelyn piped up.

"If that's true, surely they would have found something by now," Kendra said. "God knows I've had every test they can run and then some."

"Still," Gerald mused, "we'd rather be safe than sorry."

"Of course." Eager to put off the conversation, Kendra flagged a hand to catch the housekeeper's eye. "May I have some coffee, please?"

"Certainly, Miss Kendra," Gabrielle said, reaching for a cup from her tray. She brought Kendra a full cup, doing her best to ignore the gray cat mewling at her feet. "Here you go," she said cheerily. While Kendra inhaled the strong, rich brew, Gabrielle added, "I have bacon and pancakes ready. Are you hungry?"

Kendra added cream and sugar to her coffee. "Just toast," she said, taking a sip of her coffee. "With a little jam." Somewhere between vomiting and getting ready to see Dr. Somerville, her appetite had vanished.

Gabrielle eyed her. "You need more than toast," she huffed. "With all these sick people around here, I don't get to cook worth a damn."

Gerald shot Kendra a look of disapproval. "Oh, for God's sake, can't you have more than toast?"

Again sipping her coffee, Kendra relented. "I'll have what they're having," she finally said.

The housekeeper nodded and then disappeared. She returned a few minutes later and placed three plates in front of the table's occupants.

Kendra nearly laughed at the amount of food. Pancakes, scrambled eggs, a pile of whole-wheat toast and generous slices of bacon, all served alongside a tall glass of freshly squeezed orange juice. Doubting she could finish it all, she forced a smile for Gabrielle's benefit. "Looks fine," she said, reaching for her fork.

Jocelyn chuckled as she eyed the food. "No wonder I'm as big as a house," she lamented. She reached for the maple syrup. "I simply can't resist these things."

Gerald frowned and eyed his wife. "Resist harder."

Kendra nearly puked again. Gerald never failed to needle Jocelyn about her weight. She knew he was cheating, having an affair with his secretary, Amber.

Kendra had accidentally walked in on them, catching them after an afternoon's tryst. She was there to pick up some papers she'd needed to settle her father's estate. She hadn't expected to discover her stepbrother and his lover, using her father's office as a love nest for their illicit affair in the middle of the afternoon.

She blinked the memory away as something she didn't want to think about. Though Gerald had later assured her his affair with Amber had ended, she was sure it had not. Her stepbrother was a cheat and a liar.

She looked at Jocelyn, a woman not so pretty or young as Gerald would have liked. A woman who absolutely adored her husband and would do anything to please him.

And I don't have the nerve to out him, Kendra thought darkly. Her hand shaking, she reached for her coffee. She missed, knocking the cup on its side. At least it was empty, the mess minimal. "Shit," she muttered under her breath.

Gerald frowned at her when he asked, "Are you all right?"

Kendra's head hurt, and an inexplicable ache thrummed in her heart. "I'm just a little shaky today," she said. "Those headaches always take it out of me."

He accepted her explanation. "Of course."

Righting her cup for Gabrielle to refill, Kendra reached for the silver and crystal jam and syrup tray in the center of the table. She slathered a thin layer of blackberry jam on her toast and took a bite.

Ignoring his breakfast, Gerald reached into his pocket for his cigarettes. Extracting one from the pack, he lit one. He inhaled deeply, coughed, and then inhaled again. "She always loads me down with too much food," he muttered. "She's trying to make me as fat as a pig." Always aware of his weight, he refused to eat more than a few bites of anything Gabrielle cooked.

Jocelyn's fork stopped midair. "I doubt you'll ever have that problem," she commented, lowering her food.

Kendra winced. After her first miscarriage, Jocelyn had begun packing on the pounds in a desperate attempt to quell her own terrible depression. In retaliation, Gerald had simply slipped out of his marriage bed and into the arms of another woman.

In an attempt to make a show of solidarity, Kendra poured thick maple syrup over the pancakes and then salted and peppered her eggs. "They say you should never skip breakfast," she said, forcing a bite of buttery pancake into her mouth. "The most important meal of the day."

Jocelyn grimaced down at the calorie-laden selections. "I suppose I should start asking for grapefruit and toast," she commented. She looked askance at her husband. "I could stand to lose a few pounds."

Gerald took a long draw off his cigarette. Its tip glowed bright red before dying in gray ashes. He exhaled a stream of white smoke as he flicked the ashes into the ashtray within easy reach. "That would be nice."

Waving a hand to clear the smoke, Jocelyn grimaced. "And if I start working out at the gym more often, perhaps you could work on giving up those noxious things."

Gerald took a deep drag off his cigarette and then said, while exhaling a cloud of smoke, "Why should I do that? I'm not the one with the problem." Lazy curls of smoke drifted upward.

Kendra felt a twinge at the back of her throat. She wished Jocelyn had the nerve to stand up and demand Gerald treat her as more than a doormat.

Not that she could say much about self-assertion. Always the good little girl, Kendra had minded her elders and tried not to break the rules. It wasn't until Michael Roberts had walked into her life that she'd gotten a taste of freedom.

"Can you two be nice to each other for just one day?" she pleaded. "I'm really not in the mood to listen to you argue over breakfast."

Jaw tightening, Jocelyn tossed her napkin onto her plate. "That's fine," she said between tight lips. "I think I've lost my appetite anyway." Pushing away from the table, she rose. "I've got to get to the office." She shot a glare toward her husband. "One of us has to lead a productive life."

Gerald flagged a disinterested hand, hardly bothering to look her way. "Whatever you say, dear."

Jocelyn stormed out, passing Gabrielle. As a high-powered ad exec, she worked long hours. She wouldn't be home before midnight, if at all.

Heading to Gerald, Gabrielle deposited the morning mail at his elbow. "Here you go, sir." She picked up Jocelyn's plate. "Is there anything else I can get you?"

"No. I think we're fine." Stubbing out his cigarette, Gerald flipped through the stack.

Forking up a bite of eggs, Kendra arched a brow toward the letters. "Anything for me?" she asked, not really sure who she expected to hear from.

Gerald flicked through the stack. "Nothing for you. Just the usual stack of bills and whatnot."

Kendra sighed. "Oh." Although she believed she had made friends throughout her life, she was surprised that none of her old college buddies ever came around anymore. Now that she was no longer a part of the gang, her friends were too busy to hang out. And why not? They had real lives. Places to go. Things to do. Boyfriends to date. Nobody wanted to spend time with someone who was a mass of gloom and depression.

She needed something to do. Something productive. Taking control of the household would be a small step. "I can start handling the bills again, if you want," she offered.

Lighting a fresh cigarette, Gerald glanced up. "I've got things under control."

Kendra pushed away her half-empty plate. "I didn't say you didn't," she countered. "I just thought it was time for me to stand up and take responsibility for things."

A hint of disapproval pulled at Gerald's mouth. "I don't think that's wise."

"What are you talking about?" she asked in disbelief.

Gerald's mouth quirked down. "Well, I didn't want to tell you this, but I suppose I should."

She stiffened. When her brother used that tone of voice, the news was never good.

He didn't blink an eye, only stared at her as if measuring her for a straitjacket. "Given your nervous breakdown and recent suicide attempt, the board has decided you're still too unstable to assume responsibility for the trust," he said.

His words hit like a blast of icy cold water. Jaw dropping in shock, Kendra shook her head. "They can't do that—"

Not one to mince words, Gerald cut her short with brutal precision. "They can, and they have."

11

An aching hollowness spread through Kendra. Would it always be like this? Her every word and action questioned? These days, someone was always watching her and, she was sure, judging her. The poking and prodding, both mental and physical, steadily fed her paranoia's insatiable appetite.

Gathering her frazzled nerves and the tangled remnants of her composure, she asked. "So you're in charge of the money, I suppose?" No supposing about it. She knew Gerald had been deeply unhappy that their father had given her primary control of the trust—a slap in the face to the adopted son Nathaniel Carter had accepted at his own but had never quite learned to love.

Realizing he'd been too abrupt, Gerald hastened to make amends. "You have always known I have been acting on your behalf. And it's only temporary until you get back on your feet. Right now you're all over the place mentally and emotionally."

Kendra sniffed to clear her throat, to breathe. A twinge of guilt hit. Since Michael Roberts had broken their engagement, she'd dumped everything into Gerald's lap. She mentally winced.

Lately she hadn't made a single appearance before the bank's board, nor attended a single meeting to make the decision as to how the money from her father's estate should be invested. Acting as her attorney and legal representative, Gerald had handled all that business for her.

Gerald, too, cleared his throat, eliciting her attention. "I'm just trying to take a little weight off your shoulders. You need time to rest and recover, sort out your life and what you want to do. Give yourself time to heal."

Straightening her shoulders, Kendra called upon all her willpower to appear calm. "It just feels like everyone is tiptoeing around me, too afraid to speak to me for fear I'll break into pieces," she said, angling a narrow look his way.

Gerald sighed. "You've dug your own hole and crawled inside since the day Dad died. Tell me, what the hell was the board supposed to conclude? Bills have to be paid; business has to be taken care of. Shutting yourself away in your room and closing your eyes to the outside world accomplishes nothing. Life still has to go on."

It felt like life had stood her on the side of a busy highway and put its foot on her ass. One push and she'd go into the oncoming traffic. She felt tears press at her eyes. He was right, of course. "I'm sorry," she mumbled. "I've been so selfish."

Seeing her tears, Gerald removed a clean handkerchief from the breast pocket of his jacket and passed it to her. "If you're worried, I don't have unlimited control of, or unlimited access to, the funds. I still have to answer to the bank, which keeps a detailed record of all transactions. We both have access to those records at any time. You know that."

Nodding, Kendra took the handkerchief and wiped away her tears, smearing black rings of mascara on the linen before blowing her nose. Giving him a thin, watery smile, she wadded up the handkerchief in one hand. "I didn't mean to accuse you of anything," she said slowly. "I just wasn't thinking."

Gerald smiled benignly, the older brother comforting a younger, confused sibling. "Maybe it's time to get out of the house a little more. Reenroll in college and finish your degree. Perhaps even switch your major from criminal justice to something you find more challenging."

His words made sense. Spent by recent events, she felt anger desert her. "That's an idea," she admitted cautiously.

He nodded. "Do something you actually enjoy, like music or art. You don't even have to stay in Philadelphia. With Father's name and connections, you could have your pick of any college in the country. You could even study abroad if you want."

Nodding, Kendra looked at her brother. She felt like a pig for saying those things to him. "That's also an idea."

"I could always get you on with the DA's office, too," Gerald mused, the thought brightening his eyes. "There's always a need for competent help, and you have more than enough training."

"You think I could get on?"

He nodded. "Without a doubt. All I have to do is make a call. I truly think you are on the road to recovery. Having a job might help you regain your confidence, give you something to focus on."

Kendra's skin suddenly felt tight. Suffocating. She clenched her left hand into a fist and pressed it into her lap. A confident person wouldn't be hallucinating a demon making love to her. "Another idea." To distract herself, she reached for one of her brother's cigarettes. Although she didn't like the habit, she'd toyed with it in college. She could use something to calm her.

With a knowing look, Gerald offered her his gold-plated lighter. "Use this."

She plucked it from his fingers and flicked it a few times until the flame caught. Her hand shook. She stared at the flame a moment before lighting the end of the cigarette and then held the lighter out to him.

"Keep it," he offered. "I have a feeling you might be lighting a few more."

"I just need something to calm me down. I don't intend to make it a regular habit."

He winked. "Right."

Kendra took a long drag off her cigarette. She was grateful for the burning rush that filled her lungs and exhaled a gust of smoke through her nostrils. The whole point of coming down to breakfast had been to grill Gerald about his recent acquisition. "How's the thing?" she asked.

He shrugged. "What thing?"

"You know." She prodded. "The book."

Gerald's eyes lit up. "Ah, that. Good, actually. I'm in the process of having it insured. Not that I think it'll be here long."

Her brows rose. "Oh?"

He leaned toward her as though to share a delicious secret. "I've already had an offer for it, doubling what I paid."

Kendra stared at him. A couple of days ago, she'd thought him insane for spending that much money on a book, no matter how old or rare. "Someone actually offered you four million?" Her hand still shaking more than a little, she took two more drags on her cigarette. Apparently Gerald was a smarter investor than she'd given him credit for.

"They have," he affirmed, smiling.

"And?"

His brow wrinkled. "I'm considering. Undecided but considering. I think if I hold on to it a bit longer, the offer may eventually double."

"Really?"

"Absolutely."

Kendra frowned. When she'd first lain eyes on the book, she'd wished it out the door as soon as possible. Confronted with the possibility it would be going, she felt her insides curdle.

Because of Remi.

But Remi didn't exist.

Except in my mind.

Curiosity prodded. "Can I ask you a question?"

Gerald studied her a moment before answering. "Of course."

Kendra swallowed back reluctance. "Do you think the book does what it is supposed to—summon demons?"

Gerald chuckled, but the sound held no warmth or mirth. "A lot of people would like to think so."

A chill of foreboding raced up her spine. "But do you believe it?"

A hint of a smile pulled at her brother's mouth. "I suppose it's possible, if you believed in heaven—or hell."

She looked at him hard. They'd both been raised in the Catholic faith, a religion filled with nothing but sermons of mortal sins and damnation. "And you don't?" she asked slowly.

"No," he answered tightly. "Not at all."

His admission stunned her. "Then you don't think Daddy went to heaven?" She shivered and instinctively rubbed her hands over her arms to still the rising goose bumps on her skin. "What about your mother?"

Gerald's face drastically paled, and his eyes took on a bleak, haunted look. "I stopped believing in the church the day Father Callahan pulled me aside and told me my mother went to hell for being a suicide," he snapped.

A painful knot formed in the core of Kendra's heart. "I didn't know." Hand trembling, she inhaled off the cigarette and then nodded. It tasted terrible.

Gerald reached out and patted her left hand consolingly. "Well, you were just a little girl. I doubt you even remember Mom's funeral."

Kendra crushed out the cigarette in the ashtray and then ran her hands down her face. "Bits and pieces."

He shrugged. "Well, it was a long time ago, I suppose."

A thought occurred to her. "Did it bother you when I moved into your mom's old rooms?"

Gerald's brow wrinkled. "No, I don't believe it did," he said. "No reason to keep them closed up. I always thought it was a shame Father closed off that wing when she died. Sometimes it felt like he wanted to deny they were ever married."

"That's just Dad, you know." She smiled weakly. "He never was big on emotions. You just bury your dead and go on."

Again Gerald nodded. "That's the Carter way."

"I suppose it is."

"So tell me again why you're asking about demons?"

Kendra had to collect her thoughts before replying. "Well, you're going to think I'm a silly idiot, but since I saw the book, I've been dreaming about them."

His brow rose. "Oh? How interesting."

She didn't think he would find it so interesting if he knew the damned thing was making love to her. Then again, he probably would. Gerald had a taste for kinky, forbidden things.

"Yes," she murmured. "It certainly has been."

"Maybe your subconscious is focusing on the book because you're still pissed I spent too much to acquire it," he suggested.

Kendra nodded. "It's possible," she allowed. Relief spread through her.

"Though I am sure more than one person has tried to use it for that purpose," he added.

Dread swallowed up the relief in a voracious gulp.

Seeing the look on her face, he amended. "But that would be stupid."

"You think so?"

Gerald rolled his eyes. "Oh, come on. Don't take it so seriously." He expelled a huff of air. "Think about it, Kendra. You've only just gotten home after a traumatic event. After all you've been through, it would be worrisome if you didn't have a nightmare or two."

Kendra's mouth quirked down. Her insides tightened. *They aren't not nightmares I've been having. More like a sexscape, rather than a dreamscape.* She shook her head adamantly. "It feels like it's something more . . . like this damn thing is trying to draw me in. Isn't that what demons do? Draw you in?"

He laughed. "And do what with you?"

She ventured an answer. "Well, maybe deceive you into thinking things that aren't true? You know, twisting your senses around so you don't know what's real and what's not?"

Gerald cleared his throat, eliciting her attention. "I would think the migraines would be the source of that problem."

Her eyes narrowed. "So you don't think it could be a demon?" she asked sarcastically.

He smiled tolerantly. "People can't think straight when they're in pain. The headaches are obviously worse than you're letting on if you think something is twisting your mind, Kendra."

She sucked in a ragged breath. "But the things I've been seeing . . . and feeling . . . It all seems so real."

Her stepbrother's eyes darkened with chagrin. "I think you need to discuss these things with Dr. Somerville. Perhaps you could use an antipsychotic medication."

Kendra exhaled heavily toward the ceiling. "I'm not losing my mind."

"So it seems," he remarked acidly.

When Gerald reached for his cigarettes again, she asked for another one. He started to say something, decided not to and quietly passed her a cigarette.

The smirking bastard.

Wasting no time, Kendra lit hers and took a long drag. "I know I've gone through a great deal of pain and suffering these past months," she said. "But what I've been experiencing lately goes beyond a migraine."

Gerald exhaled a stream of bluish smoke through pursed lips. "Like what?"

She burst out, "It's fucking me!"

Gerald released a snort of exasperation. "It's fucking you?" He waved his cigarette back and forth as he spoke. "As in, having sex with you?"

He thinks I'm a nut, Kendra thought miserably. *And I'm giving him all the ammunition he needs to have me declared insane.*

"It's not funny," she snapped. "This thing is doing things to me. . . ." Heat creeping in her cheeks, she bit off the rest of her sentence. She didn't want Gerald to know what Remi was doing to her once she shut her eyes. The idea of being screwed while unconscious smacked of force. Or rape.

Her cheeks grew hotter.

Not that she'd been exactly unwilling.

In fact, she'd been pretty damn eager.

Her stepbrother's features remained lit with amusement as he snuffed out the remains of his cigarette in the ashtray. "I think I know what your problem is," he announced gravely.

The hand holding her cigarette began to tremble. Suddenly her throat felt closed, blocked by the intense pounding of her heart. "What?" she croaked.

Gerald reached out and stroked her arm, touching her not the way a brother would touch a sister, but the way a man would touch a woman. "I think you need to get laid." He winked. "And if you want to commit a little incest, just let me know."

Kendra jumped up and flung her cigarette butt at him, trying to get her muddled brain to decipher whether his insinuations were hurtful or just plain insulting. "Asshole!" she snarled. Trembling, her voice almost guttural, she added, "Pervert."

Gerald's attempt to fend off the flying butt had been clumsy. He'd shot to his feet when the missile had dropped to his crotch and burned a small hole in his black Armani trousers. "Come on, Kendra."

Kendra's heart slammed against her chest wall and then seemed to rise and lodge in her throat. Her blood turned to ice, while her skin felt afire. "I thought I made it clear I'm not interested in you that way."

He feigned innocence. "What way?"

She was half tempted to slug him and probably would have if she didn't feel so shaky all of a sudden. "You know."

Gerald spread his hands. "You know I'm just joking around with you," he chided impatiently.

Kendra shot him a hard look. "It's not funny anymore." She wanted to believe he was joking, but her instincts warned her there was a hell of a lot more than playful kidding behind his advances. Ever since they were kids, Gerald had done his best to press his sexual desires on her: Peeking into her room as she undressed. Catching her alone and pressing his body just a little closer than decorum between siblings should allow.

True, they shared no blood. But his advances always made her feel dirty. Tainted. It was like he wanted to be in charge of her.

A fierce stab of alarm heated her insides. *All of me.*

Control. How well Gerald utilized it.

Kendra's hands settled at her sides, balling into fists. She wished she had the power to take control's reins, too. Somewhere deep inside her, that ability, that inherent stamina, was presently taking forty winks. What would it take to awaken it? Certainly not whining or feeling sorry for herself.

Or letting Gerald bully or intimidate her.

I'm not afraid of him, she thought.

But she knew that wasn't exactly true. Gerald was lying to her. He was hiding something from her. Something important.

And for the first time in her life Kendra didn't think her instincts were misleading her.

12

Kendra paced the private waiting room like a caged animal. As she walked, she told herself repeatedly she would rather be anywhere but here where the silence and absence of another person only served to magnify her anxiety.

I am not having a nervous breakdown.

Coming to a halt, she brushed aside bangs damp with perspiration. Her skin felt tight. Suffocating. She clenched her left hand into a fist and pressed it against her purse, the weight of which made the strap dig into her shoulder.

The door behind her opened.

"Miss Carter?"

Kendra whirled on her heels, balling up the tissue in her hand. She had to be strong. She gulped back another rise of panic. Showtime was near.

Her knees trembled. "Yes?" she managed to choke out.

"Dr. Somerville will see you now. Are you ready to come in?" The nurse gave the room a quick scan to make sure all was well.

Kendra offered a tentative smile to show she was fine. "I'm ready." It was time to play the games.

Dr. Marcus Somerville sat in his high-back leather chair. He was a trim man in his late thirties, a commanding presence who sometimes unnerved her. Not because he'd plumbed the depths of her mind in rehab, but because he was too incredibly good-looking to be believed. Broad shoulders. Lean hips. Abdomen-rippling muscles. His dark hair was gray at the temples, giving him just enough of a mature look to be enticing to young women. He'd truly missed his calling in life. He should have been a cover model.

As he opened her file, Somerville's deep-set hazel eyes regarded her over the rim of his designer glasses. He leveled a look at her, one penetrating enough to make her fidget. His unblinking stare and the silence teemed with accusation. It was all she could do not to ask to have the appointment canceled and leave.

In defense of his unspoken censure, she blurted, "Hello, Doctor."

Somerville finally let her off the hook. "Have a seat, Kendra," he invited.

Kendra gulped back another rise of panic. Time to give the performance of her life. Time to show she'd gotten her shit together and bagged it.

If you can't dazzle the doctor with beauty, baffle him with bullshit.

She feigned nonchalance. "Sure."

Feeling vaguely uncomfortable, Kendra stretched out on his longue. It always felt strange that therapists expected patients to lie flat on their back, unable to see the person to whom they were speaking. Then again, considering that she was baring herself to Dr. Somerville in a deeply personal way, she doubted she would want to look into his face as she spoke.

After all, therapy could sometimes be as intimate as sex. Sometimes even more so.

A riffling of paper interrupted her thoughts. "How have you been, Kendra?" Dr. Somerville asked.

Kendra shrugged. "Fine, I guess." God, spitting out an answer was like having teeth extracted—a painful procedure.

"Not more than fine?"

Knowing he expected more to her answers, she tried again. "Pretty good, I think." She tried to add a laugh but couldn't quite manage it.

"How have things been since your release?"

She let out a shuddery breath. "Good," she said. Her voice shook when she answered. "It feels good to be home."

"Any twinges?"

Twinges. Meaning her nightly glass of wine.

Angry that he refused to reaffirm her assessment of herself, she fumed a little. "I'm dry," she said. "I haven't had a glass of wine in more than a month."

"Made your first AA meeting yet?"

Not something she wanted to do. Despite its promise of anonymity, nothing about AA was anonymous. It wouldn't be long before word got out that Judge Nathaniel Carter's daughter was a falling-down drunk.

Kendra shook her head adamantly. "I'm still looking into that," she hedged.

Dr. Somerville clicked his tongue. "I thought we discussed that before your release, Kendra. You agreed to go."

Crossing her arms over her chest, she huffed. "I know I said I would. I would have jumped off the damned roof if it would have gotten me out of there any faster."

"I'm sensing some hostility here," Somerville remarked. "I know it's difficult to open up, but I want you to know you can tell me anything. Anything at all. If it helps, you're not the only one out there with problems to solve. Lots of people need help. Admitting you need that help is the first step to getting well."

Thanks to her stay in rehab, she recognized the plot counselors and shrinks used to draw out undesirable emotions, emotions probably best left untapped.

"Of course I'm feeling more than a little antagonistic," Kendra burst out. "You think I liked being locked up in a psych ward for seventy-two hours, accused of trying to do something I didn't?"

"You were found unconscious from an overdose," Somerville reminded her. "Something like that is a cry for help."

Her mouth turned down in frustration. They'd been over this a thousand times before. Each time it made her angry. "I told you before, I didn't try to commit suicide."

The sound of pages turning floated into her ears as he checked his notes. "Then what were you trying to do?"

Kendra's brow wrinkled. That was the damn trouble: she didn't know. Everything about that night was still a great big blur, like someone had inserted a tube and drained every memory out of her head. Realizing her hands had suddenly turned icy, she rubbed them together. "I told you I don't remember."

Somerville cleared his throat as he glanced through the papers in the folder. He prodded. "Maybe you don't want to remember."

Slumping on the longue like a rag doll, Kendra again searched her mind for the vital memories of that night. That specific time remained disjointed, the few fragments she could locate lingering tauntingly at the periphery of her mind. From the moment she had awoken in the hospital, her memories were touch-and-go. One thing remained the same, however: she couldn't figure out what it was she'd done to herself.

What did any of the people who believed she'd tried to kill herself know about her? She feared death and its corrosive state. The rotting away of the flesh and the insects that would feast on it. The mere image of such decay happening to her was more terrifying than anything she'd yet to experience. She wanted life. To live as she believed she should. Happily ever after.

Without physical or mental pain.

Except that life without pain was life without feeling.

She cursed under her breath. *Damn.* "Believe me, the moment I know, you'll know." She trembled.

"Well, no one can make you go to the meetings, Kendra. It wasn't a mandatory part of your release. You completed the program, and that's been an excellent start."

"Glad you think so," she grated.

"I simply suggested the idea of AA, feeling that it would be a good outlet through which you could associate with others who share your problem."

"I'm not a common drunk," she protested. "And I don't want to hang around with other people moaning about how damn terrible things are."

"People have listened to *you* moan," he pointed out.

She shook her head. "Let's not get started on the selfish and self-centered aspects of my personality, please."

A heavy sigh. "It's your dime," he said. "So what would you like to talk about?"

A knot lodged in her throat. Maybe it would be better not to mention the migraines . . . and the strange effects the damn things were having on her mind.

Then again, maybe Dr. Somerville would be able to offer an explanation, a solution.

Kendra cleared her throat. "Well, I've been having a little problem with headaches."

"Oh?"

Swiping her tongue across dry lips, she nodded. "I'm not

quite sure how to explain it, but I seem to be losing bits and pieces of time. And things are happening to me that I don't really comprehend."

"Such as?"

Reluctance nipped at her heels. She was picking up some odd vibes. "I'm seeing things."

"Can you describe these things?" He didn't sound convinced.

"Oh, yeah. I certainly can."

Kendra relaxed in her chair, remembering the way Remi had planted tiny kisses down her neck before his lips had found and encircled a waiting nipple. A hungry, white-hot passion raced through her. She could almost hear him whispering in that sexy voice of his, urging her thighs to open so his hips could fill the void.

Clit throbbing with desire, she pressed her legs together to still the desperate ache. Had she been alone at home, she would have slid her hands into her panties, touching herself until climax eased the longing. She wanted to feel the heat of a man's erection entering her slick warmth.

Just as Kendra was about to spill her guts, a chill passed through her. Darkness appeared at the perimeter of her vision. It closed in, tunneling her view at the end of the longue. Appearing from thin air, a wavy shadow began to form, growing and shifting as it took shape.

Kendra gaped in stunned disbelief. Blinking rapidly, her heart hammering at an alarming rate, she gripped the sides of the longue.

Oh, God, don't let this be happening again!

It was.

13

When the image sharpened into focus, Remi stood in front of her. Stark-ass bare, he wore nothing but a grin.

The demon gave her a little wave. "I'm here."

Her stomach flipping over twice at the sight of him, Kendra groaned. *Oh, no,* she mouthed. Remi was back. In the flesh. In more ways than one.

She glanced toward Dr. Somerville, sure he'd be shocked by the sight. He didn't blink an eye.

Somerville cleared his throat, very obviously annoyed. "Did you hear my question?"

Hesitating through an endless minute, and then two, Kendra numbly shook her head. He was waiting for an answer she didn't want to give him. "Ah, no, I—I didn't," she stammered. "What did you say?"

The good doctor was totally oblivious to the presence invading his office like a disease, insidiously undetectable to the naked eye but deadly nevertheless. "I asked you to describe the thing you are seeing."

Trying not to think about the naked demon, she gulped—as if that thing weren't standing at the foot of the longue. "I, ah, it's not exactly a man," she began to explain. "I'm sure it's a demon."

Remi eagerly rubbed his hands together. "Oh, looks like I arrived just in time. You're talking about my favorite subject." He waggled his brows. "Me."

Kendra's mouth drew down into a vexed frown. "Go away," she hissed through clenched teeth.

"What did you say?" Somerville asked, startled.

Blowing out a breath, she quickly coughed into her hand. "Uh, nothing. Just a little tickle in my throat."

This can't be happening. I'm awake. To reaffirm the thought, she gave her cheek a little slap.

Somerville looked at her with bemused fascination, like a person would regard an alien insect impaled on a pin. "Is something wrong, Miss Carter?"

Kendra quickly shook her head. "No. Nothing's wrong." Her fingers curled around the cross at her neck. Apparently, it wasn't going to help keep Remi away. He obviously had the ability to follow her. Anywhere he wanted.

Somerville resumed his questioning. "We were talking about this thing you think you see."

Kendra looked straight at Remi. She would have smiled if the sight of him hadn't completely thrown her for a loop. "I don't think I see him," she corrected. Frustration, mingled with disbelief, snarled through her. "I know I see him."

As if to reaffirm her words, Remi raised his arms and turned his fingers inward, gleefully pointing at his tattooed body. "Oh, you see me, all right. Every delicious inch is here for your pleasure."

Or my displeasure, she thought sourly. There were times when a six-foot-tall, heavily tattooed demon just shouldn't show up in the buff.

"This demon," Somerville asked, blissfully ignorant, "what exactly does it do?"

Kendra blushed, cheeks going furnace hot. It was hard to keep her eyes off Remi. Harder still not to remember what he'd done to her. Reluctant to answer, she scrubbed her hands over her face. "Sex. It has sex with me."

"Physical relations?" Somerville asked, clearly intrigued.

Kendra gulped, struggling to take in fresh air. "Yes."

Somerville flipped through his notes at top speed. "In our previous sessions, you told me the desire to be intimate with a man wasn't there because of the scars. Have you changed your mind about that lately?"

Huh?

Kendra wrenched her gaze off the naked demon. "What do my scars have to do with having sex with a demon?" she demanded.

Somerville slipped off his glasses. "Perhaps this demon is a manifestation of your desire for physical companionship."

Remi grinned. "Hmmm. Sounds logical to me."

"That's not logical," Kendra snapped, not sure whose comment she rebutted.

"And this demon," Somerville continued, "does it do anything else when it comes?"

Kendra looked directly at Remi when she answered. "He says he will show me things." Nerves shimmered beneath the surface of her skin. She was barely holding on to her composure.

"What kind of things?"

"How about things like this?" Remi said, his answer unheard by any ears but her own. One hand slipped toward his waist. His fingers circling his penis, he started to caress himself.

Kendra's eyes widened in shock. The hairs at her nape prickled. With each pass of his hand up and down his length, Remi's cock grew harder. Longer.

Her heart thudded in her rib cage. Her stomach clenched

with an aching need. He had no shame, cheerfully masturbating right in front of her.

"Only you can see me," he moaned and stroked harder. "All this is for your eyes only."

Lucky me. "Please don't," she whispered, more than a little bit embarrassed.

Somerville believed she was speaking to him. "Don't what?" he asked.

"Don't talk about sex." Kendra let herself go limp, leaning forward until her face rested on her knees. Her hands were locked around her head, a parody of a woman expecting a head-on collision.

It was during this time a strange phenomenon occurred. Silence descended. Time faded away. A cold, biting breeze passed through her.

Aware of a subtle shift around her, Kendra raised her head. Dr. Somerville had vanished.

Only Remi remained.

Still stroking his erection, he leered down at her. "Maybe we should show the good doctor exactly what we've been doing."

Kendra's jaw tightened. "You fucker."

Remi gave his erection another long stroke. "Oh, you have no idea." He chuckled. "I'm going to fuck you in so many ways."

Kendra made a scoffing noise. "I'd like to see you try."

"Like this?" Reaching down, Remi grasped her ankles, pulling her toward the edge of the longue and spreading her legs.

So much for being in control, came her thought wryly.

Kneeling between her spread legs, Remi's hand slipped under her skirt, pushing it up around her thighs. Pressing his fingers against her crotch, he stroked her through her panties.

Unable to resist his touch, Kendra dragged in a breath of air. "Why are you doing this to me?" she gasped.

Remi stroked a little harder. Fiery darts of pleasure sent a prickle of goose bumps across her skin. "Because I can." He laughed softly. "I'm going to make you come right here in your doctor's office."

Hovering like a helicopter in flight, all Kendra could do was feel. Every thought in her head vanished when Remi's fingers slipped under the elastic, his fingers making instant contact with the small hooded organ between her legs. The touch of skin on skin sent a spear of fire straight into her core. Desire whirled through her body with growing intensity.

She'd do anything to satisfy the ache.

Kendra panted. "Please stop. I can't take much more."

With a knowing smile, Remi flicked the tip of one thick finger against her clit. "You don't really want me to stop now, do you?"

Kendra's fingers dug into the sides of the longue. She writhed against the cushion, half in pain, half in pleasure.

"Yes," she grated. Then, "No."

"I thought so." Remi eased two fingers inside her pussy. Inner muscles automatically flexed, tightening around his thick digits.

She moaned her reply.

"You like that?" Remi whispered, his voice sultry, dripping with heat.

"Damn you," she panted. "I do."

"Then you'll love this." Pushing her back on the recliner, Remi expertly slipped her panties over her legs. Discarding them, he added the soft pressure of his lips to Kendra's aching clit. As his talented tongue worked at her most sensitive flesh, his fingers slid in and out of her creamy sex.

Kendra's hips danced with every gliding motion of Remi's fingers. The friction was almost too much to take. "Damn," she bit out.

Remi lifted his head, kissing the softness of her inner thigh. "I told you I could make you come."

He was right.

Tremors engulfed her, small quakes that gradually became frenetic convulsions. The sensations were so exquisite Kendra never wanted them to end.

Adding a third finger, Remi thrust against Kendra's sensitive clit, doubling her pleasure. An intense rush of fiery tentacles wrapped themselves around her body, dragging her into an abyss of pure, unadulterated pleasure.

Before Kendra could catch her breath, her vision faded. For a moment everything in the room seemed to wink away, vanishing.

Then reality came crashing back.

14

_____

Somerville's hand lay heavily on her shoulder. His rough voice sliced through the chaos in her mind. "Kendra? Are you all right?"

With a jerky heave, Kendra opened her eyes. She felt as if she had awakened with a serious hangover. Her muscles were cramped, her skin stretched too tightly over her bones. Remi was gone, and she hadn't budged one single inch.

Gingerly straightening up, she rested her head against the edge of the longue, too drained to do much else. The office was chilly, strangely quiet. She gulped several times to keep her stomach's contents from rising into her throat and blinked. Her hands and feet were cold, as if her circulation had come to a stop.

She struggled to sit up; her entire body trembled with the effort. "What happened?" The previous few minutes had vanished, slipping through her fingers like so many grains of sand. As though she'd temporarily slipped into an alternate dimension, Remi's pleasure had happened. Just like that. Vivid-colored images of the fragmented remnants of the visitation traipsed across her mind's screen.

She glanced down. Her skirt was perfectly in place. Not hiked up around her legs.

"You seemed to go into some kind of a trance for a few minutes," Somerville said.

Kendra blinked. Minutes? It had taken Remi only minutes to induce orgasm?

Her mouth wide open, she breathed laboriously for a few seconds and then locked eyes with the shrink. "I—I'm sorry," she apologized.

His brow wrinkled. From the look on his face, he was just as puzzled as she was. "Have you had these sort of, ah, episodes previously?"

Growing more numb by the second, Kendra nodded. "A few times, yes."

"This is definitely something we're going to have to look into."

Hope flared. "Then it's not normal?"

"Certainly not."

The flame grew a little brighter. "Could it be from the accident?"

"Neurological is a possibility."

Hope now disintegrating into ashes, Kendra shook her head. "I've had dozens of tests. Everything comes up normal."

Crossing his office, Somerville opened a small dorm fridge and retrieved two bottles of water. "If we rule out physical damages, it's definitely psychological. The issues you have locked in your subconscious mind are going to have to be brought out and dealt with." Opening one, he handed it to Kendra.

She smiled gratefully. "Thank you."

He settled back into his own chair. "At this point, it's all speculation," he muttered as he downed his water.

Kendra wrapped her hands around the plastic bottle to keep from shaking. Its cool surface was soothing. "I'm not sure what's going on," she admitted. "I just know something's wrong. Really wrong. I just wish I could explain it better."

She lifted the bottle to her lips and drank deeply. The water was like a balm on her soul. She'd forgotten how refreshing cold water was to a feverish body.

Setting his water down, Somerville checked his notes. "Let's go over the last few minutes, during your episode. When you blanked out, did anything happen?"

Kendra drew back her shoulders and called on all her inner willpower to appear calm. Her stomach was churning. *If I tell Somerville what just happened, he'll have me committed.*

But if she didn't say anything, no one could help.

If nothing else, Kendra knew she needed help. Desperately. Something terrible was going on inside her psyche. Because Somerville couldn't peer inside her skull, examine her actual thoughts, it was difficult to make him understand what was happening—something she didn't dare think, nor even speak aloud.

That she was, indeed, losing her mind.

When that might have happened or why, she didn't know. She only knew it scared the living shit out of her.

Her fingers tapping the plastic, Kendra nodded stiltedly. "Yes."

"Oh?"

Teeming with frustration, Kendra's throat suddenly felt blocked by the intense pounding of her heart. "The demon came back," she admitted slowly. Now that the confession had slipped out, she really wasn't sure it was wise to share it.

His eyes narrowed with interest. "It was here?"

She nodded. Tears pressed for release. She blinked, refusing to let them fall; she was afraid if she undammed them, her confusion would loosen what remained of her control.

The doctor leaned forward, interest on his face. "What did it do?"

Pulse jackhammering, Kendra stiffened her back. "It, ah, he had—" She swiped her tongue across her chapped lips. "It had sex with me."

Somerville nodded thoughtfully, but his eyes remained narrow with disbelief. "The demon had sex with you? Right in this office?"

"Yes." Kendra suddenly felt two inches tall. She wished a crack would open in the floor, devour her. She released a strangled laugh and gave herself a mental kick in the ass for even telling Somerville about Remi.

She had no more than mentioned the demon, and Remi had appeared.

This time she hadn't even called his name. He seemed to be getting stronger, appearing where and when he wanted. Doing whatever he wanted. To her.

Setting aside her drink, Kendra lowered her head to rest on her clasped hands. Releasing a tremulous sigh, she stared at her lap through the gap of her arms. It was as if someone had led her to the top of a cliff and then, without warning, pushed her off. Somehow she'd managed to catch the edge, but she was still left dangling helplessly high above the ground.

After a few moments, she finally lifted her head. "Yes," she admitted. "He had sex with me." Her voice betrayed her unease, holding an edge that tweaked her already exposed nerves.

Somerville's brow wrinkled in consternation. "What did the demon do?" He cleared his throat. "Exactly."

Caught off guard by the deeply personal question, Kendra stared at her psychiatrist. A tic of frustration tugged at the corner of her mouth. She fought to retain her composure, clasping her hands together until her knuckles became white from the pressure.

Did she want to tell him that?

Not really.

In the face of her silence, Somerville persisted. "What did the demon do?"

Like yanking a Band-Aid off a wound, she thought she might as well spit it out. "First, he masturbated."

"He exposed himself?"

"He was naked," she filled in.

"And then what did he do?"

That answer was a little harder to spit out. "He pulled me to the edge of the longue and pushed up my skirt." Embarrassed to be sharing such intimate details, she lapsed into silence.

Somerville impaled her with a scowl. "And?"

Ignoring his baiting tone, she sighed. "And then he pulled off my panties and made me come," she snapped loudly.

"Hmmm. Interesting." Scribbling on his pad, Somerville ignored her outburst. "Tell me, did he bring you to climax with his cock?"

The silence hanging between them prompted her to finish. "His fingers. He used his fingers."

"He didn't use his penis?"

Kendra stared into the shrink's eyes for a long moment and then sighed as though all energy had deserted her. "No. He didn't."

"Did you want him to use his cock?"

Her jaw tightened. "He's used it before," she gritted out.

"And did you enjoy it? The climax?"

What kind of cockeyed question was that? She'd just told her psychiatrist she'd been masturbated to orgasm by an invisible supernatural force, and all he could do was sit there and ask for all the dirty little details?

At the moment, she felt only numb, and she shook her head. "No," she barked. "I don't enjoy having a demon appear out of thin air and fuck me."

Somerville cocked a brow, scribbled some more. "Then you don't enjoy sex?"

Kendra rolled her eyes toward the ceiling. *Heaven help me.* "Yes, I like sex."

His brooding gaze never left her face. "But you haven't had sex since the accident, correct?"

Kendra stared blankly at him for a few silent seconds. Knowing it and hearing it spoken added crushing weight to the reality of her breakup.

She closed her eyes to rally her rapidly thinning patience. "No. No sex."

"Let's talk about your fiancé, Michael. Is he the last man you made love to?"

Kendra drew in a deep, fortifying breath. "I know you think I'm crazy, but it happened. As fast as that. It's like he's everywhere around me."

He stared at her with an expression shadowed in skepticism. A mocking smile appeared on his mouth. "Michael, or the demon?"

Kendra forced herself to breathe deeply through her nostrils to still her stomach. "The demon, damnit."

Somerville scratched his scraggly beard. "Have you ever considered the fact that Michael and the demon are one and the same?"

The good doctor made a few notes on his pad. As it stood, the good doctor would mostly like pin the apparition's existence on her own starved libido. A young woman, only twenty-three, should be having loads of sex.

"This is going to take time," he commented more to himself than to her. "We're going to have to continue working through your sessions until you find the root of what's bothering you." He made a few more notes. "I know you've seen a great deal of pain in your life, but you must realize getting well isn't your enemy."

Kendra's eyes narrowed with chagrin. She had the feeling Somerville was totaling up the extra dollars he'd earn from putting her through extensive sessions of psychotherapy. She could imagine what he'd written about her: *Hysterical, repressed female. Needs a good screwing.*

She rubbed her eyes and drew in a shuddering breath. Were Remi's manifestations truly a part of her own deranged psyche? Somerville probably believed she'd benefit if Remi kept appearing. That's all most men seemed to think was wrong with a woman. All a female needed to set her straight was a nice fuck.

Mortification scalded her face.

Losing her mind had suddenly become more complicated than she'd ever imagined.

The bad thing about this was she didn't know if the demon would ever stop stalking her. Appearing when he wanted. Having sex with her any time he pleased. His ability to manipulate not only her, but those around her, was scary. No one else saw him or sensed him.

And that made him dangerous.

Kendra felt apprehension surge through her veins like chips of cold steel. She inwardly flinched. *What if it never stops?*

Somehow she had a feeling she didn't need a psychiatrist.

She needed an exorcist.

15

By the time Kendra managed to escape Dr. Somerville, the clock was headed on a downward arc toward four in the afternoon. It was too damn early to go home. And, truth be told, she didn't really want to.

Still unsettled by the intense session with her therapist, Kendra had the cab drop her off downtown. Though she owned a car, she hadn't driven herself since the wreck. Even though she hadn't been driving, she didn't feel confident behind the wheel.

Time. It was going to take time to get well. Somerville had made that perfectly clear.

Slipping out of the cab, Kendra paid the driver with a twenty. *Dr. Somerville thinks I'm a freak.* Her brow wrinkled. *A sexually repressed freak.*

Kendra didn't want to be a freak. Not today. She wanted to be normal again. Have a normal day.

The day was perfect for shopping. People milled about, smiling, laughing, enjoying the warm summer day.

Kendra walked along the boulevard, pausing to look at the

displays that caught her eye. She was on the prowl for new items for her wardrobe—she'd let herself go for months slopping around in the same old jeans and flannel shirts until Gerald had threatened to burn them all. She was due to check in with the course counselor at the college in a week to decide the course of her degree. That is, if she even decided to go back when the new semester rolled around. She wasn't sure. Gerald had offered her a job. The position might just be an entry level in the secretarial pool, but he'd assured her she wouldn't stay on the bottom rung long. She had a good head on her shoulders, common sense and ambition.

A career in law hadn't exactly been appealing when Nathaniel Carter was alive. He'd bullied both his children into pursuing legal careers. Gerald had dutifully followed in his stepfather's footsteps, first by getting his law degree and then by getting a job in the district attorney's office as an assistant prosecutor. His goal was eventually to climb up the bench and then into politics.

Just like their father had. The rural community from which Nathaniel Carter had hailed was fiercely clannish. Strangers were not welcome or trusted. A midnight boy in a sunset town, he'd long ago left behind the dusty back roads and miles of farmland: it was a place to be born, but not to die. He'd never looked back, nor gone back.

Though law hadn't been Kendra's goal, that was exactly the course she had pursued. She hated it, felt stifled by it. She'd wanted to pursue the piano—the one thing she knew her mother had done and done well. Before her marriage to Nathaniel, Renee Jessup had been a concert pianist, a star in the Philadelphia Orchestra. At the time, the match had seemed a good one. A rising young lawyer and the socially prominent WASP he'd snagged for a wife.

But Kendra's father had forbade her musical career choice, to the point of refusing to pay for her education past high school. It was his way or the highway. Like Gerald, she'd knuckled under to his wishes and enrolled as a freshman in criminal justice.

Kendra hadn't played the piano since the accident.

Maybe it was time to seriously consider the option, while she was still young enough to pursue the rigorous studies mastering the instrument would take. Though she played well, she was nowhere near the level of a maestro.

Perhaps concentrating on the piano, tackling a new challenge, would take her mind off the thing that seemed to be bedeviling her recently.

Remi.

Kendra walked on, enjoying the feel of the sun on her bare skin. In the bright light of day she could swear the demon's visitations were exactly what Somerville suggested: her mind's way of reminding her body it needed physical release, the touch of another human being.

She didn't doubt that. More than eleven months without sex had left her libido hanging. Masturbation was fine, but it certainly didn't take the place of the things a partner could do.

Kendra drew a deep breath. *It's time to let go of the past.*

Stopping to buy a frozen mocha latte at a corner coffee shop styled in a fifties theme, she continued her quasi-quest to shop. She was twenty-three years old, and for the first time in a long time, the future stretched ahead as bright as the Thursday afternoon.

A big sale sign in one window caught her attention. Fueled by caffeine and sugar, she hurried over to take a look. The mannequins in the display were clad in the latest fashions, sensible but stylish for the modern young working woman. The suits were exactly what a legal secretary would wear, the styles professional and polished without coming off matronly—open and approachable, yet giving a sense of youth and freshness. She couldn't decide which she liked better, the sensible navy-blue blazer, blouse and skirt or the charcoal-gray pantsuit.

I could take the job, she mused. An office was a perfect place to meet new people, make new friends. Widen her horizons.

She'd just decided on the navy when a familiar voice interrupted her thoughts.

This time it wasn't Remi.

Tanned arms enveloped her in a hug. "Kendra, my gosh, it's been a long time."

Gingerly extracting herself from the hug, Kendra stepped back to eye the newcomer: Beatrice Evans—her former college roommate and the woman responsible for dragging her off to see a new band playing a gig just off campus. Yes, Bea Evans had been responsible for introducing her to Michael Roberts, unwittingly setting Kendra up for the romance of a lifetime—and the heartbreak that would follow.

Kendra forced a smile. "How have you been?"

Bea smiled. "Good. I've been good." She caught Kendra's hand. "You look good. Really good. They did a nice job."

For some reason her words didn't sit well with Kendra. She felt a chill crawl down her spine. She couldn't put a name to the feeling, exactly. She just knew it was uncomfortable and annoying.

"Thanks." She shrugged. "All put together again." Nice and normal.

Except she didn't feel nice. And definitely didn't feel normal.

Bea smiled. "I haven't seen you in so long. It seems like you've dropped off the face of the Earth."

Since the accident, she'd done just that. Taking a sip of her latte, Kendra shrugged again, an attempt at nonchalance. "I've been busy," she hedged. Who the hell wanted to admit they'd just gotten out of rehab after a suicide attempt? Not exactly the subjects of a fun conversation. She felt like the worst kind of freak, an outcast. She should crawl right back into her hole and hibernate some more. She just wasn't ready to face the world again.

Bea laughed. "Oh, me, too." She clapped excitedly. "I've got a new job I'm just wild about."

Kendra tried to look interested. "Oh?" Though Beatrice had come to visit her in the hospital, their friendship had faded when the common interests of grades and boys were no longer shared. Bea wanted to go out, do things, have fun.

Kendra had to admit that after the accident, she hadn't exactly been a barrel of laughs. In fact, the only thing she'd been was a pile of gloom and doom. "What are you doing now?"

Beatrice cast her a bright smile. "I'm modeling now." She grinned. "And get this—I've got an agent. I'm moving to New York, too." She rolled her eyes. "Isn't that wild?"

Kendra wanted to bite off her own tongue. Bea was dressed in a pair of cut-off blue jeans that showed her slender legs to their best advantage, paired with a white blouse tied at the midriff and a pair of open-toed sandals. She'd left a few buttons on the blouse undone, showing just a hint of cleavage. With her darkly tanned skin and cute blond shag over sparkling blue eyes, she was pert and pretty.

"That's wild," Kendra said. "Just awesome."

Bea just had to rub it in. She shoved out her left hand. "And, look. I'm engaged."

Seeing the familiar design, Kendra's stomach clenched into a thousand tight little knots. The ring was the same one she'd chosen for her own engagement to Michael Roberts. After Michael had proposed, she and Bea had flipped through jewelry catalogs for hours, picking out the perfect ring.

Kendra felt her temper begin to simmer. *Bitch*. Couldn't even pick out her own damn ring design. "Congratulations," she mumbled dryly.

Bea chuckled. "Thanks. We're getting married next May. On the first."

That one really made Kendra want to puke. A May Day wedding. How original. They'd probably planned an outdoor shindig, complete with tossed petals and dancing in a ring around a maypole.

"You're invited, of course," Bea added.

Kendra smiled thinly. She mentally drew a bow, took aim and fired. "I think I've got an engagement of my own that day."

Bea's eyes widened in pure innocence. "Don't tell me you and Michael picked the same day!"

Kendra hated the fact Bea's words sounded more like an accusation than a question. An evil thought occurred.

And here is where the earth opens up and swallows Bea down like so much snack.

She smiled at the thought. "Actually, Michael and I broke up."

"Oh, that's sad," Bea said. "What happened?"

Not sure how to answer, Kendra caught a glimpse of herself in the department-store window. Thought she didn't look terrible, the accident had clearly taken its toll on her face, etching a few lines around her eyes and at the corners of her mouth. She looked older than twenty-three. She frowned, her mind walking the same well-trod path.

Must every waking minute center around what happened months ago? She'd played and replayed their breakup ten thousand times in her head. There was no point going back over it again. He was simply a creep.

Call it fate. Call it karma. Call it just plain bad luck.

In her dreams Kendra managed to escape the accident unscathed—something impossible for her to have managed in real life. She'd had no notice, no time to react. Strangely, getting tossed out of the car had probably saved her life. Tossed out of the mangled wreckage, she hadn't been trapped the way her father had been when the tractor-trailer had slammed head-on into the wreckage.

No way she'd admit to Beatrice Evans that Michael had dumped her flat on her ass. She still had a little pride. Not much, but a little.

Kendra raised her head, leveling her chin. "I caught him fucking a groupie and dumped him," she said.

Bea looked absolutely dumbfounded. "You dumped Michael Roberts?" she asked as if the idea were unthinkable. At the time, Michael and his band, *Mind's Awry*, had been on the verge of signing with a major record label.

Kendra smiled sweetly. "Wouldn't you?" she countered, turning the question into a challenge. What sane woman with any amount of self-respect would put up with a cheating boyfriend?

Bea nodded, agreeing. "Of course," she said. "Who wouldn't?"

Kendra flagged a disinterested hand. "And, really, I didn't have time for marriage." She cleared her throat. "Seeing as I'm starting my own business and all."

Not exactly a wild lie, either. She even had a name for her idea: Gofer It.

She'd first conceived the idea when recovering from her injuries at home. Though she'd had home-care aides, a lot of people didn't have the resources she did, and it had occurred to her that there might be a demand for a different kind of temping agency, one to do the small jobs people couldn't or didn't have time to handle.

To her surprise, Bea winked. "I've got to hand it to you, Kendra. You always were the one with the brains."

Kendra eyed her quasi-friend critically. Her temper faded. Bea was just being her usual scatterbrained self, always putting her foot in her mouth, oblivious to whom she might offend. It had been part of her charm as a roommate. Bea was pretty but about as bright as Bozo the Clown.

Kendra flashed a smile. "It's a start," she said pleasantly. No reason to be upset. People were people. You took them as you found them, part of living on planet Earth.

Bea nattered on. "Now that Michael's history, are you back in the dating game? How long has it been since you had a good orgasm?"

Kendra's eyebrows shot up. "Good grief! What a way to talk."

"Well, it's true. Come on, Kendra. You're pretty, young and attractive. Surely you've seen a few guys you'd find interesting?"

The words conjured the image of Remi with his long hair and compelling eyes. He was a magnificent beast—tall, lean and sculpted. Her heart lurched, sending her mind into a surreal sense of overdrive. When he'd brought her to climax in Dr. Somerville's office, every molecule in her body had felt as if it would explode.

She feigned disinterest, giving a slight shake of her head and sticking out her bottom lip. "Haven't met anyone." Lie. Lie. Lie.

But neither could she admit that the man recently capturing her attention also happened to be a demon—who she might or might not have cooked up in her own needy mind.

"All work and no play makes us dull," Bea reminded. "When was your last date?"

Kendra swallowed the lump in her throat, the one threatening to cut off her air and strangle her. "I haven't seen anyone since Michael and I broke up. . . ." Her words trailed off.

Bea impulsively placed both hands on Kendra's shoulders so they were eye to eye. "Don't bullshit a bullshitter, girl. You didn't die when that car hit you. You must still have feelings." She cocked an eyebrow. "Needs."

Kendra relaxed and shook her head. "My, ah, needs, are on hold at the minute."

"It's only because you want to do it all," Bea grumbled. "You always did everything one hundred percent. No wonder your grades were always straight As. You need to take a break."

Anger against her former friend dissipating, Kendra held up her hands. "I'm just getting back on my feet. Romance is the last thing on my mind."

Bea waved an accusing finger. "I'm not saying anything about romance. I'm talking about a nice roll or two in the hay with a hot piece of eye candy."

Kendra rolled her eyes. Her spirits unaccountably brightened. *If only she knew. . . .* "I get what you're saying."

Bea made a megaphone out of her hands. "But are you listening?"

Heat creeping into her cheeks, Kendra hollered back, "Yes! I am!"

"Good. Don't forget what I've said. A few kisses might do you a world of wonders." With a grin of mischief and a hearty laugh, Bea bustled away on her way to a new life.

Kendra watched her go.

Despite the fact that the conversation had had its bad side, it hadn't been entirely terrible. For the first time in a long time, she felt good. Really good.

Maybe the orgasms have helped. . . .

If only Beatrice knew the kind she'd been having lately. It would blow her mind.

Literally.

The sharp ring of her cell jolted her rudely out of her fantasy. Kendra fumbled for her phone. Its display read *ASSHOLE*. Gerald. After leaving for her appointment, she'd changed his name in her cell's address book. She was still more than a little pissed with him. His bad joke this morning hadn't set well at all.

She sighed. Couldn't ignore him forever. "Hello?"

The asshole spoke. "Where the hell are you?" he demanded

in that way that said he'd gone past irritated and into ballistic. "I've been waiting over an hour for you to get home."

Her temper prickled, but she decided not to bite back. You caught more fucking flies with honey. "I decided to go shopping after my appointment," she said airily. "And I ran into Beatrice Evans, my old college roommate. Remember her? We shared a dorm room my junior year."

"Beatrice? Yeah. I remember her. She had a really nice ass."

Typical Gerald. A womanizer to the core. Of course he'd remember Beatrice. He'd put the moves on the poor girl every chance he'd gotten. Might be part of the reason she'd stopped coming around to visit.

Kendra ignored the lecherous comment. She'd figure out a way to get even with him. Later. She sucked up some more latte, enjoying the rich flavor of the chocolate syrup mixed in the coffee drink—a double shot. She'd had a great orgasm in Dr. Somerville's office, and now some chocolate.

Hell, every day should be this damn good.

Remi was certainly living up to his job as a demon of a revelation.

"Part of getting back out and doing things," she said to Gerald. "Or something like that came out of your own mouth this morning."

"True," he acquiesced. "Very true. I think it's wonderful you're actually having a day out. Did you get anything?"

"Shoes," Kendra lied. "I got some new shoes. Red. High heels."

"Well, get your pretty little red shoes and then come home. I've got some paperwork for you to sign."

Suspicion raised its head. As always, the dark shadows looming deep in her mind threatened to drag her back into the abyss of despair. Sometimes she thought of Gerald like a shadowy specter, always lurking like some kind of omnipotent puppet master, jerking the strings so she'd dance to his tune.

She had no earthly idea why she thought of him that way. She just did.

The chill inside her stomach inexplicably widened. "What paperwork?"

"Insurance papers," he said brusquely. "I'm having the policies updated on the house and its contents. It's all routine stuff, but I need your signature on the policies, too."

16

Several men with video recorders were going through the house, intent on their job of taping every valuable item.

Unwilling to be caught on tape, Kendra dodged past the intruding lenses. "Where is Gerald?"

One of the men lowered his camera. "I believe he and Mr. Montgomery are in the library."

Kendra's stomach cramped with anticipation. An inexplicable chill clutched her heart. She hadn't gone into the library since her first encounter with Gerald's newest acquisition.

As if on cue, her stepbrother poked his head out of the library. "Ah, I thought I heard you come in." He made a motion with his hand. "I need you for a few minutes, please."

She took a few deep breaths to steady herself. "I'm on my way." Nonetheless, her guts tightened as she walked toward the library. Her high heels echoed on the white marble floor. She'd promised herself she'd never go back into the room. Not that it mattered—Remi's reach seemed to have no limitation. Apparently, the demon could get to her whenever and wherever he wanted.

Entering the library, a surge of panic reared inside Kendra. Inexplicable mental alarms went off. A primordial voice from deep within her subconscious shrieked that she should run and not look back. Run away from this place before—what?

She shivered and instinctively rubbed her hands over her arms to still the rising goose bumps. The library was icy, a cool breeze winnowing out of nowhere. She glimpsed a shadowy movement, dark and stealthy, from the corner of her right eye. Stiffening, she turned her head but saw nothing to warrant her burgeoning sense of unease.

Had the movement been a trick of the light?

No.

Kendra was sure she could feel something else in the room. Some*thing* threatening, although the basis for that eluded her. It wasn't Remi but another sort of force. A beast she couldn't quite drag out into the light and expose.

But only Gerald and the insurance agent were present, and neither man appeared to be aware of anything unusual.

Gerald looked up from his paperwork. His gaze was penetrating beneath half-lidded eyes, almost intimate in their appraisal. He didn't conceal the fact he was pleased by what he saw. A smile turned up one corner of his mouth, and one eyebrow arched appreciatively. "Kendra, quit dragging your feet and get over here. Mr. Montgomery hasn't got all day."

Remembering Gerald's not-so-subtle suggestion this morning, Kendra nearly lost her composure. Her heart raced. She wished the floor would collapse beneath her. At least the rubble would offer her a place to hide until she could get her emotions under control. She knew by the way her stepbrother had looked at her that he desired her. And she knew if she'd just crook her finger his way she could have Gerald in her bed in no time flat.

But that was wrong. They'd grown up together. As brother and sister. Crossing that line from platonic into sexual would be wrong. Dead wrong. And however much Gerald disliked the fact . . . well, she would just have to stick to her guns.

Rallying her composure, she cleared her throat. "Of course."

She walked over to Gerald's desk. The lectern loomed in the background. The precious grimoire it held remained under glass, frozen.

She eyed the newcomer, a relatively familiar face. Dane Montgomery was one of her father's closest cronies and had handled all the family's insurance needs for years. He was a trim man in his late fifties, his face round and cheeks unusually ruddy for his pale complexion. His dark hair was sprinkled with gray.

"Hello, Mr. Montgomery," she said. "It's good to see you."

While Dane Montgomery opened a file he held, his brown eyes regarded her closely. "Good to see you looking so well, Kendra," he said. "Gerald tells me you're getting around, maybe going back to college soon." His features were guarded, his eyes strangely intense in their perusal.

Heat surged into Kendra's face, and she gripped her purse to steady herself. She smiled thinly. "Yes, I'm looking into things now."

"She's doing well," Gerald added. "Out shopping today with one of her old college roomies."

Montgomery's gaze narrowed on her as though she was a hardship he had to force himself to accept. "Good for you. Your father would be proud to see how you've picked yourself up."

A sickening, acidic feeling churned in Kendra's stomach. "I hope so." She looked at the folder he held. "Gerald said you have some paperwork for me to sign."

Montgomery nodded. "Yes, I do." He didn't elaborate.

Gerald stood up, offering her his seat. "Here, sit down."

Kendra sat. There was a disquieting air about him. She suddenly didn't relish the idea of being anywhere close to him.

Montgomery presented her with a pile of paperwork. "If

you would, just sign where the markers are." He offered her his pen.

"Certainly." Just as Kendra began to reach for the pen, a vein in her temple began to throb. A shard of agony lanced through her head. Icy pain squeezed her brain. She gasped and then gritted her teeth. A heavy layer of sweat broke out on her forehead. Her mouth went dry. She could not swallow.

She scowled and pressed two fingers to the pulse, fighting an internal battle to control the migraine that threatened to consume her mind. She must fight it with every ounce of strength. She could not succumb. Not now.

Every time she got a headache, Remi came around.

"Not now," she gasped, unaware she was speaking out loud. "Not now."

Montgomery raised a brow. "Excuse me?" he asked, puzzled by her outburst. "Is something wrong?"

Kendra shook her head. "No, I'm fine." Her words were a lie. Her breathing was heavy and painful. She was suddenly nauseated, trembling so hard her eyes could barely keep focused. Her punisher and tormenter never failed to rear his ugly head at the most inopportune times.

"Well, if you would just sign the papers, we'll be done."

Kendra again reached for the pen. Her entire body trembled with the effort. Nevertheless she drew back her shoulders and called on all her willpower to appear calm. "What am I signing?" she asked, dimly aware she didn't have a clue as to what had been shoved in front of her.

Gerald hastened to answer. "It's just a routine updating of the policies. Now that Dad's gone, he's no longer a policy holder. Everything's being transferred into our names, so we can keep the house, the vehicles and ourselves insured. I've also drawn up the paperwork giving you power of attorney over my health care, should I be unable to make such decisions for myself."

Kendra brushed the tips of her fingers over the paper. It was rough to the touch. "Isn't that something Jocelyn should handle?" she asked, surprised.

Gerald frowned, clearly searching for the best words. "As my sister, I would rather you handle that type of thing."

She shook her head. It was sheer misery to think, but she couldn't slow the course of her thoughts. "Still, that's something a wife would want—"

"Let's just say there's a chance Jocelyn won't be around"— he reached into his pocket, drawing out his cigarettes—"in future times."

Shaken by this turn of events, Kendra held out her hand. "Let me bum one, please." Wasting no time, she lit up. God, oh, God. This pain. If it got much worse, she'd surely take another dive into the floor.

Gerald started to say something, decided not to and quietly passed her a cigarette. Already he was a two-pack-a-day smoker, and that number was increasing with each passing day.

Kendra took a deep drag; a pacifying rush of smoke filled her lungs. "I'm sorry to hear that," she said. "I like Jocelyn."

Gerald took another long draw on his cigarette. Its tip glowed red before dying into ashes. He flicked them toward the ashtray. He missed, and they dropped to the floor around his feet. He guiltily brushed at them with the tip of his shoe, leaving long gray streaks on the white marble tile. "We're working on things," he said tightly. "Meanwhile, I want things in order. Just in case. Accidents happen, you know."

A knot wedged in Kendra's throat. Leaning forward, she placed her elbows on the table and massaged her eyes with her fingers, not caring whether or not her makeup was ruined. As much as his words stung, she was not deluded enough to deny them.

Accidents happen, she repeated silently. *Shit happens.*

She smoothed a few stray wisps of hair behind her ears. "Yeah," she said quietly. "I know."

Gerald released a rush of smoke through his nostrils. "It's not about Dad," he said quietly. "Something else has happened."

Kendra glanced up. "What's happened?" She drew in a deep breath. "Is it bad?"

"It's worse than bad," Gerald said. "In fact, it's almost too terrible to think about."

"I guess you had better spit it out."

Snuffing out his cigarette, Gerald released a tremulous sigh. He reached for the newspaper, lying folded in half on his desk. Opening it, he pointed to a brief headline: WOMAN MAULED TO DEATH BY PIT BULLS. The paper wasn't a local Philadelphia paper but one from Los Angeles.

Kendra quickly skimmed the story. A chill of foreboding raced up her spine. "Terrible," she agreed. "But what does that have to do with you?"

Gerald exhaled heavily toward the ceiling. "That is the woman who sold me the *Delomelanicon*." He took another long drag off his cigarette and then exhaled a stream of bluish smoke through pursed lips.

Kendra felt the blood draining from her face as she shook her head. She laughed in disbelief and then sobered when she realized he was serious. Trembling, her voice almost guttural, she said, "Tell me you're kidding, please."

Gerald lit a second cigarette off the remnant of his first. His hand shook—more than a little. "Not that I'm insinuating anything, mind you. It just seems odd that she should have been killed by her own pet dogs within days of selling me the book."

Ice-cold blood spread through Kendra's limbs. Dropping her cigarette into the ashtray, she again massaged the throbbing vein at her temple. Perspiration broke out on her skin, and her sweater clung uncomfortably to her body. "And you think because you have it now that something will happen?"

A terrifying stretch of silence.

Kendra had the distinct impression he was hiding something

from her. Gerald was too tense, uneasy. "Tell me," she insisted quietly.

Gerald shook his head, bringing a tumble of hair onto his pale forehead. He flicked the strands to move them out of his eyes. "When I bought the book," he finally admitted, "the former owner warned me that it came with a curse."

A fierce stab of alarm heated her insides. "W—what kind of a curse?"

Gerald shook his head. "She wouldn't tell me. She only said she hoped I wouldn't find out."

Kendra placed the back of a hand to her clammy brow. A choked sound escaped her lips. She already knew what came with the book.

Demons. The grimoire was riddled with them.

White-hot pain suddenly zinged through her mind, blinding in its intensity. Kendra gasped, trapped within the confines of her own skull, grasping claws pulling her down, down into what she dared not contemplate. Somehow she knew the woman's death was connected to her, and she also knew Gerald's purchase of the book had been a grave mistake.

"Kendra?" She looked up to find her stepbrother standing directly over her, concern warring with curiosity in his expression. "What in the world is going on with you?" he asked.

She blinked. "What do you mean?"

"You went very pale."

Kendra lowered her hand. "I'm fine. Just tired, I guess. It's been a long day."

"If you feel the need for medical attention, a physician can be summoned."

Kendra stifled a nervous laugh. "No. I just need to lie down."

Montgomery stepped in. "If you could just sign the paperwork, Kendra, I can be on my way."

Kendra glanced up. She'd totally forgotten his presence. "Oh, certainly," she mumbled. Reclaiming his pen, she quickly scribbled her name in the places indicated by the colored sticky notes.

"I don't believe in such nonsense," Gerald said. "But still, it's safe to have all your ducks in a row in case something happens. Imagine being attacked and mauled to death by your own dogs."

"That's a shame," Montgomery said, scooping up the papers she'd just autographed. "But dogs like that have a bad reputation for turning on you in the blink of an eye."

A wry smile appeared on Gerald's mouth. "Undoubtedly," he agreed. "An accident, however tragic."

A choked sound came from Kendra as she rose to her feet. She needed to get out of the library, away from that damned book. She had a feeling the former owner's death wasn't an accident.

It had been a deliberate punishment.

For what, she didn't know.

Again, a strange force pushed to the forefront of her mind. A thought caught her unawares, and she cringed at the force of it as it lanced her mind.

Once the grimoire and its demons latched on to someone, they never let them go.

17

Feeling sick to her stomach, Kendra ran to her room. Locking the door behind her, she sat on the bed. She winced as her headache intensified, pain gripping the back of her neck and spine.

Her day had started off badly and progressively gotten worse. On the brink of collapse, she placed a hand to her clammy forehead, desperately trying to will away the sensations incapacitating her. Damnit. Now was no time to be on the edge, coming apart at the seams.

Hugging herself, she rocked back and forth, fighting off the blackness flowing across her vision like ink over paper. A curious sensation passed through her, something akin to a cold hand clasping her spine from the inside.

She tried to summon saliva into her parched mouth. None came. Icy pain squeezed her brain so fiercely a growl of a moan escaped her.

As with her experience in the library, Kendra was vaguely aware of a physical shifting, as if the room around her were somehow reshaping itself. Time spun away, vanishing as a strange sensation of numbness overtook her senses. Her pain began to drizzle away.

Fading. Thankfully fading.

Her eyelids drooped. Darkness crept closer.

Kendra forced them up again, blinking hard, struggling to regain her vision. A shiver passed through her. It was all she could do not to bolt from her bedroom.

Go where?

Beyond the window across from her, the sun began to sink into the west. In the distance, black clouds were gathering like a swarm of pissed-off hornets. From the looks of the sky, the weather was in for a drastic change. A storm was closing in, presaged by unnatural stillness. Not a leaf stirred. It was as if the wind were deliberately holding back, the dead calm a harbinger of what was to come. A silent, slinking darkness overtook Earth as the last light of the day succumbed to night.

Just as the last of that light drizzled away, Kendra thought she detected the dulcet tones of a man's voice. It was drifting from the adjoining room, soft and enticing. She listened for a time, the words not loud enough for her to recognize the speaker.

Inexplicably drawn to it, she hurried across her room.

The voice whispered steadily on, slightly muffled by the closed doors separating her bedroom from her sitting room.

Hugging herself, Kendra crossed to the door separating the two rooms. She hovered uncertainly, an ear to the wood. The melodious voice wove its way through her, around her.

Beckoning her inside.

Kendra looked down as she closed her fingers around one of the crystal knobs. It was cold to the touch, unnaturally icy. Surprised, she jerked her hand away. She considered leaving and would have, if not for the knowledge of what lay on the other side of the door. An image of her unearthly tormentor glided into her mind.

Remi.

She drew back, closed her eyes and fought against a rising tide of fresh panic. *I need to know why he's here, why he's latched on to me.*

Taking several deep breaths to calm herself, she reached down and again grasped the doorknob. It turned smoothly under her hand. She eased the door open, praying the hinges would not give away her presence. She continued to push the door until the room came into full view.

Despite herself, Kendra stepped inside. As if pushed by a phantom hand, the door shut behind her. Locked itself.

She looked around the familiar room. Two walls were lined with book-laden shelves, her own collection nowhere near as large as Gerald's, but satisfying nevertheless. Beneath the vaulted ceilings, several long couches covered with crocheted quilts invited one to stretch out, as did comfortable longues with high-backs and leather upholstery. Tables were at hand, sporting newspapers, magazines and coasters to hold drinks. An easel, sketch pad and chalk were situated near a window seat that afforded a view of the estate's back acreage and the magnificent sunsets that waltzed across the lawns as night descended.

A disconcerting feeling further came over her, this one a feeling of not being alone, of playfulness. She thought she heard a man's breathy sigh, felt a caress across the back of her neck.

Squeezing her eyes shut, Kendra breathed deeply. There was no mistaking Remi's scent.

She turned, half expecting to see him behind her. But there was no one there. Her eyes automatically drifted to one of the pictures on her wall, a beautiful, sun-drenched tropical landscape.

She immediately noticed the change. Where before the portrait had shown only the vaguest hints of pigment, she could now clearly see that color was bleeding and blending, bright and vibrant, bursting with an energy that seemed to come from within the canvas itself. Stranger still was that the other paintings around the room were slowly losing their color—as if they were being sucked dry by the forces centered on this one.

More incredibly still, Remi stood inside the portrait. Inside his newly multihued realm, he beckoned for her to come closer.

At this point, all logic completely fled.

"Kendra," he said. "Join me." Though his words were a bit muffled, she could hear him perfectly.

Kendra shook her head in confusion. His invitation made no sense to her. As though caught in the ties of a strange dream, she lifted her arm, reaching out to touch the canvas. Tension coiled inside her. "Why are you doing this to me?"

Remi laughed. "Because I can."

"It's to make me crazy," she gasped.

His grin grew wider. "If you would call seduction making you crazy, I suppose I am. First, with enticing words and then with a beautiful place to make love."

Nothing about this made any sense. Somewhere between going into her room and sitting down on the bed, she must have fallen asleep.

Except—she didn't feel asleep. In fact, she felt very wide awake and aware.

A shadow of doubt crossed her features. "Nothing makes sense," she allowed slowly. "The beautiful place—it's a picture hanging on my wall. Or don't you know that?"

"I know it." Remi spread his arms as though welcoming her. "A demon knows no boundaries."

Letting her hand drop, Kendra shook her head. A human did have boundaries. "Stop playing with my mind, Remi. You're driving me insane."

The demon's merry laugh drew her eyes back to the landscape. "Perhaps I am keeping you sane," he countered with another devilish laugh.

Kendra shook her head. "Impossible."

"In my world, all things are possible," he said and gestured again. "Come. See for yourself."

Even though she wanted to resist his invitation, Kendra took a step toward the wall. Her limbs seemed to have taken on a life all their own, ignoring her commands to turn and run away.

"Stop doing this to me," she muttered more to herself than to him. "I don't want to."

Remi gestured again. "Yes, you do."

It was utterly impossible for her to resist his command.

She experienced a sense of urgency, of compulsion in his presence. His faraway figure continued to entice her. She was aware of the beating of her heart, the air she drew into her lungs. How could she be unconscious yet so aware at the same time?

"Come to me," he urged. "Come with me."

She released a disparaging puff of air and shook her head. "I don't want to."

Despite her refusal, Kendra took another step forward and then another, gliding through the wall and into the picture as if she were a sylph made of smoke.

Before she knew what had happened, she was enveloped in deep shadows dancing around her in the most alarming manner. It seemed they were clutching at her, drawing her into the depths of she knew not where. A strangled gasp erupted from her throat. Moments later, she felt buoyant, as if floating out of herself.

She panicked, trying to step back, but grasping fingers pulled at her, refusing to let go. Her gaze shifted to the eerie mist swirling around her with dizzying speed. The mist pulsed with life, changing from reddish yellow to white to gray to black before going to reddish yellow again in mere seconds.

Something within called to her through a link with her

mind, threatening to love and slay her all in one seductive instant. Remi was the center of the dimensional universe he'd beckoned her into. To manipulate or to be manipulated was all he existed for.

As suddenly as she'd gone into the darkness, Kendra found herself standing on a velvety green region set against wooded hills. A soft summer's breeze swept across her face and ruffled her hair. The sun in the crystal-blue sky over her head dappled the leaves of the trees and grass. In the distance was a gently bubbling stream.

Confused by the unfamiliar landscape, she lifted a hand to shade her eyes from the glare. She felt the sun's warmth on her skin, heard birds chirping, smelled the fresh scent of air untainted by any trace of civilization.

Looking around, she quickly surmised that she was completely and utterly alone in the vast expanse. Could she believe what she was seeing, or had she gone completely out of her head?

A stir behind her caught her attention. She heard Remi before she saw him.

"Kendra. My beautiful Kendra."

She spun around, her gaze searching for and then settling on the familiar figure. A breath hitched in her throat. Instead of his usual loincloth, Remi was naked. Hardly a surprise. He seemed to spend most of his time in a complete state of undress.

A furnace blast of pure lust made her mouth go cotton dry.

Not that Kendra minded. With his wide shoulders, rippling abdomen and long, lean legs, he was the perfect male specimen, right down to the cock she couldn't possibly ignore even if she wanted to. Even when flaccid, his penis managed to impress. His blond hair with its fiery red and copper highlights hung to the middle of his back, its length pulled by the wind surfing through the trees.

Kendra felt her blood pressure rise. He was breathtaking. "Absolutely beautiful."

Remi's mouth arched upward with a contented smile. "As are you." An impish gleam lit his gaze as he eyed her from head to foot.

Not that there was much to see.

Kendra followed his blatant stare, realizing for the first time that she was as naked as the day she'd been birthed.

Blushing hot, she let out a groan. "Don't you ever get enough?" She glanced up. His steely eyes were stormy with a heat transcending lust.

Remi shook his head. "I'll never get enough of you." He sighed, a sound of longing. "As last I have finally found a woman I truly desire."

Kendra swallowed with effort. For an instant, she thought she read torment in his expression. The kind of torment seen in the face of someone in desperate need of affection but unable to express themselves verbally. She blinked a bit dazedly at him. The intensity behind his perusal was beginning to unsettle her. "Y—you desire me?"

He met her gaze. "I do. Very much." He brushed his fingers across her breasts, across the ridges of the scars marring her skin.

Kendra felt the pull of his touch all the way to her groin. Her legs wobbled, her knees going weak. She started to wrap her arm around her chest in an instinctive move to cover the ugly things.

Remi gently caught her wrists, holding her hands away from her body. "Only you think the scars are ugly. To me they are your glory, your trial by fire." The heat in his gaze burned away her trepidation.

For the first time, Kendra looked, really looked, closely at the tattoos inked into his skin. It was then she realized the symbols hadn't been etched into his skin—they'd been branded there, deep enough to raise thick ridges on his flesh. Like her, he was scarred.

Punished.

She reached out, outlining the path of one dark arch. She couldn't be sure, but, more than a design, the tattoos seemed to be lettering. Some kind of ancient lettering. "What do they mean?"

Remi moaned softly as her finger traced the sensitive area. "They are the marks of my damnation. I will wear them through eternity until the end of my time."

The constricting tug around Kendra's lungs tightened. Sweat beaded on her upper lip, and she drew in a reedy breath. "Then you weren't always a demon?"

His stare growing somber, he shifted uncomfortably. "In the beginning, no." He drew in a breath and released it slowly. "Once, a very long time ago, I was a seraph."

Kendra shivered at the implication behind his words. Demons weren't the souls of humans gone bad but of angels cast out of heaven for defying God. Fear, sick and clammy, oozed through her bowels. "Are you . . . ?"

Seeming to read her mind, Remi's eyes darkened subtly. "One of the fallen?" He nodded slowly. "Once, I was an angel who sat at the Creator's right hand. To worship and adore was my only reason for being."

Knowing her bible lessons well enough, Kendra shivered. "But it wasn't enough." Not a question.

Remi looked as if she had driven a stake through his heart. "Always a god's heart hungers for more."

Kendra clamped her teeth against the cold nausea of her dread. One need not believe the story of conflict between the celestial beings and mankind to know how it had played out. "And so men were created."

Remi nodded. "And for him, woman."

Deeply disquieted, Kendra eyed him warily. "But more than being created to worship, man was given something the angels could never have."

"Free will," Remi murmured. "The right to choose your own destiny. To make your own choices."

Kendra glanced at him again. She knew how the story ended. "And the angels' jealousy and envy of humans got them all cast out."

Remi looked deeply into her eyes through a guarded expression. "We were thrown away, down into an abyss of fire and ice." He slapped a hand on his shoulder and down his arm, as if slathering it in oil. "Our skin, too, was marked with the wretched symbols of our blasphemy—a despised and accursed thing to bear. As a further curse, we were given the hearts of humans and the minds of demons. Our revenge for such eternal damnation is to prey on mankind, expose the weaknesses of body, mind and spirit. Always we prey with the intent to introduce a rot into a victim that will decay—and destroy."

Kendra's heart pounded hollowly inside her chest. She saw through his eyes a land mantled in eerie mists that brought neither day nor night. A land of fiery molten lava boiling amid vast barren fields of pure ice.

She swept her tongue along her lower lip. "Is that why you've latched on to me?" she asked, voice barely above a whisper.

Remi's eyes lit up with a crafty glint. "Exposing your weak spots, glutting myself on your insecurities. As a demon, it is my mission."

Fear hit her again. She started to take a step back, away from him, but her limbs wouldn't obey her silent command, leaving her rooted to the spot. Open and vulnerable.

"To drive me insane," she murmured.

Remi stared at her for a long moment and then reached out and brushed his fingertips tentatively across her lips. His touch heated her skin. "There you are wrong," he said softly.

Desire flared to live once more.

Kendra closed her eyes against the tremors of awareness slithering through her veins. Remi affected her on more than the physical plane. He'd not only gotten inside her head, he'd delved deep into her psyche, and that made his control over her even more dangerous . . . and explosive. "I don't understand."

He paused a beat and then answered. "I stand before you now, not as a demon commanded to destroy you, but as a man desiring a woman. Though it may seem unclear now, the bond between us is growing, strengthening. Give yourself to me, and I will not betray you."

18

I will not betray you.

An unexpected tremor shimmied down Kendra's spine as Remi's words whirled in her mind. Closing her eyes, she swallowed over the lump in her throat. "How do I know you're not lying to me?" She whispered the question, barely daring to speak the words aloud. "After all you've done . . . how do I know I can trust you not to hurt me?"

Remi reached out, smoothing long strands of hair away from her face, running his thumbs over her cheekbones. His sun-warm skin chased away the chill penetrating her bones. "You don't," he murmured. "You must have faith."

Strange sensations moved through her body as though slow, sensual circles were being drawn around the tips of her nipples. *I'm totally enchanted with this man,* she thought crazily.

But it wasn't logical. Remi was a demon. A deceiver of human senses.

Kendra hardly cared. What mattered to her was the here and now. She wished her heart would stop pounding before it cut off her breathing altogether. "My faith has been awfully thin lately," she whispered, voice going hoarse.

Remi leaned toward her, reaching out and tipping back her head. His warm breath tickled her face. "Just accept that it's real," he said. "That I will be with you as long as I can."

Kendra opened her eyes. "Why me?"

Remi dipped his head until their lips almost touched. "For the first time in my eternity, I have found a woman worthy of my heart," he said against her mouth. "And I will defy all damnation to keep you safe."

His words squeezed her heart. His conviction was strong, his words solid to the core. It was easy to believe he meant exactly what he said.

Even if he was lying to her.

Closing her eyes, Kendra metaphorically took another step into Remi's world. Like a rope ladder in the wind, it quivered but held firm.

Pulse pounding in her temples, she leaned into the caress of his warm breath against her lips. His mouth crushed hers, hot, hungry and wet. Their kiss wasn't a whisper, a gentle meeting of mouths, but rather a shout. Hungry, grasping and desperate.

Remi tasted sweet and musky, like a fine old port, well aged in the cask of a dark cellar. His lips moved to her neck, teeth nipping at the pulse point in her neck as if to get at the fragile vein below her skin. His hands slid up her hips, cupping her breasts.

A shiver chased through her. She was on fire, her core an aching, boiling mass of something she couldn't quite fathom. *I'm falling in love with him. . . .*

Nibbling her lower lip, Remi continued to cradle her breasts. "Let me please you." His hands rubbed gently, squeezing and fondling. A growl of need rumbled deep in the back of his throat.

Kendra drew in a breath, arching her body closer to his. His mouth came down over hers again, his hands sliding around to cup her behind as though to prevent her from escaping him.

She had no thought of escaping his hold. Pushing up to the tips of her toes, she pressed her mouth back against his, her tongue eagerly entering into the duel. Her arms circled his neck, her fingers delving into his long, thick hair to pull him closer.

Everything became jumbled in her mind after that.

Somehow they dropped to the ground, and she was on her back in the warm grass. On top of her, Remi had total control, exploring her body with eager hands, trying to taste, lick, bite and suck every inch at once. His weight was half on her, one of his thighs nestled between her spread legs, holding them apart.

His free hand stroked down her firm belly, reaching for the creamy warmth between her legs. "This is what I have been aching for. To taste your sweet cunt again and then feel it closing around my cock."

Her blood heating under his touch on her bare skin, Kendra willingly tilted her hips to allow him free access. "Like I haven't been dying to feel that cock of yours inside me again."

Remi slid his hand toward her mound, delving through her silken curls and then her moistness as he caressed her clit. "I need you, Kendra," he groaned, smiling down at her with an arousing intensity that set her heart afire.

Kendra's brain was fogging, but she didn't care. She only knew she wanted to make love to this magnificent beast. Whether it made any sense, she didn't care. She was only thinking of now. "Then take me."

"Oh, I intend to." Remi pinned her hands to the ground. "Over and over." He lowered his head to her chest.

Kendra gasped when his mouth closed over one hard peak. A quiver ran through her body. Breathless little sounds escaped her lips as his tongue expertly painted the sensitive little bead.

A smile twitched at her lips. "Oh, that's nice." The caress of his tongue around her areola gave life to a swirling ribbon of lust that coiled deeper and tighter inside her core.

Remi raised his head long enough to give her a lazy grin. Kendra's heart beat rapidly in her chest. His hands held her wrists pinioned tightly, forcing her body to ache and strain with need. She closed her eyes, picturing him mounting her, aiming his delicious cock at the center of her sex and then diving in with one long, deep thrust. . . .

Her breath caught again, her back again arching when he again captured one pink nipple. He gave the little nubbin a soft nip, bringing a soft flash of pain.

Kendra let out a quick rush of air. "I wasn't expecting that," she breathed. "Not fair. . . ." The way he could make her body feel defied description. Hard and hot as a branding iron, his cock strained against her inner thigh, harder and more insistent with each passing minute.

Letting go of her wrists, Remi moved lower. His lips brushed over the soft planes of her abdomen. "I want to make every way I touch you enjoyable."

Kendra recognized his intent. Remi grinned at the sight of her, spread open for the taking. The heated, moist sensation of his tongue lapped against her exposed sex.

Kendra's hips bucked. A series of tremors began to shimmy throughout her body, the waves continuing to engulf her until all her senses were swamped in a pool of unending delight.

His mouth still dancing around her most sensitive nerves, Remi slipped one thick finger inside. Making oral love to her clit, his finger slipped in and out of her eager sex.

The heated, moist sensation of his mouth nuzzling her as his fingers invaded her sex sent white-hot darts of need shooting straight down Kendra's spine. Everything he did felt magnificent.

She let out a loud moan. The thunder of her heartbeat was so strong she almost felt as though she'd pass out from the sheer pleasure he instigated. As if on his command, she started to shake. A thrill blazed through her, spreading and growing like wildfire across dry prairie grass. Screaming in delight, she climaxed.

Remi slowed the pace. No longer thrusting with his finger, his thumb still worked its magic on her clit. "I enjoy seeing you take pleasure at my touch," he murmured.

Still trembling from head to foot, Kendra opened her eyes to find him staring down at her. His masculine features were so perfect, the satin veil of his hair parted simply down the middle to fall in a curtain around his shoulders. She would have been content to look at him forever, except that every circle of his thumb on her sex made her hotter and hornier than ever.

So far he'd done all the hard work.

It was time to give the gift of what she'd received.

Sitting up, Kendra slid her hands over his chest, savoring the feel of his skin under her palms. She felt the hot sun beating down upon his naked flesh. "Let me touch you."

Remi's lips turned up at the corners in a slow grin that set her pulse to beating in her ears. "I would be pleased if you wanted to."

Kendra's hands sank lower. "I've been dying to get my lips around this," she confessed. Glancing up at him, she coquettishly grinned, wrapping her fingers around his erection. Fully engorged, his cock was long and thickly veined. The crown flared, wide and broad, as ripe and firm as a peach under the sun. A moist drop of pre-cum seeped from its head.

Remi shivered when she gently ran her closed fist up and down his length, tugging and teasing. His head fell back, and a strangled sound escaped his throat.

Kendra grinned. "Feel good?" He was powerless in her grasp. Even if she was to deliver great pain, he would not have been able to stop her. She could do with him as she wished, and he would welcome it.

Closing his eyes, he clenched his teeth and fought to keep control over his impulses. "Very good," he managed before another moan overtook him.

She gave him a wicked grin. "Relax," she warned him. "Don't come too soon."

"Keep touching me like that," he half gasped, half moaned, "and I will most certainly come."

Kendra laughed, pushing him onto his back and straddling his legs. Positions reversed, she was in control. With her thighs spread across him, she was determined to have her way with him. The tightening of his muscles and the tensing of his nerves gave her a wonderful sensation of power.

She bent and, with slow, deliberate circles, traced his engorged tip. Her tongue flicked over the broad crown before slowly swirling down his length.

Control melting like hot wax, Remi gave himself to the moment. His hips bucked upward, desperate to satisfy the aching need clearly undulating through his body. His big hands slipping into her hair, he held her head, clearly hovering on the brink of a delicious climax.

Kendra felt his tremors begin, small waves at first, and then totally swallowing him up in an intense convulsion of pure pleasure.

There was no way she was going to let him leave her behind.

Lifting her mouth away, Kendra shifted her body over his straining erection. Unable to keep himself at bay another minute, Remi immediately grabbed her hips and pulled her down on top of his rigid erection even as he simultaneously thrust up inside her slick heat.

Startled by the size of him coupled with the intensity of his entry, Kendra arched in agony, unleashing a cry into the air. His demanding lunge had let her know exactly what he intended to do to her.

Leaning forward, Kendra's nails dug into his flesh. "How could I forget how damn big you are?" she gasped.

Remi lifted her, pulling almost all the way out. "But you like the pain," he said.

She hitched a much needed breath. "God, yes . . . I can feel every damn inch."

He grinned. "Just like I can feel every inch of you around me." He moved his hips upward, slowly easing into her silky depth. "Mmmm. No woman has a right to be that damn tight."

Kendra ground her teeth together. The tip of him was smooth, but with every thrust she felt the rough, veined ridges of his cock. The friction, delicious as it was, bordered on unbearable. "No demon has a right to be hung like a stallion either," she gritted.

Beneath her, Remi started a slow and easy stroke. The action brought their bodies together until they weren't just joined but were united as one. "Relax."

Kendra glanced down. From the look on his face, she could see he was fighting to keep control of his own needs. "You're the one who needs to relax," she breathed. Rocking her hips against his, she allowed him even fuller and deeper access. Her initial pain faded into something far different, something delicious, creating an agony so exquisite she called out for longer, harder strokes.

Between them they began a rhythmic undulation that grew more frenzied and eager with each passing moment.

Kendra gave herself to the exquisite sensations of his hips pounding up against hers, hammering her as soundly as iron would drive nails.

With every lunge of his hips beneath hers, Remi went farther inside her. The crown of his erection shuttled in and out until the friction was enjoyably unbearable as they both approached the edge of orgasm.

The peak of absolute release came without warning, sweeping both of them away.

Remi went over the edge first. Groaning, his fingers dug into her thighs even as his hips surged up into her a final time. His cock spat fire, sending out a stream of hot semen. Kendra willingly followed in his wake.

The fast and furious pace ceased.

Her body trembling with aftershocks, Kendra tugged a breath into her burning lungs. She doubted she would ever breathe normally again. Remi was still inside her, thrust so deep it felt like they'd be connected together forever.

The demon again grinned up at her. He surprised her by giving one nipple a playful tweak. "I should let you take control more often." His hands cupped her breasts; his fingers circled her nipples, slow and steadily. "No other woman has ever put me beneath her."

Kendra's hard little peaks tightened deliciously. She sucked in a ragged breath. His unique scent, a spicy mixture of sweat and musk, filtered through her senses. If she'd been in danger of losing control, it didn't matter anymore.

She'd gone over the edge.

And liked it.

Her palms still spread across his heaving chest, she returned the favor, brushing her thumbs across his dusky, flat male nipples. "Just goes to show you I fully deserve to be on top." Giving him a wicked wink, she flexed muscles deep inside her abdomen.

He gasped at the feel of her inner muscles rippling around his length. "Do that again, and I'll have you again," he sighed with satisfaction.

Her pulse still pumping at an accelerated rate, Kendra shot him a mock stern glare. As she looked at him splayed beneath her, her stomach muscles contracted with need. "I don't think you can handle it," she said, tongue firmly in cheek.

Remi slipped his hands behind her. His warm palms settled on her ass, spreading her open. A roguish light glinted in the depths of his gaze. "Oh, I intend to," he rumbled. "No part of you will be virgin by the time I am finished with you."

Catching his meaning, Kendra gasped. "I've never had—" she started to say. Her brows knit; her mind churned. Accepting the thought wasn't easy. Thinking about the territory he hadn't yet explored made her words end in a slow groan.

His gaze never left hers. "Don't worry. I know how to fit a very big thing into a very small space."

19

Darkness stood its own vigil over Kendra's slumber until something prodded her awake. At least, she thought she was awake. Her mind was sluggish, her eyes scratchy and dry. Her muscles and joints ached as though she had been jogging several miles.

Opening her eyes, she peered into the inky blackness. A quick look around told her she was still in her very own room, asleep in her very own bed. She strained her ears, listening for the voice. Outside her windows, branches scratched at the panes like sharp fingernails raking across a chalkboard. The wind howled in a creepy whine, raising gooseflesh on her arms.

Somehow the hours had slipped by with mind-boggling speed—almost preternaturally.

The demon had again come and gone, leaving her arms empty and her body aching for his touch. The memory of what he'd done to her still lingered in her mind, as bright and as vivid as if it had actually occurred.

Of course, it hadn't.

She knew why she was having trouble concentrating. Remi. The damned thing had insinuated himself into her world, crept into her mind, and now she could not get him out. He could be silent for hours at a time, but it always felt as though he was there with her. Watching. Listening. Judging even her thoughts. It was her paranoia, of course.

Sanity and insanity warred for domain as she told herself the demon had to be an illusion, some strange trick her mind was playing on itself. She could only pray her final descent into madness would be a gentle one.

Something behind her moved, jarring the mattress.

Kendra sat up, eyes agog at the sight.

Remi was stretched out beside her in all his naked glory.

This was it. She'd just gone around the bend.

He was asleep, his features slack, unguarded in slumber. Despite his age, which must have numbered in centuries, he looked very young. Vulnerable.

Unaccountably, Kendra's heart swelled at the sight. *He must have been one of the most beautiful angels.* Even his scars—those terrible symbols burned into his skin—did nothing to detract from his looks. They belonged to him, were a part of him.

Just as her scars were a part of her.

A disembodied voice caressed her ears. *We can't change the past or who we are,* it said. *We can only accept what we have become and go on.*

Needing to touch him, Kendra reached out and stroked her hand across the broad expanse of his hairless chest. His skin felt real, solid under her hand. The simple touch gave life to a twirling ribbon of need that pulled her in deeper.

Remi opened his eyes. Smiled. "Mmmm. You can keep that hand going downward, if you like."

Kendra's gaze strayed to the center of him, to the penis nestled snugly in a tight thatch of blond curls. His cock twitched, a sure sign of his arousal.

Drawing a deep breath, she met his gaze with determination. "I thought I imagined you. Everything we've done."

Remi yawned and stretched. "A little mind fuck can be nice." A slow grin began to simmer on his fine lips. "But I want you to be wide awake and aware when I take that tight little ass of yours."

Kendra gasped with surprise, covering her mouth with a hand. "Uh-uh," she said between her fingers. "This is all just an illusion."

Remi slowly shook his head. "Oh, it is all too real, my dear. And you remember what I told you the first day I arrived?"

Blushing, Kendra nodded. "That I would have to submit to you."

He nodded. "Totally and completely."

Cold fingers clamped around her heart. Squeezed. "Please . . . I've never . . ."

Remi's hand slid down his abdomen. His fingers curled around his shaft, no longer flaccid or inattentive to the situation at hand. "I want that now, Kendra. To have you totally and completely."

A new wave of anxiety flowed through her. She felt as if her world had risen up and tilted sideways, knocking her off balance all over again. "Why are you doing this to me?" she asked, her mind still not fully functioning or able to grasp his reemergence.

His palm stroked his cock, and Remi's gaze searched hers. "I'm going to possess you in every way possible," he breathed. "And when I have done that, you will belong to me, Kendra. Only to me."

Although the idea of being taken in such an unnatural way frightened her a little, she couldn't resist trying to imagine what it would feel like as Remi claimed her. All of her. She wanted all her senses to feel alive, and she wanted to experience making love with him again.

Heat again surfaced in her cheeks. "Will it hurt?"

A sardonic smile twitched on his lips. "I can make it hurt as much or as little as you like."

His words gripped her spine like icy claws.

Kendra's gaze settled on his cock. He was larger than any man—human or not—had a right to be. A poorly suppressed shudder worked through her. The air surrounding them was charged with electricity. It was easy to imagine the pain he could deliver—and the pleasure. Somehow she had the feeling she must endure his demand, however frightening or distasteful. For the sake of her sanity.

For the sake of my soul.

"I won't force you," Remi said softly. "But if you agree, I won't hold back." The concentrated look on his face vanished, replaced by one even more intense but equally sexy. It was the kind of look that made her nerve endings tingle.

Kendra exhaled the breath she hadn't been aware she was holding. "Yes," she said. "Do it."

Cock still in hand, he graced her with a lazy grin. "I've been waiting for that tight little ass of yours."

Kendra couldn't help shivering. "What is it about anal that turns you on so much?"

"Penetration of the forbidden aside, I need you to trust me—without doubt. Can you do that?"

She nodded. "I think so."

"Good. Then take off your clothes."

Kendra's brows rose. "What?"

"Take off your clothes," he repeated.

She looked down, realizing she was still dressed in the same skirt and sweater she'd put on earlier in the day. "Oh." Suddenly embarrassed, she slipped off the bed. "Just a minute."

He sat up. "Where are you going?"

She pointed toward the adjoining bathroom. "To undress."

Smiling, he shook his head. "Undress right here. Where I

can watch you." He settled back on the pillows. "Take off your sweater."

Kendra tugged at her sweater, trying to work the expensive fabric over her head with a modicum of grace. It caught on her necklace, causing her to tug harder. The thin chain holding her cross snapped. Jewelry tangled in the weave, and she let it all drop to the floor in a heap.

"Sorry." She grimaced. "Not sexy."

"That's what you think." Remi's hand traveled the length of his penis and then back down again. Damn, but between flashes of lightning his cock seemed to grow longer and harder with each pass of his hand. In the shadows it looked at least a foot long. Maybe more.

Imagining that iron-hot bar up her ass, Kendra gulped.

Her skirt was easier to manage. Reaching to the zipper on one hip, she lowered it, slip and all, and then stepped out of the pile.

Remi eyed the last of her ensemble. A sexy red bra hugged her breasts, just as matching lace panties cupped her ass. Garterless stockings in a sheer flesh tone hugged her legs. Her heels, while not super high, gave her legs a nice, shapely curve.

Remi grinned. "Now that's what I've been waiting for."

Kendra started to unhook her bra.

"Don't." Sliding to the edge of the bed, Remi pulled her between his spread legs. His cock arched against his lean abdomen, eager to feed. He traced the lacy edging over one breast. "Nice."

Kendra's nipples pushed against the taut confinement. While not exceptionally large, she wore a B cup and filled it quite well.

Expert hands unsnapped the front catch of her bra. The cups fell away. Her nipples jutted out, proud and hard.

His hands circling her hips, Remi pulled her forward. His mouth closed over one tip, giving life to an ache that was as sweet as it was demanding. As he suckled the sensitive nubbin,

Kendra was aware that his penis surged between them, just inches away from her creaming slit. He was huge, more than aroused, and the thought of him penetrating her on any level turned her insides molten.

Moaning softly, Kendra slipped her fingers through his long, silky hair. She offered him her other nipple. "Please," she murmured.

Remi obliged. His lips closed around the rosy, hard tip.

Pressing her body even closer to his, Kendra groaned into his hair. Her pelvis arched nearer to his cock, her dew soaking the crotch of her panties. "Damn, I want you."

Slowly, languorously, Remi slipped off the edge of the bed. His mouth slipped over the slope of her breast as he trailed his lips down her rib cage. Lips pressed against her vulnerable skin, and he slipped his fingers into the edge of the panties. The silky fabric slid over her ass and down her thighs.

Kendra gasped. The feel of her panties going down her legs was one of the most sensual she'd ever experienced. Her insides boiled, her core going past molten to atomic.

One strong hand slid up her inner thigh, finding the cleft concealed by the short thatch of intimate curls. "I know you're wet." His lips stroked her abdomen. His tongue dipped into her navel. "Ready to be fucked."

Kendra shivered when his fingers found and stroked her clit. Each slide of his thick fingers over the sensitive bundle of nerves stoked an ache she doubted could ever be sated. "I am."

His hands on her hips, Remi turned her around. "Kneel in front of me."

Far beyond refusing him anything, Kendra knelt. What he intended to do, no other man ever had. It was almost too intimate to consider.

A gentle pressure at her back. "On your hands and knees."

Kendra planted her hands palm down on the carpeting. "Like this?"

"Perfect." Remi knelt behind her, parting her ass cheeks. He pushed the tip of one finger into her soft, pink anus.

Kendra gasped from the sensation that aimed straight for her core. Without thinking, she tightened her cheeks, automatically trying to keep out the invader.

"It will hurt more if you don't relax," Remi said softly.

"I've never . . ."

Sensing her hesitation, Remi drew his finger away. "You need some relaxing."

Seconds later, her cheeks parted again. This time his warm tongue invaded the cleft of her ass. His mouth was soft and warm, his searching tongue sweeping inside her most intimate places.

Her clit pulsing with pleasure, Kendra pressed back against him. "Oh, my," she gasped. "I never knew . . . That feels so . . . ." The ability to speak coherently left her. With the storm as their only music, his lips expertly pleasured her.

When the warmth of his mouth drew away, Kendra drew in an unsteady breath. There was no mistaking her body wanted him. Wanted *this*.

His cock slipped between her ass cheeks, and Remi nudged against her wet flesh, groaning. "Relax. I'll do the rest."

Biting down on her bottom lip, Kendra hesitated. "Okay." Her fingers dug into the thick shag carpeting. "Now."

Remi pushed a little harder. The crown of his penis felt broad and hot as it pressed against her tight anus. "Press your hips back against me," he moaned.

Closing her eyes, Kendra eased her body back against his hard shaft, concentrating to open herself as wide as physically possible.

A slow, long groan broke from Remi's throat. His erection broke through the tight clench of muscle, sliding inside her tightest crevasse. "Ah, paradise. . . ."

Kendra breathed through her mouth as she slowly took him into her depth, sinking back against his hips until she'd consumed him to the balls. His cock was heat, breadth and a spike of sheer pulsating pleasure. . . .

He was seated deep inside her. One of Remi's hands circled around her hip, fingers probing between her legs. His thick fingers found her slit and then sank deep inside her eager sex. "Now, I own you," he gasped.

Kendra didn't care. She rocked forward, then back. Remi's shaft pulled out. Ah, relief. She pushed back, and it slid back inside her willing anus. Rapture held hands with the dazzling edge of a throb that must be sated. . . .

Remi filled her cunt even as his cock filled her ass, and he again groaned. His hips undulated against hers, driving his cock the way a workman would push a jackhammer into concrete.

Kendra risked a glance over one shoulder. Twisted with fierce passion, his features didn't look human. The intimacy of such a carnal act sent a bolt of fire burning straight into her core. The scent of two aroused bodies intent on chasing pleasure intoxicated her.

The potent thought of being taken by a demon added a fearsome edge of the forbidden to her sinister gratification.

Remi moaned, and his free hand slid around to cup Kendra's left breast. "There. I have you completely." He pulled at the engorged nipple.

Kendra writhed with a fierce, rapacious need that stunned her. Breast fondled, cunt stuffed, ass conquered—Remi had her just the way he wanted.

A weak moan of unsettling enjoyment escaped her.

Remi growled. He thrust hard, grinding his cock deeper into her. His fingers invaded, taking liberal advantage of her dripping sex. "There's no getting out of it now," he rumbled.

Conquered as she'd never imagined, Kendra moaned in dismay. She couldn't think much further beyond the cock reaming her ass or the fingers stabbing her depth. That Remi had found a way to fuck her completely slashed a violent rip of feral gratification across her heart. Though she fought against it, she felt the unexpected and vicious ascension of the blistering pressure that signaled imminent climax.

A shiver raced through her. A reverberating, almost fluid snarl vibrated up her throat, boiling over her breath-scorched lips. Each calculated lunge goaded her, forced her to take him deeper. The swelling pressure in her ass threatened to explode.

Kendra moaned, scratching and digging at the carpeting with her fingernails. Like a hot iron rod, Remi's cock stretched her past all endurable limits. "Damn you," she cursed.

Remi chuckled darkly. "I'm already damned." His hand left her breast. A wide palm settled across one ass cheek with stinging intensity. "I'm going to come. Hard." Another punishing slap followed. "It will hurt, though only for a moment."

Kendra felt his erection grow bigger. Longer. Hotter. "If there's any way to send you back to hell," she threatened, "I'll find it."

Remi growled his answer, as unintelligible and fierce as the storm outside. His cock surged, spilling liquid fire.

Kendra gasped and then stilled as searing heat and startling pleasure came together, mingled and then detonated.

Orgasm followed the first assault, a maelstrom of bone-shattering intensity. Her body convulsed around his shaft, and Kendra barely had time to gasp before another wave of intense delight picked her up and shook her like a rag doll. Rapture shimmered through her veins, unexpectedly intensifying with a gut-pounding velocity.

She had no time to process the sensations crawling over and through her like a billion tiny stinging ants. Through the pain there was pleasure. And through the pleasure—

Her limbs buckled beneath her, and she dropped to the carpet. Remi followed, covering her with his sweat-soaked weight. Bodies still joined, they lay in a heap, exhausted but well sated.

Remi was the first to stir. "Wow." His warm breath tickled the nape of her neck. "That really rocked the world."

Kendra drew a shaky breath. "I've never done anything like that." Her body still trembled with the aftershocks of climax and the impact of what they had just done. The numbness in her abused rear began to subside, replaced by delicious warmth.

Remi nuzzled the damp hollow between her neck and shoulder. "I hope you enjoyed it."

Kendra felt her face warm with a blush as his lips brushed a sensitive spot just behind her ear. Her clit responded with immediate interest, pulsing with a series of powerful spasms.

A brief thought arrowed through her dazed mind. *I can't get enough of him.* What they had just done hadn't been enough to sate her carnal hunger.

She wanted more.

20

As it was, being pinned to the floor beneath a hundred-and-some-odd-pound demon wasn't unpleasant, but it did tend to get a little uncomfortable, given that the carpeting was scratchy, and Kendra was beginning to itch. She wiggled. "You mind?"

"Not at all." Bracing his palms against the floor, Remi raised his weight off her back. His hips continued to press into her rear, his not-quite-flaccid penis still snuggled firmly between her butt cheeks. He gyrated. "In fact, I think I'm about ready to get started again."

Kendra quickly wriggled out from under him, rolling over onto her back. With legs sprawled open, she was naked, save for hose and heels. "If you don't mind," she groaned, "I think I've had enough ass play for one night." Her rear ached. Not unpleasantly, but it wasn't an experience she was eager to have a second time.

Remi eyed her. A grin spread across his face. "Missionary will do."

Kendra groaned. "Good grief. Don't you ever get enough?"

"Enough sex?" He shook his head. "No, I can never get enough sex."

She lifted her head, peering across her naked body at him. "You seem to be able to get sex any time you want."

He sucked in a breath. "Only if a woman is willing." A pause. "And not many are."

Kendra's eyes widened. "Why can't you just take what you want?"

Remi reached out, caressing the inside of her leg. "I'm a demon," he said sulkily. "Not a rapist." His fingers inched higher. "I do have my standards."

Kendra's breath lurched to a halt. His touch was warm and firm, his hand inching up her thigh toward her sex. The relentless, pounding beat of desire was building all over again. She licked dry dips. "I didn't know demons had standards."

His fingers brushed her damp labia. "This one does."

Drawing in a ragged breath, she forced back a moan. "You don't ever stop, do you?"

Remi grinned and moved between her legs. Supporting his weight with his elbows, his lips hovered just above her mound. "Nope." His head dipped. His tongue slithered between her sensitive folds, a wet and hot glide against her most sensitive nerve endings.

Kendra gasped, joyfully aware of his tongue probing every hidden spot. Her vaginal muscles tightened, the beginning of a glorious sensation she couldn't believe herself achieving yet again: not one, not two, but three glorious climaxes in one night.

A sound of unrestrained pleasure broke from her throat. Her shoulders going limp, her head dropped back onto the carpeting. "I can't—" she gasped but got no further. Her breasts throbbed, the nipples rock hard. She was so eager to climax again she hurt.

"Squeeze them," Remi urged. "Touch yourself while I please you."

Kendra reached up, timidly circling the rosy areolae with her fingers. The muscles deep in her belly instantly curled, sending a spiral of heat straight between her thighs. "Mmmm, that feels nice."

"Harder." Remi's voice was deeper, strained. "Pull them."

Kendra pulled. Her body pulsed with need, blood thrumming through her veins at a furious pace. "Make me come again," she whispered on a vibrating sigh.

Following her plea, Remi's lips closed around her clit, teeth scraping with the most delightful pressure. He slipped two fingers into her dripping sex, thick and deliciously hard.

Her vision suddenly going cloudy and unfocused, Kendra bucked and writhed as his mouth and fingers worked her swollen flesh. Hot breath scorched her lips as she panted for breath.

Sensing her needs, Remi pushed his fingers deeper even as his tongue caressed her pulsing clit. Finding just the right rhythm, he stroked and stroked, pushing her perilously close to the edge of total abandon.

Beyond refusing him anything, Kendra twisted her own nipples, begging him with shameless words to give her the sweetest release. The thrill rose in a wave. Crested. "Now!" she panted. "Give it to me!"

Remi thrust a final time, stabbing as far as physically possible. His knuckles ground against her clit even as his tongue did the most amazing dance.

Blood pounded at her temples as Kendra jerked and arched her back; a tidal wave of sensation washed over her. Pressing her hips against his face, she groaned, long and low, determined to wring every last sensation out of the moment.

Long seconds ticked away, the silence invaded only by the sounds of the storm outside.

Kendra shuddered, slowly opening her eyes.

Remi hovered above her, grinning like a fool. "That was magnificent." He lifted his fingers to her mouth, smearing her cream across her lips. A spicy kiss followed when his lips captured hers.

Kendra opened her lips to the invasion of his, tasting her own sexual juices when his tongue swept in. Accepting his offering, she stroked back, eager to take everything he had to give. Her hands settled around his shoulders, the feel of concrete-hard muscle flexing under her palms.

Remi's mouth lifted from hers. "I enjoy seeing you take such pleasure in my touch," he said.

Still shaky from her wonderful climax, Kendra curled her toes. "And I took it." She laughed shakily. "Over and over again." She swiped a hand across her sweaty forehead. "But I hope you'll forgive that I don't think I've got another in me. I'm totally wrung out."

He eyed her naked, sweaty form. "You're not too tired for a nice bath," he said, one brow arching with the innuendo. "You know—hot water, lots of slippery bubbles . . ."

Meeting his lecherous gaze, she couldn't help but laugh. "And your hands sliding all over my naked body? Yeah, I think I get the picture." She cocked her head. "Are you sure you're not a sex demon?"

Remi shook his head. "That would be a succubus. I am a demon of revelation."

Kendra sucked in air, trying to think through the fog shrouding her brain. "So far the only thing you've revealed is your fabulous body." She met his gaze and swallowed. "And that very big cock of yours."

He climbed to his feet and then bent over and scooped her up as if she were nothing more than a kitten lolling about on the floor. "Which you seemed to enjoy." His deep, throaty voice was filled with desire, an indication of his own delight.

Her arms automatically circled his thick neck. Damn. He was strong, no doubt about it. He could probably snap her like a twig if he were so inclined. She'd hate to see him angry, imagining he would be a force to be reckoned with if prodded the wrong way.

Remi carried Kendra into the bathroom. Candles set throughout burst into glorious flames, the flickering light casting sensual shadows on the walls around them. As he approached the tub, the taps automatically turned on, sending a blast of steaming, hot water into the porcelain depth. A bottle of bubble bath uncapped itself, tipping itself over in midair. A white, foamy layer formed on top of the water. Lavender-scented steam fogged the air.

Kendra nodded appreciatively. "Nice. I could use that ability."

Remi laughed. "One of the small benefits of being a demon. Telekinetic abilities."

"So my wish is your command?"

Remi shrugged. "Or something like that."

He bent, lowering her toward the water.

Kendra glanced toward the water. And froze. A bloody red froth churned beneath her, waiting to swallow her up.

A strange buzzing sensation passed through her body. Her heart raced, and her brain crackled with a surge of energy as if she'd stuck her finger straight into a light socket. Her olfactory sense picked up a faint scent of sulfur.

As Remi bent toward the water, she was vaguely aware of a brief, tingling shake, wrenching her out of her body. A new vision overtook her senses, bringing with it a rush of unbidden images.

In the blink of an eye, Remi changed, morphing into a darker, more threatening entity.

Another chill snaked up Kendra's spine as her gaze again

shifted. Hovering across from the scene, her vision zeroed in, and a breath hitched in her throat when she realized the intent behind its actions.

Her unconscious body was being lowered into the tub.

Blinking in disbelief, she told herself she had to be hallucinating. This couldn't be happening. The sight was almost too terrible to be endured.

Murder.

Dread coiled around Kendra's heart as she watched her doppelganger sink beneath the steamy water. She wanted to scream, stop the Reaper from committing its terrible act, but her throat was frozen, her mouth locked open in a silent scream.

She watched with dreaded fascination as the water churned around her body, the frothy red bubbles turning a queasier shade of blood. . . .

Then the psychic link severed, and everything went blank. Dead white.

The strange blip squeezed Kendra's brain so fiercely a moan escaped her. She gasped painfully, feeling herself tipping into a dark void. "No, please, don't hurt me—" Weak, breathless and exhausted, she began to struggle, fighting to break free of the arms holding her.

If she went into the water, she would die.

A vague thought rose through the morass. *Just like the first time,* a faraway voice echoed.

An obscuring fog manifested and overtook the room. Lost, her conscious mind slid toward the empty abyss hovering at the edge of her vision. She was trapped within grasping shadows, vicious claws pulling her down into a terrible place she dared not contemplate.

A moment later, Kendra felt cool tile beneath her.

She immediately slumped into a heap, head resting on the edge of the tub. "My God," she murmured. "I—I can't believe . . ."

Even as her mind struggled desperately to process what was happening, it was fading away as if her brain were a sieve full of too many holes to hold a coherent thought.

An unseen someone knelt beside her. The darkness receded, creeping away.

A block of ice formed around Kendra's heart. The danger was back. She heaved herself up, throwing out a hand, ready to strike against the predator manipulating her senses.

Recognition crept in. More fissures of light broke through the cloak suffocating her senses. "Remi." She blinked at him, her mind still not fully functional.

His expression tense with concern, he nodded. "Something happened to you?"

Kendra heaved a ragged breath and rubbed her cool, moist brow with the heel of her right hand. "I'm not sure," she said, voice shaking, barely above a whisper. "But I think I just stepped out of my body."

"You don't remember?" The demon's eyes glowed like coals in the candlelight, enigmatic little ribbons of fire seeming to crawl within the steely depths.

Fire that's burning my mind to ashes. . . .

Kendra clamped her teeth against the nausea tying her stomach in knots. Was it her imagination, or did his face look crafty? Once again he'd woven some strange spell around her wits, and she hadn't even been aware of his manipulations.

All she knew was that this time he'd taken her not to a plane of physical bliss but of absolute, heart-stopping terror.

She drew a steadying breath. "No. It was there, and then it was gone. Like a door opened up and then slammed shut. I got a peek, but only that. It happened as you lowered me toward the water. I saw—" She hugged herself as another chill coursed through her. "I'm not sure, but I think I died."

Remi reached out, stroking her face. "Whatever it was, it deeply disturbed you." The feel of his hand on her skin jolted her. It was a light touch, but the heat from his fingers soaked right through her skin, straight to the bone.

Her back stiffened. A small hiss slipped through her lips. "You're the one doing this to me," she accused. "Pulling me in and out of reality into places I can't possibly be in or go to. You're twisting my damn mind, making me see things that aren't there." Her throat tightened. "Feel things that didn't happen."

The words flew out, a knee-jerk reflex to fear and panic. Ever since this nightmare had begun, she couldn't tell where reality ended and fantasy began.

It has to end, she thought. *Before I lose my mind completely.*

Remi's hand dropped away. "You do not see it now," he whispered, "but I am only trying to help you."

Kendra slumped back against the tub. "Stop helping me," she breathed. "I can't take it anymore."

A wounded look flashed through his expressive eyes. "Do you really mean that?" he asked softly.

Squeezing her eyes shut, she nodded. "Get thee behind me, demon."

21

After another fitful night of disjointed dreams and tossing and turning, Kendra stirred from slumber, cramped and uncomfortable.

Vaguely aware of a cool breeze caressing her skin, she rolled onto her side, curling into a ball. Still half asleep, she reached out, intending to pull a blanket over her chilly body. Her hand reached out, grasping nothing.

Her eyelids cracked open. A vast white expanse of shag carpeting met her blurry gaze. A familiar object, long and faintly phallic, began to take shape, floating out of the blur as her vision sharpened and focused. A bottle materialized. One with the familiar label of a vintage she adored.

Alarmed, she shifted her head. A second bottle gradually floated into view. And then a third. Her clothes were scattered nearby, tossed onto the floor with no thought of getting anywhere near the hamper.

Recognition kicked in, and her heart skipped a beat. Oh, no. A familiar dull throb beat an accompanying echo at her temples, a reminder of the countless times she'd woken up dazed and confused.

Despite her initial grogginess, she sensed something in the room, something out of the norm. She had a distinct and unsettling feeling someone was, as always, watching her.

Closely.

As though confirming her suspicions, a pair of black leather boots topped by a pair of sharply pressed charcoal-gray slacks stepped into her line of sight.

Kendra grimaced. She didn't have to guess who wore the pants. A groan of dismay slipped past her dry, cracked lips. Her hand shielding her eyes, she glanced up at the towering figure. Gerald Carter leaned over her, his lips curled in a mocking smile.

Oh, boy. Definitely not a good thing.

The shit was about to hit the fan.

Gerald shoved his hands into his pockets and rocked back on his heels. "Looks like you had quite a party last night," he commented drily, surveying the disarray in her room. He rolled one of the bottles under one foot, turning it so he could see the label. "A 2005 Antinori Solaia. A full-bodied wine with a delicious hint of blackberry." A little kick sent the empty bottle rolling her way. "Right out of our very own wine cellar."

Forcing her gaze away from the damning bottle, Kendra ran her tongue across her lips. Damn. She didn't even remember tasting it. The thought of a glass of her favorite wine made her throat constrict with thirst.

Lowering her hand, she shut her eyes. She lay, panting, weak and utterly spent. Her party of one had worn her down to a nub. Another long, slow groan escaped. The hangover certainly felt familiar enough. In past times, she'd woken up in just the same condition.

Practice apparently made perfect.

Except that she didn't remember drinking the wine. Surely she would have recalled going down into the wine cellar and selecting the dusty bottles off the shelves in a perfectly temperature-controlled room.

Still, guilty was as guilty did. The evidence was more than ample, the empty bottles pointing at her like damning fingers of accusation.

She hastened to explain, attempting to clear up the entire misunderstanding. "I didn't drink it," she breathed. "I swear. I never touched a single drop." But searching her mind was like looking into a shattered mirror. There were too many pieces missing to make sense. All she remembered was Remi making sultry, passionate love to her. . . .

Then nothing else.

She looked around her room. There was no sign of her nocturnal lover. Once again the demon had crept away, unseen by any eyes except her own.

Fear, sick and clammy, crawled through her gut.

It was almost like he had never existed.

Kendra swallowed thickly. She had apparently dreamed the whole steamy encounter. The night of mind-twisting, no-holds-barred sex had never happened.

His expression devoid of sympathy, Gerald knelt. "No use lying about it," he said, his voice tight with displeasure. "It's your favorite and quite a rarity at three hundred dollars a bottle. I hope you're proud of yourself. In one evening you managed to suck up almost a thousand dollars' worth."

Panic flushed through Kendra's veins like acid as the dots connected into a terrifying picture. Sweat beaded on her upper lip. It was beginning again. The blackouts. Losing time. The great gaps in her memory. All the classic signs of the chronic alcoholic.

Kendra pressed three fingers hard against her temple. "I don't want to hear it," she moaned. "Please, I have too much of a headache to argue with you."

Gerald grinned. "Blame the booze, not me." His gaze slipped over her body, visually exploring every inch. "Tell me, do you still masturbate with the bottle when you're drunk?"

Masturbate with the bottle? The breath froze in Kendra's lungs. No. Surely she'd never done that—

Belatedly putting two and two together, Kendra struggled to sit up. Her worst fear was quickly confirmed. Except for her stockings and shoes, she was completely naked. Totally exposed.

Kendra's hands flew up to cover her chest. "Oh, God," she mumbled numbly. "What happened to me?"

Her pulse skyrocketing, images of Remi undressing her flashed across her mind. She hadn't even been responsible for removing her own clothes (if Remi existed), but there was no way to tell Gerald about her nocturnal lover.

Think, she ordered herself. *Concentrate.*

But it was no use. Fragmented memories blurred and dimmed each time she made a grab for one. She strained to capture them, but trying to pull all the pieces together just sent the vision tumbling out of her grip.

Grinning like a Cheshire cat, Gerald pulled his brows together. "That's easy. It looks like you fell off the wagon with a thud." He eyed her again, his gaze lingering on her breasts before slipping down to the vee between her thighs. "But I love the way you fall." The intimacy behind his gaze jolted like a cattle prod to the ass.

Kendra blushed. Instead of offering her something to cover herself with, Gerald would take the chance to stare at her liberally. There was no telling how long he'd been ogling her before she'd woken up. *The letch.*

Drawing her knees up to her chin, she curled her arms around her legs. "Get out," she gritted.

He laughed. "I don't think you're in any position to order me around right now."

Unwilling to get up while he watched, Kendra tightened her arms around her knees and swallowed back a wave of queasiness. She shifted to the side so she wouldn't be so exposed, giving him a view of her back. "Just leave me alone," she pleaded. "I need to lie down for a little while."

Her dismissal pissed him off. Majorly.

His fingers curled around her upper arm. Muscles rippled under his gray shirt as he yanked her to her feet. Geez. He was stronger than he looked. "No way I'm going to let you crawl off into bed and sleep off your hangover," he growled under his breath. "You're going to get off your lazy ass and get yourself cleaned up. Your days of sleeping in until noon are over."

Caught by surprise, Kendra lurched back, stumbling as she tried to break out of his iron grip. "Leave me alone!" she snapped. "I don't need your help!"

Ignoring her protest, Gerald grabbed her around the waist, hoisting her up in front of him. He was so damn tall and so damn strong only the tips of Kendra's heels touched the floor, skidding uselessly as she tried to gain enough traction to escape his hold.

She squirmed, doing her best to escape his punishing grip. "Stop it, damnit!"

Gerald held on. Marching into the bathroom, he flung open the shower door. Flipping the cold tap on at top blast, he pushed her inside. "This ought to sober you up."

Ice-cold needles blasted Kendra's bare skin, piercing so deeply the breath temporarily vanished from her lungs. She scrambled to escape the arctic attack, but Gerald shoved her back. "Stay there," he ordered.

Heels skimming on top of the slippery tile, Kendra barely managed to grab the safety rail to keep herself from falling flat on her ass. Every inch of her stung from the intensely frigid temperature of the water.

Breathe, she thought. *Just breathe.* She gasped for air

through the subzero assault, but her throat felt paralyzed. She gasped again, managing to suck in oxygen through a mouthful of water.

Close to passing out, a wobbly reflex tightened her grip around the rail. Vision wavering, she was on the verge of total collapse when the water abruptly ceased.

She breathed a sigh of relief. Thank God.

Naked, teeth chattering and more than a little confused, Kendra sagged back against the wall, trying to gather her strength. Her thigh-high stockings clung to her skin like a layer of slime, and her expensive pair of designer heels were water-logged under her feet, uncomfortably squishy. Her nipples were taut, hard little beads.

"Enough," she gasped. "I've had enough."

Gerald cruelly reached for the tap again. "You sure?"

Soaked to the skin and then some, she nodded. "I won't do it again," she promised, not really sure that she had done any-thing to feel sorry about in the first place. How could anyone forget drinking not one but *three* bottles of wine?

"You're damn right you won't," he snapped. "I've worked too damned hard to get you back on your feet, and I'm not going to have you slipping away now. Why are you doing this to yourself?"

Some element in the tone of his voice made her feel guilty. She looked at his face. Worry and anger warred in the depths of his blue gaze. Tears welled up. Each breath hitched in her throat. "I wish the hell I knew," she said, exhaustion weakening her voice. Being caught passed out drunk and naked was more than horrid. It was mortifying. Humiliating.

Even worse was the fact that she seemed to have lost total control over her own actions. Everything about her world had become terribly skewed. She no longer knew where fantasy ended and reality began. Her world had taken on a surreal quality. It was like living in a phantasmagoric realm, her mind continually shifting from one spectacle to the next.

Unable to think of anything more to say to explain her actions, she stared at her stepbrother as a feeling of hopelessness once more closed in around her. Soon her mind would slip away, would plunge her back into a realm of darkness.

Gerald's gaze softened, and a half smile appeared on his lips. Stepping into the shower, he brought up his right hand to caress her cheek. It was just a light touch, but the heat of his fingers seeped right through her skin, entering straight into her blood, warming it. "All I've ever wanted is to take care of you," he murmured. "Why won't you let me do that?"

A shiver passed through Kendra. It was all she could do not to bolt from the shower. His touch was stirring wild sensations behind her breast. His play of concern expertly strummed her sexual awareness.

For a moment her senses blurred, and she received the distinct impression that it was Remi standing in front of her, touching her, reassuring her. Confusion replaced control. The two looked so much alike, it was hard to tell one from the other . . . . "Is that what you really want?" She swallowed thickly. Heat suffused her. Her legs were becoming jelly. "To take care of me?"

Gerald's intense gaze locked on her mouth. "Yes." He chuckled softly and then brushed his lips across hers in a kiss meant to claim. "In fact, I know just the way to take care of your hangover." In the blink of an eye, he changed, concern morphing into something lewd, something vicious and predatory. He nibbled at her left earlobe while his left hand cupped and kneaded one of her breasts.

A new wave of anxiety shot through her.

Realizing his carnal intent, Kendra pushed against his chest. "Stop it, Gerald!" She felt as if the world had tilted sideways, sliding out from under her feet in the blink of an eye.

Her stepbrother didn't budge, pinning her back against the shower wall with little effort. His hand slipped lower, pressing between her legs. His mouth assumed a seductive smile. "I could have you here and now."

Fighting against a fresh rise of panic, Kendra squeezed her eyes shut. Gerald was a big man, tall and almost twice her weight. Thick fingers slid through her slippery folds. "I bet if I stroked your clit, you'd go off like a rocket."

Kendra gritted her teeth. "Pig!" she spat. The single word flew out like a knee-jerk reflex, sudden and concisely delivered. She shoved again, concentrating as much power in her arms as humanly possible.

Gerald hardly budged. "Come on, Kendra," he purred, cupping and stroking one breast. Outlined against the front of his slacks, his erection strained for release. "You know you want it. I can give you something a hell of a lot better to suck on than a bottle."

Kendra angrily swiped a hand across her mouth to erase the imprint of his kiss. "I'd jump off a cliff before I'd fuck you."

To her chagrin, Gerald just laughed, its deep, rich sound echoing all around her. "You'd better be careful with what you say. Someone might mistake your words as a suicide threat." Grinning like a wolf eyeing a tasty snack, he circled the tip of her erect nipple with his thumb. "I'd sure hate to have to send you back to the sanitarium, if you get what I'm saying."

Her stomach twisting into knots, Kendra inwardly cringed. Oh, she got it, all right. He was blackmailing her, twisting her words around to extract what he wanted. "You bastard," she said, the words barely able to escape through her clenched teeth.

Gerald tugged the tender nubbin, sending a spike of pain straight through her. "And I intend to prove it in so many ways," he said.

Kendra's breath froze in her lungs. It would be easy to just give in, to give him what he wanted. But in the back of her mind, she knew that once wouldn't be enough. If she gave in, he'd be back. Again and again. Whenever he wanted. More than that, giving in would be worse than having it taken from her. Then she wouldn't be a victim. She'd be an accomplice. She swallowed back a wave of queasiness. Giving in would be unacceptable on so many levels.

Tired of being the prey of his unwanted advances, she resorted to the sole defense a woman had against a larger, stronger man. Managing to free an arm, her left hand dropped to the front of his pants, deftly, boldly circling his erection.

This dog needs a little training.

Tipping her head back, Kendra stared into his eyes with a dare. Gerald was a big man, but a man's penis was sensitive territory. Handling it wrong could be painful. Very painful. Given her present state of mind, she wouldn't mind hurting him. A lot.

Kendra's fingers tightened around his cock, digging deeply into his vulnerable flesh. "Know what, asshole?" she breathed sweetly.

His back stiffening, Gerald wisely held still. His expression went from desire to dismay in the blink of an eye. "What?" he asked, careful not to move one inch.

"I don't want to fuck you." She delivered a little twist to his taut flesh, enough to make things more than a bit uncomfortable. "Not now. Not ever."

He winced and nodded. "Understood."

Her brow wrinkling, frustration brewed inside her like hot lava. Too bad she couldn't rip off his dick and beat him senseless with the stump. "Are you going to leave me alone?"

His tongue came out, wetting dry lips. "If that's what you want."

Keeping her glare aimed on his face, she nodded. Her fingernails were pressed so deeply into the front of his slacks she'd probably punched holes in the material. "It's what I want," she grated, grip tightening another degree, just to make her point clear. "Get the hell out and leave me alone."

His mouth arced into a rueful smile. "If you don't mind . . ."

Kendra reluctantly released her grip on his penis—not so hard and ready for action as it had been a few minutes ago. All his desire had apparently vanished. "Next time I won't be so gentle," she purred.

Gerald immediately scrambled out of the closed space of the shower, putting a good amount of distance between them. His blue eyes narrowed, glacial with anger. "Frigid bitch!" he cursed.

Kendra crossed one arm over her bare breasts. Angling her body toward the wall, her other hand covered her privates. Hardly enough, but it was all she had at the moment. "Better than being a raping son of a bitch!" she yelled back at him.

His gaze raked over her naked flesh like razors. "You'd better be careful about the accusations you throw around." He smirked. "Hung over and naked isn't exactly the way to build confidence in your recovery."

Her already erratic pulse skipped another beat. "I didn't do anything wrong."

Gerald raised a skeptical brow. "So you're claiming those bottles just magically appeared in your room?" His lips twisted into a sneer. "Such a clever excuse. It sounds exactly like something a drunk would say."

"It's true," she said, hating him for making her feel weak, stupid and foolish. She was sick to death of it. Sick of being judged. Sick of being ridiculed. Sick of being called a liar when she hadn't done anything wrong. She'd worked hard to gain her sobriety.

Apparently, nothing she could do or say would change Gerald's opinion.

Not when there's three empty wine bottles, and you're passed out cold on the floor, she thought bitterly.

Had the scene not been such a familiar one, it would have seemed like a setup.

His lips curling with disgust, Gerald eyed her. She flinched when he raised his hand abruptly. "You're pathetic."

Kendra clenched her fists at her sides. "Just get out!" she snapped, voice cracking with frustration and anger. She was having trouble breathing, as though she was on the edge of a seizure. "Get out and don't ever come back in my room."

Tossing his head back in defiance, Gerald narrowed his eyes as he snagged a towel off the rack. "I'll do what I goddamned well please." He threw the scrap at her. "Meanwhile, you had better watch your step. You never know when the past is going to come around and bite you in the ass." His attitude and body language clearly indicated she was dismissed. Turning on his heel, he slammed out of the bathroom.

Hands shaking, Kendra had barely managed to catch the towel. Fumbling, she awkwardly wrapped it around her naked body, grateful for the small amount of coverage it offered. It was better than nothing, and she was glad to have it.

Relieved Gerald was gone, she sagged against the wall. She drew a deep breath and closed her eyes. Her heart still beat double-time against her ribs. *What the hell just happened?*

Her brow furrowed. Nothing made sense anymore. It was like she'd taken her brain out, set it down and walked away. If her head weren't attached to her shoulders, she'd probably lose it, too.

She felt squeezed, trapped between the rock that was Gerald and the hard place that was Remi. Between her predatory brother and one horny demon, it felt as if she were swimming with the sharks. Both wanted to take a bite out of her ass.

Her head slumping in her hands, her shoulders sagged. God. There had to be a way to get off the out-of-control carousel her life had become. She was disintegrating, slipping beyond all hope of salvation.

One more wrong step, and her next fall might be a fatal one.

22

Two hours later, Kendra went downstairs. By the time she entered the living room in search of her stepbrother, she'd made up her mind things were definitely going to have to change. She wasn't putting up with any more harassment from him, on any level.

Enough was enough.

Fury boiling in her chest, she looked around. Only Jocelyn was present, curled up on the sofa with a pint of Häagen-Dazs triple-fudge ice cream. She was still dressed in her pajamas, and her hair was a matted mess; her eyes were red and puffy. Saying she looked like hell was an understatement.

Gerald, of course, was nowhere to be found.

Seeing her sister-in-law in such distress, Kendra swallowed back her anger. There was no reason to jump Jocelyn for being married to a male chauvinist ass. "Where's Gerald?" Kendra asked, trying to put a casual note in her voice.

Jocelyn barely glanced up. "Who gives a shit?" she snapped, clearly fighting to keep her own temper under control.

Kendra's stomach tightened. Wow. "Sounds like someone's seriously pissed."

Jocelyn downed a spoonful of the decadent dessert. "I am."

Realizing her debacle wasn't the only one in the house to be dealt with, Kendra forced herself to tamp down her anger toward her brother. "You must be if you're blowing your diet."

Once Kendra caught up with Gerald, she would ream his ass up, down and sideways, too. But there was no reason to drag Jocelyn into the fray between Kendra and Gerald. The poor woman already had enough trouble on her hands with her womanizing husband.

Jocelyn swallowed and then dug into the carton again. "Again, I don't give a shit." She pressed her lips together, but not before Kendra saw her bottom lip tremble. "What's the point of trying to keep your figure for a man who doesn't want to have sex with you?"

Kendra drew a breath and closed her eyes. The last thing she wanted to hear about was Gerald's sex life. She already knew he was a horn dog. The fact he'd just put the moves on her was ample proof.

"I thought you guys had a pretty good sex life," she commented vaguely, wishing this conversation could be avoided. She really didn't want to know about her stepbrother's intimate relations. What she already knew was bad enough.

Jocelyn plunked the empty carton down on the end table and then dropped the spoon inside. "My husband hasn't touched me in almost a year," she said matter-of-factly. "He says it's the stress—too many things to take care of since Nat died."

Kendra fought to keep a straight face. She knew for a fact Gerald's libido was alive and kicking. Her sister-in-law would probably freak out if she knew Kendra had recently had ahold of his penis.

Then there was the matter of Amber, Gerald's secretary. . . . Yet another warped piece of the already twisted puzzle their lives had become.

"I'm sure that's it," Kendra hastened to say. "We've all been under a lot of stress."

Her face strained and tense, Jocelyn reached into the pocket of her housecoat. "Then explain this," she said, displaying a flimsy wrapper.

Kendra didn't recognize the thing. "Uh, what's that?"

Her brows puckering, Jocelyn wiggled the thin thing back and forth. "It's a condom wrapper," she said solemnly. "Which I found in my husband's pocket when I pulled his clothes out of the hamper to go to the dry cleaner's." She flicked the spent wrapper into the empty carton of ice cream. "A Trojan, lubricated with spermicide. Apparently his little bitch isn't on the pill."

Yep. He was still seeing Amber.

A wave of sympathy rolled through Kendra, along with a fresh rush of anger toward the insensitive jerk she called her brother. She suppressed the urge to spill her guts. *What the hell am I supposed to say?* she thought, casting around for something that would sound reassuring.

Nothing came to mind.

"I don't know what to tell you," Kendra hedged. The last thing she wanted was to get in the middle of a disintegrating marriage. She already had enough trouble with her stepbrother. The fact he'd tried to get into her panties just this morning didn't help matters one bit.

She decided then and there that her decision to move out was definitely the correct one. She planned to begin looking for a suitable apartment this afternoon. It was going to be the first step toward taking charge of her life. She no longer wanted to live in her father's house, whether or not half of it belonged to her. It was time to get out on her own, restart the life she'd put on hold since the accident. She'd been to hell and back in more ways than one.

Jocelyn lifted her shoulders. "Neither does my husband." She sighed, wiping her hands up and down her face. "Can you believe he had the nerve to deny everything? He looked me right in the eye and said he didn't know how a used condom wrapper got into his jacket pocket." A laugh crept out, edged with a touch of hysteria. "Christ, he wouldn't even give me the dignity of telling me the truth to my face. I mean, I can handle he cheats. I've suspected it from the beginning but never had any evidence. But why lie about it?"

Kendra's gaze couldn't quite meet Jocelyn's. "To spare your feelings?" she ventured. That's why Kendra had never said anything about Gerald's affair to begin with. He was a good-looking man, a real piece of eye candy for the ladies. His choice of a bride had stunned those who knew him. Jocelyn Eggers was moneyed, pedigreed and well educated. What she was not was beautiful. Gerald hadn't chosen Jocelyn for love but to continue the climb up the social ladder.

For her part, Jocelyn had been thrilled to snag a rising young attorney. Five years older than her groom, she was already past thirty and wasn't getting any younger.

Jocelyn shook her head. "My feelings apparently don't mean a damn thing to him."

"So what are you going to do?" Kendra asked.

Shaking her head, Jocelyn drew a deep breath. "I don't know yet," she said softly. "All I do know is that things have got to change. I can't go on living this way."

Hallelujah! Kendra couldn't have put it better herself. She nodded. "I understand completely."

Snapping up a tissue, Jocelyn wiped at her red-rimmed eyes. "So what did you want with my husband? Your face was brewing a thundercloud when you walked into the room. For a minute I thought lightning bolts were going to shoot out of your eyes."

Might as well spill. It wasn't like Kendra had anything to hide. Well, not much anyway. She drew a long breath and slowly exhaled. "I'm moving out."

Jocelyn looked surprised. "You are? When?"

Kendra's mouth flatlined. "As soon as I find a suitable apartment."

Jocelyn indicated the walls around them. "Why? This is your house. If anyone should pack and move, it's probably me and Gerald."

Kendra shook her head. "Technically, it belongs to both of us, to live in for the rest of our lives, if that's what we want. If we decide to sell, it's to be an even split. As long Gerald wants to live in the house, fine. Should he want to sell, I'll have no reservations." The house was a prime piece of real estate valued at two million. And though she'd grown up in the house, it didn't hold a lot of happy memories.

Jocelyn cocked her head to one side, giving Kendra a queer look. "So you don't want to live here anymore?"

Taking in the entire room in a single, sweeping glance, Kendra shook her head. "No, I don't."

"Why?"

Kendra shrugged. "I want my life back," she explained. "I want the life I had before the accident. To be a nice, normal, sane person. That's not happening here. I'm not getting better. I'm just spinning my wheels."

Jocelyn nodded seriously, skewering her with a pointed look. "That makes sense," she said. "I was hoping you'd get your head screwed on straight."

Was it her imagination, or did Jocelyn seem slightly relieved at the idea she'd be moving out?

Kendra tightened her grip on her purse. "I don't know that

my head is on straight, but I've made up my mind that it needs to be. I have enough of an inheritance to take care of myself quite nicely. And sitting around here doing nothing isn't part of the plan anymore." If she didn't decide to return to college, she already knew for sure that she wanted to travel. Doing Europe sounded absolutely divine, and she wouldn't mind seeing some new sights—perhaps even indulging in a love affair or two.

"I think that's excellent," Jocelyn said. "I'm sure Gerald will be happy to help you get set up."

That knotted her guts like a pretzel. "As for the trust, I've already decided to petition the bank's board to allow me to resume control as primary trustee and executor. Though my father was very specific as to how it was to be invested and managed, I believe it's time for the money to be divided."

Jocelyn gazed up at the ceiling and closed her eyes. "I don't know that it's going to be that easy," she warned. "Given your recent, ah, breakdown, I don't see how that's possible."

Kendra grimaced. "I'm not crazy, Jocelyn. It's true, I slipped, and I fell. Badly. But I'm getting my life back together, and I deserve to have that chance." Truth be told, she no longer felt comfortable having Gerald handing the money. A clean break was preferable—and more than reasonable. Nathaniel Carter had been wise, investing well. The estate he'd left behind had been conservatively estimated to be around thirty million at the time of his passing. Splitting the money down the middle with Gerald would be more than fair.

It's time for us to break up, she thought. *I've got to move on.*

Jocelyn shook her head. "I don't think Gerald's going to see it that way, Kendra."

Kendra drew a deep breath. "If I have to take it to court, I will."

"That's a threat he won't take lightly."

Kendra snorted. "I don't want things to get nasty, but I will if I have to." And she'd use every bit of ammo she could lay her hands on against Gerald. Even if it meant telling his wife the truth about his infidelities.

Flashing her a skeptical look, Jocelyn placed a hand on her chest, fingers tightening in the folds of her robe. "You really think you can stand up against him?"

A bitter smile laced Kendra's lips. "It's no secret Gerald wants absolute control. Like our father, it's his way or the highway. There's no middle ground, no compromise."

Jocelyn gazed at her in all seriousness. "Isn't that the truth?"

Kendra's lips quirked up. "In retrospect I realize a lot of that is my own fault. Yes, the accident incapacitated me—but I recovered. What I hadn't recovered from was my own guilt. At the time I felt it was right to punish myself, flog myself repeatedly with my own remorse and regret. Mourning what had slipped through my fingers. In reality, I never had a firm grip on things to begin with."

"And you think you've got a clench on things now?"

A thrill of excitement, unexpected and unaccountable, rushed through Kendra's veins. "Yes," she said firmly. "I think I realized this morning that I don't like the direction my life is going. Kind of like a dash of cold water in the face, if you will."

An awkward silence lurched between them.

Jocelyn tapped her fingers on the leather upholstery of the couch. "Been dashed many times."

Remembering her recent trip to the shower, Kendra tightened her jaw. Gerald had had no right to manhandle her like that, no matter how angry he'd been. She still couldn't even remember drinking the wine, damnit.

She cleared her throat of the lump building there. "Moving out will be the most important part." She inwardly flinched. "Did you know I've never lived alone, never been completely responsible for making my own decisions? Even in college I had a roommate and an allowance. I've never even worked a part-time job." Thanks to her father's determination to control her every action, from education to the choice of a suitable spouse, her entry into true adulthood had been delayed.

Grimacing, Jocelyn shifted uncomfortably. She wasn't exactly the poster girl for self-confidence. "I pretty much guessed the men in this family ran over the women," she commented, face darkening. "Why are women so weak and stupid when it comes to good-looking men with big cocks?"

Kendra drew back her shoulders, raising her hands palm out as if pushing away the past. "No more being a damn doormat." She narrowed her eyes. "Maybe it's something we should both think about."

Instead of standing up for herself and making her own decisions, Kendra had allowed others to pull the strings. First her father. Then Michael. Then her stepbrother. All three men had pulled her in different directions, each with their own agenda. She'd tried to please them all and had ended up pleasing no one.

Least of all herself.

With so much pressure hitting her from all sides, it was inevitable something would snap, that the cogs would cease to function smoothly when one was jarred out of place.

In a roundabout way, the materialization of the demon had been the glue helping her put things back together. In trying to sort through the chaos muddling her brain, she had begun to take a closer look at the people around her. Her recent clashes with Gerald had snapped her eyes open. It was possible that what she had imagined to be a demon was, in fact, her subconscious mind's manifestation of the sexual tension buzzing between them. She certainly couldn't deny she'd once found Gerald attractive. She'd even considered giving into his advances and sleeping with him.

But that had been before he'd married Jocelyn, before Kendra had taken up with Michael. Sex between them had never happened.

Her mouth quirked down. *And it never will.*

She was getting her ass out from under the same roof as soon as possible. Once she had some space to breathe, she was sure things would come together in her life.

And maybe Remi would leave her in peace.

Whatever response Jocelyn might have had was interrupted by the bleating of a cell phone. A familiar ring filled the room: a few guitar riffs from a popular rock song.

Kendra dug in the side pocket of her purse, pulling out her cell and checking the display. *PRIVATE.*

Probably a damn telemarketer.

Blowing out a frustrated huff of breath, she flipped open the phone. "Hello?"

"Kendra?" A familiar voice filled her ear.

Her heart missing a beat, Kendra felt her throat tighten. All the oxygen left her lungs. "Michael?" Her hand shook to the point that she almost dropped the phone.

"Yeah, it's me," Michael Roberts said.

She struggled to breathe, to sound calm. "What do you want?"

Jocelyn made a *who is it* motion with one hand. *Gerald?* she mouthed.

Her brows drawing down, Kendra quickly shook her head and covered the mouthpiece. "It's Michael."

Your ex? Jocelyn mouthed back.

Shooting her a keep-quiet glare, Kendra nodded.

Jocelyn motioned for Kendra to slam down the phone. "Hang up," she said aloud.

Michael's voice sounded faraway through the slight static of the carrier's signal. "You still there?"

Turning away from her sister-in-law, Kendra stepped out into the hall. "Uh, I'm still here." A pause. "What do you want, Michael?"

His reply came through a second later. "I've been thinking about you, babe."

Fighting to keep her composure intact, Kendra stood rooted in place. She felt absolutely awkward. Tiny beads of perspiration popped out on her forehead. Shit. It suddenly felt like someone had cranked up the heat from warm to sizzling. Walking barefoot on the surface of the sun would have been more comfortable.

She hadn't talked to Michael in at least six months, maybe more. The last time they'd spoken had been, well, the last time. No long good-bye, no prolonged breakup.

"Okay," she said and then cringed. Lame. Oh, what a total loser. She considered hanging up, but the sound of his voice curled around her heart, drawing tight. A mental picture of his thick dark hair, high forehead and absolutely sensuous mouth flashed in front of her eyes.

Michael laughed, ignoring her guarded reply. "Anyway, I've been thinking it might be good to see you, you know? Maybe get together and talk over old times."

Her lungs froze. The tightness returned. Listening to his beautiful voice, it was hard to breathe. "You want to get together with me?" she croaked, back stiffening at the very audacity behind his request. *Old times. What old times?* "With me?"

He laughed again. "Why not?"

The bonds holding her heart captive loosened a little. "Maybe because you dumped me flat on my ass," she retorted. The fact she had to say the words caused another hard knot to form in her throat. Her vision blurred.

Embarrassed to be pushed to the point of tears, Kendra angrily swiped at her eyes with her free hand. Damnit. She wasn't going to cry.

She heard Michael suck in a ragged breath. "Maybe I didn't

have a choice," Michael countered slowly. "Maybe someone else made that decision."

An image of her father, angry and shouting, flashed across Kendra's mind. Her stomach doing cartwheels, her mouth dropped open. "W—what do you mean?"

"Not over the phone," Michael said. "I'll tell you. In person."

A rush of pure adrenaline coursed through Kendra at the possibility. One door had shut in her face. Was it possible another was about to open? People did change their minds. Couples did get back together.

The storm clouds overhead seemed to be breaking. She suddenly realized she wanted Michael to want her back. Dare she hope . . .

"When?" she asked breathlessly.

23

North Philadelphia wasn't the best part of the city to live in. Populated mostly by poor minorities, the neighborhoods were ramshackle. Garbage was strewn everywhere, and shuttered factories cast shadows over the populace they'd once employed. Teens and adults alike lingered on corners just hanging out, looking listless. Run-down buildings were covered with graffiti, and it wasn't unusual to spot drug dealers working in broad daylight, making rapid hand exchanges with their customers.

Kendra double-checked the address Michael had given her. "Are you sure this is the right place?"

The cabbie nodded. "Sure am."

Looking out the window, Kendra eyed the building. It didn't look like any place that should be inhabited. In fact, it looked like it had been condemned a long time ago, but no one had told the residents to move out. Or maybe they had been told to move and had instead hung on because they'd had no other place to go.

The driver noticed her hesitation. A well-dressed woman

stuck out like a sore thumb in this neighborhood. "You want me to wait?"

Kendra considered telling the driver to move on and get her out of the neighborhood as soon as possible. Instead of saying that, she shook her head and handed the driver a fifty to cover the trip. "Keep the change."

The cabbie grinned. The change meant he got at least fifteen dollars out of that fifty. "Thanks," he said, tipping his hat. "If you need a ride again, call the company and ask them to dispatch Wally. I'll be right here to pick you up."

"Thanks." Kendra opened the rear door and slid out of the cab. "I'll do that."

Leaving the curb, the cab sped away.

Stepping over the cracks in the sidewalk so as not to catch a heel, Kendra walked toward the steps leading into the apartment building. A couple of dark-skinned men lolled there, smoking and drinking beer. They didn't look friendly or welcoming of a stranger in their midst—a stranger who obviously didn't belong.

Kendra cleared her throat. "Uh, does Michael Roberts live in this building?" she asked, hoping they had never heard the name. If not, it would give her an excuse to leave. As soon as possible.

One of the men sucked his bottle of Bud Light. "Yo, man, you know this Michael dude?"

The other man bobbed his head. "Yeah, he owes me a twenty and a pack of smokes." He eyed Kendra. Only a blind man would have missed her necklace and watch. "You his girlfriend?"

She shook her head. "Just a friend."

The man cackled. "Well, if you be a friend o' his, you tell him to get his scrawny white ass down here and pay me back. Said he'd pay me last week, and all he does is dodge by when he see me comin'."

Kendra couldn't imagine Michael being hard up. When they'd broken up, his band had been on the verge of signing with a major label. The advance, as she'd heard it, had been quite nice.

Apparently, things had changed in Michael's life. For the worse. Nobody chose to live in such a neighborhood, much less have to dodge lowlifes over a stinking twenty-dollar bill and a pack of cigarettes.

Kendra dug into her purse, cautiously inching out another fifty. It probably wasn't wise to let the men know she had any cash on her, but since they'd just seen her pay the cabbie off, that was a moot point. If one of them pulled a weapon, she'd just toss her purse and run like hell. They could have the money; it wasn't worth losing her life for a few hundred dollars and some miscellaneous items.

She handed over the fifty. "Will this cover it?"

The man grinned. "Oh, yes, ma'am," he said, bobbing his head politely. "More than 'nuff."

Kendra relaxed. "Which apartment is Michael's?"

The man pointed. "Up there, number twelve. Third floor." He paused and then added. "You goin' to have to take the stairs. 'Vater's been broke quite a while now."

Kendra nodded. "Thanks."

Easing past the men, she made her way into a cruddy, garbage-strewn lobby. True to his word, the elevator was out of order. There was no way the thing could work. It had no doors and had obviously been used as a receptacle for human waste on more then one occasion.

Wrinkling her nose to escape the stench, Kendra hurried up the stairs. Locating the third floor, she headed down a hallway lit by a few naked light bulbs. Most of the others had been broken or burned out.

Jesus, this is bad.

She knocked on the door of apartment twelve. At least, she

hoped it was the right one. The little metal numbers adhered to the door had fallen off, leaving only a vague outline.

"Who is it?" The voice calling out was familiar.

Kendra leaned toward the door. "Michael!" she called. "It's me. Can you let me in? Please."

A chain rattled. A bolt slid back. The door cranked open.

Kendra glanced up at the tall, rangy figure outlined in the doorway. Thick brown hair hung past his shoulders. Brown eyes stared out of a face half obscured by the scraggly beginnings of a beard. Bone thin, his body was all planes and angles.

Kendra gasped, staring at him as if seeing a ghost. Little remained of the man she'd fallen in love with. Had it not been for the familiar lines of his face and the intelligence burning behind his gaze, she wouldn't have recognized Michael Roberts at all.

Seeing her, Michael grinned. "Come in, come in." He stepped back, allowing her to enter.

Kendra cautiously stepped over the threshold. Inside, the apartment almost mirrored the disaster of the building outside. Graffiti covered the walls—what few remained. Most of the inside had been torn down, so it was all just one big open space.

Trying to keep her face carefully blank, Kendra looked around. A mattress covered with a blanket rested in one corner, bracketed by a few packing crates that served as tables. More crates were placed around the room at odd intervals, interspersed with familiar pieces of furniture well used and well worn. A hot plate and dorm fridge on a counter served as the kitchen's only appliances. Only the bathroom seemed to offer a bit of privacy and sanctuary.

Despite the shabbiness, the apartment was clean. Neat as a pin. A few homey touches had been added here and there, making it a bit more welcoming to a woman's eye. A couple of the crates had been covered with cheap plastic tablecloths, and a few throw rugs covered the bad spots on carpeting that should have been ripped up and thrown away ages ago.

Michael shut the door, relocking it. "Not exactly as good as the last place I had," he said by way of a greeting.

Remembering his uptown loft with its snazzy art-deco furnishings and musical equipment crammed to the ceiling, Kendra quickly averted her eyes away from the shambles. "It's definitely a change," she said, casting about for a way to say something without insulting him.

He shrugged. "It's a roof over my head. At this point, having a place to go is all that counts."

She cleared her throat. "You've changed. A lot." She made a gesture toward her hair. "Your hair is really long."

Michael pulled at one greasy strand. "Haven't had time to get down for a haircut," he mumbled. "Last place I was at didn't exactly offer a lot of personal grooming choices."

More adrenaline pumped into Kendra's veins. "Kind of gives you that streetwise look."

Another shrug. "Well, in this neighborhood you gotta blend in with the trash to survive." His brown eyes raked over her. There was an element of masculine appreciation in his gaze that made her pulse flutter. "You haven't changed. You look great." Catching her in a rough embrace, he gave her a tentative hug. "It's good to see you," he murmured into her hair.

Kendra looked up at the man who'd once made her emotions flip every which way. Though her blood pounded in her temples, she was surprised that seeing him again didn't make her knees go weak.

She drew a breath. Getting over the hurt wasn't going to be easy. But she was willing to try. God, how she wanted a chance— any chance—to make things better.

For both of us.

"You think so?" Her hand started to stray toward her face, toward the scars carefully touched up with makeup. She caught the action and halted it midway. She'd taken care to look good, making sure she looked as perfect as possible. She wanted him to see her looking her best. Prove to him she wasn't just damaged goods, repackaged and put back on the rack at a reduced rate.

Michael caught her move. "You can barely see them," he said. "In fact, I wouldn't notice them at all if I didn't know they were there."

Ignoring the way her pulse picked up speed, she swallowed back the rise of self-doubt. "Thanks. I've gotten used to them." She eyed his figure. Desire, sneaky and hot, kicked her in the gut. Despite his thinness, there was still something attractive in his bohemian appearance. "You've, ah, lost some weight." At least twenty pounds. Maybe more.

Stepping away from her, Michael shrugged. His posture was strained, tense. "It's that jail food. Damn stuff is tasteless and bland. Shit, the slop they serve is more punishment than just being behind bars."

Kendra felt her blood pressure plummet. "I'm sorry about that," she said softly.

Ambling over to retrieve a pack of cigarettes, he eased out a round cylinder and lit it with a match. "Yeah, I was, too." He tossed the burnt-out match in a small cracked ceramic dish serving as an ashtray. "But I guess your brother rubbed it in."

Every muscle in Kendra's body tensed. "He said you were picked up, but I didn't know how long. I thought you'd be out in a few days on a misdemeanor." Her words came out raw, tinged with betrayal.

Michael shot her an annoyed look. "I would have thought the son of a bitch would be crowing all over the place," he said sourly. "After all, he's the assistant DA who convinced the judge to bring the hammer down hard on my head. Instead of getting probation, I got a year in the county lockup." He rolled his eyes. "I'm a fucking felon for getting caught with some weed."

Kendra's hand flew over her mouth. Shock rattled her entire body. "Oh, shit, Michael. I didn't know. I had no idea."

He eyed her, a sad little smile crossing his lips. "Well, you couldn't, I suppose. You were still in the hospital."

Kendra felt nauseated, cold and numb, as if someone had dumped her in an icy pool. "Is that why you broke up with me?" she asked slowly.

Michael slowly exhaled a stream of white smoke. "Yeah. I didn't want you to know I was on my way to jail when I came to see you that last time."

Kendra felt her world begin to spin, the air around her suddenly sucked away. On the verge of collapse, she staggered toward the couch, sinking down onto cushions barely offering any support. Still, they were better than the alternative, which was hitting the floor. "Gerald never told me." She began to shake her head. "I had no idea. None whatsoever."

Walking to the couch, Michael sat down beside her. The poor old couch groaned, barely sagging under his pitiful weight. He reached out. The tips of his fingers barely touched her cheek. "I know you thought I broke up with you because of the accident. But I want you to know I'm not that lame or shallow. Your brother told me to break off our engagement, that I'd only be dragging you down with me." He shrugged. "Guess I'm lucky. Could have gone to prison for up to three years. As it was, I served only nine months, with time off for good behavior."

A fresh surge of anger toward her stepbrother rose. *What a fucking rat bastard,* she fumed. "If only you would have let me know, I could have talked to Gerald, maybe gotten him to ease up. At the very least, I could have helped you fight the conviction—maybe even had it overturned. The marijuana wasn't even yours to begin with."

Something she said made Michael turn his gaze away. "That's not exactly right," he mumbled.

Kendra dragged in a breath. Her brow puckered in a confused frown. "What?"

Michael pulled his fingers through his long, matted hair. "The pot was mine," he confessed in a rush. "I was dealing a little on the side to keep the band going. The equipment, the van, the travel—shit, it isn't cheap to get a career going."

Hearing his words, Kendra slumped back. Oh, hell. She'd been dating a drug dealer. Exactly as her father had told her just minutes before his car had made the fatal turn onto the exit. Nathaniel Carter had accused her of having stars in her eyes, mooning over Michael Roberts because he had that bad-boy, rock-star appeal.

She couldn't help but remember her father's words. The judge had flat-out told her she lacked good judgment, that rushing into marriage with the first man she'd ever made love to was a mistake she'd regret. He'd wanted her to wait—at least a year, maybe even two. But at the time ten minutes away from Michael seemed like an eternity. She was young, in love and had wanted to marry him as soon as possible.

"Shit," she muttered. *Dad was right.*

Michael reached for her hand. Cool fingers closed around hers. "I wasn't seriously into it," he tried to explain. "We needed the extra cash—just until the band got a break."

As she looked into his eyes, Kendra's throat tightened. "It doesn't matter that you were just doing it to get extra money, Michael. Dealing drugs—any drug—is wrong. It's illegal. Dad was just doing his job when he came down on you." She swallowed thickly. "So was Gerald. They were just trying to protect me."

His gaze flashing with irritation, he pulled his hand away. "So you're going to take their side?" he snapped.

Her spine stiffened. "In this case, yes, I am." Another thought occurred to her. "If you were lying to me about the dealing, what else were you lying to me about, Michael?" Her thoughts swirling, she pulled her brows together. "The groupies? You said you never fucked any of those girls who hung all over you.

Did you, or were they just something you dabbled in until the band got a deal?"

Michael pushed off the couch. "Christ, Kendra. If I had thought I was going to get a grilling, I wouldn't have called." He rolled his eyes. "It's not like I wanted to get back together or anything."

His blunt statement took Kendra aback. Her blood going cold, her heart skipped a beat. "You don't?" she asked, dread mounting in her chest. Disappointment burned through her. She felt like such an idiot.

Michael looked at her as if every marble she possessed had just rolled out of her head. "God, no. I don't want to get back together," he groused and then added, "Your family has caused me more than enough trouble, thanks."

Kendra cringed. "Then why did you call?"

Michael blew out a frustrated huff of breath. "I need a loan," he stated bluntly. "Something to get me back on my feet." A shrug of exasperation followed. "I thought you might be willing to help me, all things considered."

Come again?

Her eyes locked with his for a moment. "A loan?" she echoed. "You want me to give you money?" The words were like an iron grip, squeezing her heart to the breaking point. Any more pressure, and it would shatter completely. Her day, which had started off badly, had just gotten worse.

Michael stubbed out his cigarette, flicking away the butt. "Just something to get me back on my feet." Bitterness turned down his mouth. "I got kicked out of the band. They signed the deal without me. Got a hundred-fucking-thousand-dollar advance."

Dismay, mingled with disappointment, bubbled inside Kendra's gut like hot lava. God, she'd spent practically the entire cab ride fantasizing about getting back together with Michael, thinking about what it would be like to make love to him again.

She sighed. Talk about being a fool. She might as well have been wearing a big fat *F* branded on her forehead. "I'm sorry you lost out on the deal," she said solemnly. "You're talented. Too much to let this hold you back. You can start over."

Though she couldn't condone drug dealing on any level, she knew in the back of her mind that part of Michael's problems had stemmed from their relationship. Nathaniel Carter hadn't liked anything about his daughter's choice of a beau. The judge had pulled every string he'd had, and then some, to make Michael Roberts's life miserable—including having the young man picked up for delinquent parking violations. That Michael happened to have been carrying his stash of weed during the pick-up was the coup de grâce.

Rubbing his prickly jaw and frowning, he stared at her. "You're damn right I'm going to start over. And you're going to help me."

Kendra wasn't sure she'd heard him right. She glanced at him warily, trying to determine whether he was joking. "Why would I want to do that?"

Michael's lips twisted into a sardonic smile. "I got screwed over royally, all thanks to the late Judge Carter and his good little boy in the DA's office." All traces of humor abruptly vanished. His jaw tightened beneath the whiskers covering his chin. "After all your fucking family did to put me behind bars, you owe me."

24

I'm stupid. Gullible. A fool.

That's what Kendra thought as she waited in line at the bank. She couldn't believe she'd actually agreed to loan—no, give—Michael Roberts ten thousand dollars.

Because I feel guilty.

She winced. It wasn't her fault Michael had been picked up for parking tickets and found holding pot. Even if the judge hadn't sent the order down from the bench to pick Michael up, he would have been arrested the next time he got pulled over for any traffic violation. It was only a matter of chance, of timing, that he'd gotten caught that time.

Kendra winced again. She already knew her father had had it in for Michael and had used his power to hurry his downfall. Her father would have done anything to discredit Michael. And he had. Though Nathaniel Carter hadn't lived to see Michael convicted for possession and dealing, it didn't matter. As assistant DA, Gerald had simply picked up the reins, following through on orders Kendra was sure the judge had already handed down. Nothing less than the maximum punishment would satisfy.

Going to jail had cost Michael everything, including his ability to make a decent living. Released from jail, he was now a felon with a record—not exactly desirable in a tight job market. People weren't beating down his door to hire him as a musician. The band he'd formed had already taken another step up the ladder of success without him. If nothing else, Michael Roberts was down and out in every way.

Clutching her purse tighter, Kendra still waited in line. Ten thousand dollars was a pittance in her world—pocket change. The money her father had left behind more than provided a source of financial support for his children. While the bulk of the assets were set up on a path of consistent growth and investment, the monthly interest was split between Kendra and Gerald and deposited in a checking account for general use. She didn't have to answer to anyone how she spent her private allowance. Because she hadn't written a check in months, there should have been quite a tidy sum in the account—more than enough to give Michael his fresh start.

"Next," a teller called.

Kendra drew a breath and walked toward the service counter. *You don't have to give him a damn thing.*

A woman dressed in a conservative dark suit smiled at her. The gold name tag on her lapel read CONNIE. "How can I help you today, miss?"

"I need to cash a check, please."

Connie smiled. "Certainly."

Kendra fumbled for her checkbook. Opening it, she hastily scrawled out a check to *cash*, signed it and handed it over to the teller.

The clerk looked at the amount. "May I see a driver's license or some other form of identification, please?"

Kendra flicked out her driver's license. "Of course."

The woman compared the names and then handed the license back. "Thank you, Miss Carter. Let me get your account information on screen." She tapped a few keys, waiting for the computer. A moment later she frowned. "I'm sorry. It appears that you don't have enough funds in your account to cover the withdrawal."

Kendra's brow wrinkled. "What do you mean, I don't have enough?"

The teller checked again. "According to our records you have a balance of only four thousand three hundred twenty-five dollars and ninety cents in your account."

Kendra shook her head. "But this account has a monthly direct deposit that's a lot more than ten thousand dollars."

The teller checked her records. "Those deposits have been stopped," she said. "Months ago."

Kendra wouldn't have felt it if the floor had dropped out from under her. "That's impossible," she countered. "My father's trust pays into that account every month."

Handing Kendra's check back, Connie shook her head. "I'm sorry. I can only tell you what the computer shows me. Perhaps you'd like to speak with one of the officers in the bank-trust department? If there's a problem, I'm sure one of them can help you." She picked up the phone and dialed.

Mortified to have her check refused, Kendra crept out of line. Something wasn't right. Though she hadn't used the account in several months, there should have been at least a hundred thousand dollars in it, maybe even more—she wasn't sure, because she'd never kept up with the deposits.

Her jaw tightened. There were a lot of things she hadn't kept up with after the accident. Gerald had handled everything.

Kendra's guts knotted even tighter. "The son of a bitch," she muttered. Somehow he'd aced her, cutting her off at the pass.

Ten minutes later a short, stocky man hurried her way. "Miss Carter," he said, offering a brief handshake. "I'm Simon

Brown, one of the bank's trust officers. I understand there's a problem you want us to look into."

Kendra eyed the portly man in his early sixties. He had a round face and olive complexion that bespoke his Sicilian descent. His hair had thinned considerably, leaving him with only a ring around his bald pate. Dark eyes regarded her over the rims of glasses. His skin was sallow from a life spent under fluorescent lighting, from drinking too much coffee and from exercising too little. Dark circles drooped under his eyes, the result of many late nights on his clients' behalf. His Armani suit was rumpled from several days' wear.

Kendra nodded. "Yes, that's me."

Brown ushered her toward his office. "If you will step inside," he said, allowing her to enter first. "Thank you." Taking a seat, Kendra watched him walk around to his desk. "When Connie called, I took the liberty of pulling the file on the Carter trust."

A little relief. "Then you knew my father?" she asked.

Brown's head bobbed. "Oh, yes. I helped Nathaniel set up everything. He was particularly anxious that you would be well taken care of."

Kendra sagged in the chair. More relief. "According to your teller, the direct deposits on my checking account have ceased."

Brown consulted his records. "Yes, those were stopped several months ago."

"Why?"

He checked the file. "According to the paperwork, the funds weren't stopped but merely diverted to another account."

Her brows rose. "Another account?"

"Yes."

The sinking feeling returned. "Don't tell me: the account belongs to Gerald Carter."

Brown nodded. "Your brother had the funds diverted after

the accident that took your father's life, I believe. At the time, he cited the reason as that you were too incapacitated to handle the funds yourself."

"That would have been somewhat true," Kendra allowed carefully. "But as I am the primary trustee, that can be reversed, now that I am back on my feet. Right? The funds can be diverted back into my account?"

Brown checked his paperwork. "Normally, yes."

"Normally?"

"In the case where two or more cotrustees serve, the trust instrument may provide that either trustee may act alone on behalf of the trust or require both cotrustees to act or sign. As your father set it up, you were the primary, requiring no signature except your own. Only when Gerald wished to tap into the assets did it require both signatures."

Kendra's lips thinned. "I know for a fact he's dipped into the principal. Why wasn't my signature required for those expenditures?"

Brown steepled his arms and laced his fingers over the file. "Because the trust instrument also provided that the secondary cotrustee shall act as sole trustee if one of the persons named becomes incompetent and is unable to continue administering the trust. With that being the case, Gerald was well within his rights once he proved you to be incapable on a legal level. Given the paperwork he presented almost a year ago at the time of your first hospitalization, the trust department agreed to his requests. That has, of course, been continued because of your recent, ah, psychological problems."

Psychological problems. His polite way of saying she'd gone round the bend. Lost her fucking mind. Though Gerald had told her something to that effect, the blunt statement took Kendra aback. "So how do I reverse that?"

Simon Brown didn't glance down at his file this time. By this time it was clear he'd been prepared for her arrival. He most likely thought he was dealing with a nut, and not one of the crunchy, tasty ones. "At this point, you can't."

The world caved in. She looked at him, certain he was mistaken. "What do you mean, I can't?" she asked stupidly.

Brown didn't blink an eye. "According to our records, you have signed a durable power of attorney over to Gerald Carter, one designating he is to act as executor in all your financial matters, including administration of the trust and its assets."

A feather could have knocked Kendra over. She raised her hands defensively, as if trying to ward off invisible blows. "That's not t—true," she stammered. "I never signed anything to that effect."

Giving her a chary look, Brown plucked a document out of his pile. His mouth pulling into a frown, he slid it across the desk. "Is this not your signature?"

Snatching the sheaf, Kendra hurriedly scanned the pages. It didn't take a legal expert to know what they were. Sure enough, her very recognizable handwriting was at the bottom, complete with the frilly little loops in the letters *K* and *C*.

Exactly where Dane Montgomery had told her to sign.

As dismay stampeded through her veins, her hand began to shake. "I didn't sign this."

Brown's brows knitted. "Are you saying that isn't your signature?"

She shook her head. "It's my signature, all right. I thought I was signing a new policy on the house and its possessions."

Brown looked at her as if she were an idiot, plain and simple. "You didn't read what you were signing?"

The moment he said the words, Kendra's heart dropped to her feet, shattering into a billion pieces. There was no way she wanted to admit aloud that she'd been so blind as to sign legal documents without bothering to read what they might entail.

Kendra swallowed thickly. *Checkmate.* Gerald's web had

closed around her, trapping her. Fool that she was, she'd walked in with eyes wide open.

Butterflies took flight in her stomach as she shot Brown a pained look. "He must have taken care of this just today," she reasoned out loud. "That's why you had the file already on your desk."

Spreading his hands over the file, Brown nodded. "Of course."

She tossed the paperwork back on his desk. "And you didn't even think to question it or contact me?"

He sighed. "Given your recent problems—which are well documented—we had no reason to. Mr. Carter has been acting as your attorney since the accident, has he not?"

Kendra reluctantly nodded. "That's true," she admitted.

"Had that changed recently?"

Kendra's lips thinned. "Not recently enough," she mumbled. She'd just decided this very morning she was going to oust her stepbrother from her business and hire an outside attorney. She'd told Jocelyn as much, that she'd fight for the right to regain control of the trust.

Gerald was simply sneakier with his maneuverings. He'd gotten the drop on her, and she hadn't even known it until now.

"The paperwork Mr. Carter presented is signed, dated, witnessed and notarized, which is all we legally required. Given that he's been acting on your behalf since the accident, we had no reason to question its authenticity." Brown hesitated a moment, clearing his throat before continuing. "And, pursuant to Mr. Carter's request, we have begun liquidating the trust assets."

Kendra cringed. The day had gone from bad to worse to apocalyptic. It couldn't possibly get any worse. "Liquidation?" she asked. "As in, cashing in all the stocks and bonds?"

Brown's lips pressed together. The man knew he was delivering bad news and clearly didn't want to. "Yes. Once all the assets have been liquidated, the cash will be deposited into his personal account," he said carefully. "To that end, the trust will be permanently terminated."

Her blood going dead cold, Kendra's whirling mind barely processed the bank officer's words. It was painfully uncomfortable to sit there and listen to him tell her she'd just been swindled out of her entire inheritance by her own stepbrother. Despite all the safeguards and hurdles Nathaniel Carter had put in place, Gerald had neatly managed to jump every last one and emerge the victor.

It was my own goddamned fucking fault, she fumed.

Frustration simmering in her chest, Kendra scowled fiercely. "And there's nothing I can do to get the money back?"

Shaking his head, the bank officer cleared his throat. "Upon the grantor's death, the primary trustee immediately has the same powers the grantor had to buy, sell, borrow or transfer the assets inside the trust in any way deemed fit. Also, the successor trustee has the right to distribute the trust's assets according to the grantor's instructions in the trust instrument. In this case your father gave you full power to manage the trust as you wished. In signing over that status to Gerald, you gave him the same rights."

Kendra's mouth dropped open, and it was all she could do not to scream. "And that probably means he doesn't have to give me a dime if he doesn't want to." Not a question. She already knew the answer.

Broke. She was dead, flat broke with a capital *B*.

Sympathy lingering in his gaze, Brown shrugged. "Exactly."

Kendra wasn't finished yet, but her heart pounded so fiercely she could barely think through the thud. "And it was all legal?" she asked, her voice barely audible. "To the letter of the law?"

Brown didn't blink. "It is—unless you can prove mental incompetence or other psychological impairment at the time the power of attorney was signed." Lowering his head, he peered at her over the thick rim of his glasses. "I'm afraid proving you were tricked into signing the paperwork would be difficult to do in a court of law. If you were out of your mind, you had no business signing it. And if you were in your right mind, why did you sign it?"

Aw, terrific. Allowing Gerald to act on her behalf had meant the bank's trust department had no reason to question the new paperwork. He was, after all, her acting attorney and had been since her father's death. Using that leverage, he'd slipped the noose around her neck and then drawn it tight. In effect, she'd hanged herself.

For ten, maybe twenty seconds, Kendra couldn't move. Her body felt paralyzed by what the trust officer had told her. Nothing had adequately prepared her for Gerald's under-handed scheme. Nothing.

She took a moment to find calm, to center herself and her thoughts. Dealing with this disaster meant slowing the rush of blood in her ears. It also meant being aware of her own actions and not letting her emotions take control. "Well," she commented dryly. "It appears my brother got what he wanted."

"Which is?" the banker asked politely.

A harsh laugh scraped past Kendra's lips. She gave herself a good, swift mental kick to the ass for being such a clueless moron. "I bent over, and he fucked me."

Royally.

25

The cab skidded to a halt, and Kendra bailed out.

Tossing a fifty-dollar bill at the driver, she slammed the door. "Keep the change!" she hollered as she ran up the driveway.

Gerald's Maserati GranTurismo S was parked in the drive. Good. That meant the fucker in question was home.

Kendra gritted her teeth. *Time to fuck him back.*

Pulling out her house key, she deliberately ran the sharp tip down the side of the car as hard as humanly possible. The exterior paint job was a custom shade called Grigio Nuvolari, a special order available only on request. The car had cost more than most people paid for their houses.

Grinning at her handiwork, she headed toward the front door. She didn't yet know what she was going to say to Gerald, but she did know she was going in fists a-flying. The idea of pummeling her stepbrother to a pulp was more than appealing.

Kendra headed into the living room. Empty. The muffled sound of a voice emanated from the nearby den. Ah—her father's sanctuary, now Gerald's place to hide when he didn't want to be disturbed. Of course the weasel would go back underground and try to hole up until the danger passed. But this storm wasn't passing any time soon. Oh, no. The wind had just begun to blow, and Hurricane Kendra was poised to make landfall with vicious force.

She charged into the den. Sure enough, Gerald sat at their father's antique desk, chatting on his cell phone. Catching sight of her, he quickly cut the conversation short. He flipped his phone off and tucked it into a pocket of his sport coat.

A shit-eating grin curled the corners of his mouth. He obviously knew she was onto him, and he didn't care. "Somebody looks fit to be tied."

Kendra's jaw clenched automatically at the sight of him. She was here to settle things with Gerald once and for all. At this point she had nothing to lose. Nothing at all. He'd taken everything from her, stripped her bare, leaving her without any resources. But she wasn't afraid; she was too damn mad to be scared.

She swallowed hard, trying not to lose her grip on her emotions. "I've just been to the bank," she said. "Seems the deposits to my account were stopped months ago."

Gerald rocked back in his chair. A smile played around the corners of his mouth. "Is that right?" There wasn't a bit of tension about him. He appeared perfectly calm. Almost too calm.

Kendra clenched her fists, refusing to be intimidated. "When I checked into the problem, I was told you diverted the funds into your personal account."

He nodded. "That I did," he said, not showing a whit of remorse.

Kendra's fists tightened, her fingernails digging painfully into her palms. Staying focused was absolutely essential. "Quite to my surprise, I was also informed I had signed a durable power of attorney giving you complete control over Daddy's trust."

Gerald pretended to think a moment. "Yes," he said slowly.

"That's how I remember it. In fact, I'm quite sure that's how Dane Montgomery remembers it, too, as he acted as witness."

Kendra refused to be intimidated. She met his mocking gaze head-on. "You set me up, you son of a bitch. All this time I've trusted you to do what's best for me, and you've been manipulating the money Daddy left me."

Reaching for the pack of cigarettes on his desk, Gerald shook one out and lit it. "What can I say?" he asked, exhaling a stream of smoke through his nostrils. "I saw the opportunity, and I took it." He was dead serious.

Kendra's jaw dropped. Her resolve fizzling into vapor, she blinked. "That's it?" she asked, blindsided by his cheerful confession. "You're admitting you tricked me to get control of Daddy's money?"

Pushing out of his chair, Gerald walked to the front of the desk. Leaning back on it, he smiled; the reflection in his eyes, though, held no mirth—only a cold, calculating, barely controlled fury. "That's exactly what I did," he said, leveling her with a look that chilled her to the bone.

"I don't understand." Her mouth felt as dry as cotton wadding. She licked her lips and wished for a drink of water. "Daddy left enough for both of us." Her voice was low, barely audible.

Instead of denying everything or trying to spin one of his tall tales into a reasonable explanation, Gerald was admitting everything. Straight to her face, with no bullshit or excuses. He'd swindled her, and didn't seem to have a bit of guilt.

Not one single ounce.

His smile vanishing, Gerald scowled fiercely. "You just don't get it, do you?" He laughed, but the sound held no humor.

"Get what?"

"It's not that he left enough money for both of us, it's that he gave a silly little bitch like you complete control."

As tough as she wanted to appear, Kendra was badly shaken.

She'd believed she had a goal to accomplish. Now she wasn't so sure that would even be possible. "I didn't make that decision," she said, confused. "Daddy did."

A harsh laugh rolled over twisted lips. "Yeah, isn't that the way it's always been? Dad made the decisions; he had the control. Everything I did was to please that old bastard—and nothing I ever did was good enough." His gaze burned into hers over the narrow space separating them. "You think I wasn't reminded over and over that I wasn't his real son, that I could never equal Daddy's precious little pet?" His voice quavered every so slightly.

Irritation twisted inside her. "Dad rode you hard because he wanted you to be the best. But you weren't the only one he jerked around. He rode me hard, too. Everything we did, he controlled."

"Control's over," Gerald snarled. "The old bastard is dead in his grave, and I'm not having him fuck me over from it. Thanks to your nice little signature, I got everything I deserved in the first place. The trust is mine, and there isn't a damn thing you can do to reverse it."

Kendra looked at him, speechless. Gerald wasn't fighting. He wasn't arguing. He didn't have to. He'd won, and he knew it. "So that's it?" she finally managed to ask. "You're leaving me with nothing?"

Stubbing out the remnants of his smoke, Gerald shook his head. "Oh, no. Half of the house is still yours. You can live here as long as you like. The place will need a caretaker, and I can't think of a better person."

"You bastard," she breathed under her breath.

Gerald pretended not to hear her. "Oh, I'm not being a total bastard at all," he said, his expression of delight unyielding. "You'll have an allowance, of course. Not as large as the one father allowed, but it will enable you to live somewhat independently."

Tension arced through her. "Doesn't sound like I'll be very independent at all." Emotion tightened her throat. "In fact, it sounds like you'll control my every move."

Pushing himself away from the desk, Gerald sauntered over to where she stood. "Of course I will." His cheerful smile quickly evolved into a lustful leer. He lifted a hand, tweaking the tip of her left nipple. "But I could be persuaded to increase your allowance if you agree to grant me certain physical liberties."

A wave of nausea rolled in Kendra's gut. The innuendo behind his words was more than insulting. It was disgusting. "I'd live in a cardboard box before spreading my legs for an asshole like you." The painful emotions morphed into anger. Her heart rate bumped up a notch. "Pervert. You're a married man, for God's sake."

In perfect control, Gerald refused to be baited. "Not much longer," he said airily. "Not only am I leaving this house, I'm leaving my wife. Ah, the Bahamas. Sun, sand and surf with a little bankroll of thirty million dollars to keep me living the high life." His words sent tiny little shivers down her spine.

Kendra trembled before she could stop the reaction. Her bowels twisted with the disgust she'd felt building for days. She hated that he'd beaten her so effortlessly.

"Drop dead," she glowered. Mentally, she admitted defeat.

Moistening his lips, Gerald clearly relished his accomplishment. "I'm not planning to do that any time soon, but thank you for the lovely sentiments." He spread his arms wide, as though he intended to embrace her. "Now give your big brother a hug and wish me bon voyage."

Before the hysteria that had set in could fully take root, a new voice cut into the conversation: "The only trip you're going to be taking is to jail."

Their movements perfectly in concurrence, both Kendra and Gerald turned at the same time toward the source of the ominous comment.

Jocelyn stood outlined in the threshold. Not a trace remained of the unhinged woman she'd been just a few hours ago. Her hair and makeup beautifully done, a confident woman stood ready to go toe to toe with her cheating husband.

Gerald's brows drew down in anger. "What the hell are you talking about?"

Walking into the den, Jocelyn smiled. She lifted her hand to show the little black satchel she carried. "I think Kendra's going to need some evidence when she goes to the police. As I heard it, you confessed to tricking her into signing the power of attorney." She waggled the small bag. "Add this little bit of evidence to my testimony, and you'll be going to prison for a very long time, Gerald."

The tension throbbed between them all for a minute. It didn't take a mind reader to know Jocelyn intended to nail his ass to the wall.

Gerald's face twisted. "Where the hell did you get that?"

A smile tugged at Jocelyn's lips. "I found out all about it when I broke into your e-mail account to read more about that little bitch I know you've been fucking behind my back."

Kendra's heart thudded so loudly she could barely hear Jocelyn speak. Just when it looked like she'd lost everything, some small saving grace had stepped in to help. A cold, damp sweat rose on her skin as she listened to her sister-in-law pick up the verbal whip and crack it over her errant husband's head.

Thank God. Someone had the power to put Gerald in his place.

Jocelyn turned to Kendra. "It seems my husband has had his getaway set up for a long time. But like most schemers, he can't keep from sharing his plans with the woman who's been sucking his dick. I've got a whole sheaf of e-mails printed up, all ready to go to the police—with this." She hefted the bag.

Kendra looked blankly at the bag. Anticipation sent her heart into a faster rhythm. "What is it?"

Jocelyn glanced toward her husband. "Gel-filled capsules of Temazepam and some nice used syringes."

Kendra drew a blank. "I don't understand."

Her gaze turning on Gerald, Jocelyn's eyes narrowed. "Oh, I bet Gerald does."

Holding his hands in front of him in a defensive posture, Gerald adopted an innocent expression. "You don't know what you're talking about, Jocelyn." He backed toward the fireplace, putting space between himself and the damning evidence. "It's my prescription, legally approved by a physician. It means nothing."

Jocelyn lifted a single inquiring brow. "Spare me the bullshit, please. I've already checked it out. This drug is one that can induce headache, lethargy and impairment of memory, particularly when mixed with alcohol." She gave him a conspiratorial wink. "Pretty clever, overdosing the poor girl until she could barely function. It gave you all the control you needed to worm your way into managing her inheritance."

If Kendra hadn't seen through her stepbrother's manipulations before, her eyes were suddenly wide open. Her heart lurching behind her rib cage, she tried to block the dizzying sensations crawling along every nerve ending. A crazy mix of fear and relief filled her. A single thought jolted.

I finally know what's wrong with me.

The trembling started deep inside her. She tried to control it, but it wasn't happening. Guts twisting with disgust, she gasped, fighting for air. "How much of that shit did you pump into me!" she interjected, her voice stretched with emotion.

Realizing his perfect plan had just blown up in his face, Gerald glowered. All the hate of hell burned in his eyes. His breathing was uneven, his movements restless.

Somewhere in Kendra's mind, a faint alarm sounded. *He isn't going down without a fight,* she warned herself.

Without warning, Gerald's hand shot out, snatching the black iron poker out of its stand.

Kendra caught his move. A new rush of fear surged through her. "Look out!" she screamed.

But it was too late.

Gerald swung at Jocelyn, bringing the heavy weapon around in a vicious arc. It whistled through the air, thudding solidly against her temple.

Reeling from the unexpected blow, Jocelyn dropped to the floor like a sack of rocks. Blood oozed from the rip in her temple. The sharp side prong of the poker had obviously penetrated her skull—fatally so. A soft *oomph* drizzled past her slack lips. The small satchel she held was still clutched tightly in her fingers. Even in death she wasn't letting go of the vital evidence.

For two beats, Kendra couldn't react, couldn't believe her eyes. Shock radiated through her. Tears burned. Hysteria bubbled up in her throat. Still not fully able to believe what he'd just done, she just stared. Even though she'd witnessed his brutal retaliation, it felt as if she were standing a million miles away. It hadn't fully registered that a dead woman lay at her feet. But as hard as she tried to block the images, she just couldn't stop them from replaying.

The poker swung again at Jocelyn. Connected. Over and over.

Gerald's burning gaze slid over Kendra. His lips thinning into a rigid line, his grip tightened on the poker. "Don't even think about it."

Realizing she'd be his next victim, Kendra turned, intending to get the hell out of the house as soon as possible. There was no time to consider her options. She had to do something. Time was ticking away.

She needed help.

Just as she put the thought into action, a powerful arm suddenly encircled her waist, lifting her off her feet. A big hand clamped over her mouth.

"You're not going anywhere, you little bitch," Gerald hissed from behind. His voice was taut, ragged with respiration. His fierce grip on her body was as tight and unbreakable as an iron chain.

Fear rocketed through Kendra's veins. She kicked, clawing at the hand covering her nose and mouth.

Gerald held on tighter, pressing harder. "It'll be easier if you don't struggle." More curses and threats punctuated his efforts to get her under control.

Kendra's vision began to blur and then waver as the pressure across her face intensified. A new rush of fear spiraled through her. Her chest seized as she fought to suck in a lungful of much needed air.

Nothing.

Her palms started to sweat. *Shit*. She couldn't breathe.

The realization pressed Kendra's panic button, pushing her past fear and into pure terror. Her lungs burned with the need to drag in a breath of air. Realizing she was close to sliding into a dark void, she redoubled her efforts to free herself. It was no use.

I'm going to die.

A dull ache began buzzing inside her skull, followed by a sensation of coldness washing through her veins. She steeled herself for the agony to come, but it was no use. A part of her understood she was dead, no matter how hard she fought or wanted to live.

Her stomach clenched as darkness crashed in from all sides.

26

Kendra drifted back to consciousness. Thankful for the light creeping through her cracked lids, she warned herself to stay awake, stay aware. But the shock of witnessing Gerald murder his wife had drained the last of her energy. She felt weak, boneless.

The sound of water running filtered through her ears, jogging her senses with its familiarity.

Struggling not to slip back into the dark void, Kendra forced her swollen eyes open as wide as possible. It took her a few moments to realize she was sprawled out on the floor in her own bathroom. The ceramic tile beneath her body felt cold, hard.

Her limbs were being manipulated, lifted. Unfamiliar hands pulled at her clothing, stripping away the layers. Her blouse and skirt were tossed in a pile. Her shoes and hose followed.

Gerald's face loomed over her. His hands reached for her bra. Unsnapping the clasp between her breasts, he tugged the garment off.

Kendra held still, trying not to panic. "What the hell are you doing?" Her words came out a mumble, barely coherent over the roar of running water. Her senses numb, her head reeled.

Gerald's hands slipped to her hips. He tugged her panties down. "Just getting you ready."

More confusion. She could barely imagine what was going on in that twisted mind of his. "Ready for what?" she gasped.

Gerald chuckled softly. "To die."

Kendra drew a deep breath, trying to clear her head. Bits and pieces of recent events floated to the forefront of her mind. She struggled to sit up, to escape her murderous stepbrother. "Let me go!"

Before she could gather the strength to scream, Gerald slapped her. Hard. "Be still!" he ordered, impaling her with a scowl.

Her face burning hot, a flurry of colored stars danced in front of her eyes. Her teeth gritted against the pain, she unwillingly sank back down. He'd stripped her bare. She was vulnerable, exposed and too weak to defend herself against further assault. "Please . . . don't hurt me."

Gerald turned, reaching up onto the bathroom sink. "Oh, I promise you, this won't hurt."

Recognizing the damning black satchel Jocelyn had discovered, she widened her eyes. A small hiss escaped her lips when he unzipped it. A syringe appeared. Filled with a clear liquid.

Uncapping the needle, Gerald checked the dose and then tapped the side to clear out air bubbles. Rolling her onto her side, he neatly slid the needle into the curve of her left buttock. His action was precise, perfectly disciplined.

And completely homicidal.

Kendra gritted her teeth against the unwelcome sting. Nausea rolled in her stomach. Dizziness suddenly swamped her. She felt woozy, numb. She couldn't seem to control her arms or legs. She forced herself to breathe. "What the fuck did you do?"

Gerald grinned. "Just a little something to help you relax."

He reached over to the tub, shutting off the taps. "Now I've drawn you a nice, warm bath." Slipping his arms under her body, he lifted her over the edge.

Warm water enveloped her, sliding over her chilly skin like silk. Her head lolled at the edge of the tub. Dreamy, oh, she felt so sleepy. *If I close my eyes, it'll all go away. . . .*

Some inner instinct warned her of the danger.

Fighting through the haze spreading through her mind, Kendra opened her eyes. "No," she mumbled. She grabbed at the edges of the tub, trying to pull herself out of the water.

Gerald pushed her back in. "Oh, no. You're staying right there. In order for my plan to work, this little scene has to be perfectly staged."

Kendra gasped, trying to take in enough air to clear her head. "What plan?" she gasped and then blurted, "I saw you kill Jocelyn." Her voice was shaky but determined.

Her stepbrother frowned. "That's not quite the way it happened. More likely, you killed Jocelyn after she confronted you about your alcoholism. It's a shame, really, that you started drinking again."

For some reason, Kendra's focus zeroed in on his hand. She saw he had a straight-edged razor blade, its exposed edge gleaming wickedly.

Her eyes widened with horror. The blade wavered but didn't disappear. *Oh, shit.* Where did that thing come from?

Gerald lifted her left arm out of the water, the underside exposed, and slashed the blade across the width of her wrist, opening the vein. Blood dripped, mingling with the warm water. His rage at her was cast in stone on his face as he found her other arm and swiftly opened the right wrist. He let her limp hand drop back into the water. And then he smiled, a cold, rictal grin of relief.

The rhythm of Kendra's heart accelerated. She'd felt the

entry of the blade slicing into her skin a millisecond before she'd felt the pain. Paralyzed, she could only watch as her blood seeped from the long slices he'd inflicted.

Little by little, the water grew redder.

Pushing to his feet, Gerald began to clean up the evidence, slipping the syringe back into the bag. "It's really too bad you couldn't live with what you've done to Jocelyn." He dropped the razor into the tub. "Can't say I'll miss the bitch, though."

An automatic denial rose to Kendra's lips, but she was too feeble to voice the words. Weakened by the blood loss, she felt herself pulling away from the scene, as if she were merely an observer and not a participant.

She began to sink. Her chin disappeared under the water and then her mouth and nose. Seconds later she felt the tainted water pouring in, filling up her nasal passages and throat. Pushing the breath out of her.

No!

Bracing her feet against the tub, Kendra forced her eyes open. Spluttering and gasping, she spat out the foul liquid even as she attempted to keep her head above the water line. She wouldn't be conscious long. The drug he'd injected was beginning to take further effect, blurring her vision, softening the edges of the pain he'd inflicted.

Snuffling like a half-drowned cat, she moaned. "I don't want to die this way."

Gerald shoved his hands in his pockets. "Seems to be the way the Carter women die around here." His eyes never leaving her face, he rocked back on his heels. "I imagine my mother looked much the same way when she committed suicide." He shook his head. "It's a tragedy. You dying the way she did in the same room."

Kendra tried to lift a hand, to reach out to him. "Please, Gerald . . . I won't tell anyone. . . ." Her blood splattered on the white tile just inches away from his feet, staining the pristine surface, seeping into the grout.

Shaking his head, Gerald tsked. "Damn. Now I'll have to have the floor redone." His gaze traveled to her face. "The blood doesn't come out, you know. It's all going to have to be ripped up. Carpeting in the den will, too, I imagine."

Losing strength, Kendra's hand slipped back into the water. "Are you insane?" Fuzzy little sharks swam at the edges of her brain. Sharp teeth bared, they closed in, eager for the feast. She drew in a labored breath. It was getting harder now, the insidious influence of the drug slithering through her veins like a poisonous snake. It was doing its work, slowly suppressing her central nervous system. If she didn't bleed to death, she'd lose consciousness and simply drown.

Gerald had made sure her death would be foolproof.

Tossing his hair away from his forehead, Gerald shrugged and smiled. "Maybe. Maybe not." He closed his eyes and grimaced. "Time will tell, I suppose." Laughing wryly, he checked his watch. "Another ten minutes ought to do it. I want to make sure you're beyond resuscitation this time. Last time you survived, damnit."

Kendra struggled, making a final attempt to raise her body out of the tub. She couldn't get a grip on the slippery porcelain, nor break inertia's hold on her limbs. Sinking back, a groan escaped her throat. "I'll find a way to get even with you," she breathed, exhausted by her brief struggle. "Somehow."

Gerald's gaze was menacing, completely devoid of any trace of guilt. He straightened his shoulders, waves of animosity emanating from him and spilling over her. Precious time ticked away. "I sincerely doubt that." He slowly shook his head. He allowed a long moment to pass as he raked his gaze over her. A mocking smile appeared on his mouth. "I'm sorry I never got to fuck you."

Her throat tightening, Kendra swallowed back the bile rising in the back of her mouth. The bitter acid burned all the way down, tying her bowels in painful knots. Her body felt heavier, as if it were floating away, leaving her behind. "Bastard," she mumbled thickly.

Little black bag in hand, Gerald gave her a wave before turning and heading toward the bathroom door. "It would have been good, babe. Really good." Clicking the lock into place, he pulled the door closed behind him.

Kendra squeezed her eyes shut, but not before hot tears slipped down her cheeks. The tiny bit of hope she'd held in her heart that he'd somehow change his mind winked out.

Panic was clawing at her soul; her heart thumped hard. She was going to die—no doubt about it. As to how Gerald could possibly explain two deaths, that was a no-brainer: He'd lie. He'd lie, and the authorities would believe him because no one knew how to spin a tale better than lawyers. Carrying her body out, the morgue team would probably shake their heads. *Poor woman*, they'd think. *She was a nut, the alcoholic who broke down. Not once, but twice.*

Her mouth wide open, Kendra breathed laboriously for a few seconds and then let her body go completely limp. No longer willing to fight against the inevitable, she felt herself begin to sink. The water closed in, claiming her. Unworldly hands dragged her toward a yawning abyss of nothingness.

Growing number by the second, light-headedness immediately swept through her like a gale. Her hands and feet were cold, as though her circulation had come to a stop. Darkness closed in at the periphery of her vision, tunneling her view toward a strange flickering illumination that lingered in the distance.

Just out of her reach.

The light was beautiful. Pure.

Kendra reached out, eager to embrace it. Life meant nothing.

A hand reached out for hers. Strong fingers closed around her, pulsing with warmth, life. But instead of pulling her into the light, it yanked her away.

Kendra's eyes snapped open. Recognition crept through the dusky greenish haze fogging her senses. She strained, barely able to make out the lines of a familiar masculine figure.

"You're back," she croaked, half in disbelief.

27

Nodding, the demon hunkered down. Extraordinarily intense eyes with irises the shade of a stormy sky peered at her. "And now we come to the end." His gaze bore into hers. "As promised, all has been revealed. All lies are out in the open, the truth stripped bare."

Kendra's heart hammered, and she found it difficult to breathe except in short, hoarse spurts. With an inner strength she didn't know existed until now, she clung to life and alertness. She struggled to lift a hand, grasping at the edge of the tub. "Is this it?" she asked. "Is this how I'm going to die?"

Remi's gaze never deviated from hers. "Perhaps." The barest hint of a smile trekked across his lips. One big hand lowered over hers. "Perhaps not. That is entirely your choice." Strange, but no sooner had the demon touched her than her weakness intensified. Her olfactory sense picked up a faint scent of sulfur.

A weird buzzing sensation passed through Kendra's blood. Her heart raced, and her brain crackled with energy. "I don't want to die."

Remi's grip tightened on her hand. "A demon is summoned

to serve." He breathed in deeply and released it through his nostrils. "But a price must be paid."

Kendra didn't stop to consider. She wasn't exactly sure what he was saying, but she knew she didn't have any choice but to agree. Whatever the price might be, she'd pay it. She was running out of time, and her options were limited. At this point she was pretty much desperate.

Her mind reeled with questions, but she pushed them back. Drawing a breath, she swallowed back a wave of nausea. She was panting. Tremors coursed through her. "Help me," she gasped. "Save me."

"Such is your will?" the demon intoned.

Kendra shuddered, heart lurching into her throat. There seemed to be no air left in her lungs. Only coldness. Stark, frightening coldness. "Serve me."

Remi nodded. "I will give you what you seek."

Standing, he bent to retrieve her limp body. One arm slid under her head, the other dipping beneath the bend at her knees. Lifting her out of the water, he held her close, cradling her against his chest. A torrent of some unknown language frothed from his mouth.

He slowly drew his arms out from under her weight. "You will be suspended," he murmured. "Do not try to fight it."

Kendra obeyed without question. Her body automatically going stiff and straight, she found herself hovering in midair. Trying not to panic, she glanced at Remi. He stepped away, out of her reach.

A black veil unexpectedly settled over her eyes, blotting out her vision. Kendra could feel her body going numb, swaying. Her stomach rolled. She swallowed, clenching her jaw, trying to fight off the sickness threatening to overtake her.

For a long moment there was silence.

Remi reached out, gently caressing her naked skin. "Relax," came his soothing voice. "Accept my entry into your mind."

His hands were warm against her chilled flesh, and every electric stroke took her breath away.

Kendra felt tiny fingers of luminous warmth rubbing her skin. Soothing waves of radiant heat easily penetrated her bone to enter her skull. Like a cleansing fire, it shimmered through her mind, attacking the slashing claws of fear, sending the creature skittering back into the dark recesses that had given it foul birth. Her body reacted instinctively. She felt tense muscles relax as the warmth slowly advanced through her from head to toe. Tension drained away, leaving only numb relief in its wake.

Her body buoyant, her mind untrammeled, Kendra was close to drifting off to sleep when a featherlight stroke across her cheek brought her eyes open.

Remi was stretched out beside her. They lay together, seemingly cushioned on a pillow of fluffy clouds. It was impossibly soft. Weightless. Comfortable.

Squirming around to adjust to the sensation, Kendra stared up at him in dazed amazement. "Where are we?" she murmured. Even though she felt no pain, her whole body was hyperaware, hypersensitized to the slightest feeling.

Remi smiled at the wonder in her voice. "We are inside your mind." He visually drank in every detail of her naked body, his hand moving to smooth tendrils of hair away from her face; then he traced her lips with the tips of his fingers. "To help you, we have to come together in every way." His lips brushed against hers. His hand drifted lower, touching her breast, circling her areola. With the lightest of touches, he ran one finger over her nipple. Hot steel encased in silk pressed against her thigh.

No use questioning the logic of how and why. It was easier to accept. Here, with Remi, she was safe.

Cherished.

Keenly aware of his arousal, Kendra shifted so his erection pressed against the soft nest of her belly. "That feels so good."

She closed her eyes against the rightness of his touch. The solid length of his muscular frame pressed against hers. "Don't stop touching me."

Remi cupped her breast, teasing the hard little bead. "I never want to."

Kendra trembled when he took her nipple between his fingers and gently pinched. She groaned deep in the back of her throat. "Damn, that feels good."

"Touch yourself," he urged softly.

More than willing to obey, Kendra's hand drifted down between her legs to stroke her clit. She was wet and ready, aching for completion.

Remi worked her breast harder, watching as she pleasured herself. She entered herself, first with one finger and then with two, pushing deeper and moving her hips back and forth. Breathing raggedly, she felt her body began to shake.

Remi repositioned himself between her spread thighs. He caught her hand and replaced it with his own. Using two thick fingers, he penetrated the fold of velvet flesh, slowly easing his fingers toward the very heat of her core. "Do you want more?"

Kendra felt his fingers disappear into her depth. "I want all you're willing to give," she answered on a moan.

Remi moved his fingers a little, pressing his knuckle against her clit. He dipped his head to taste her rosy flesh.

She trembled and pressed down harder on his hand. Her clit sang with pleasure as he circled it with his tongue and lips.

Remi lifted his head. His own breath came in ragged bursts. "How far do you want me to take you?" With a single finger, he stroked her damp, sensitive center.

His touch wrung another soft moan from Kendra's lips. Her gut throbbed with need. "All the way." This brand of lust was still new to her, exciting and exalting. Their lovemaking possessed an urgency that would not let her do anything but give in.

Erection in hand, Remi ran the head of his penis between her nether lips. Without waiting, he thrust in hard and deep, hands gripping her hips and taking all control.

Kendra moaned, and he pulled back, starting a steady rhythm of hard strokes. With a sigh that came out as a whimper, she met his every thrust with one of her own. Eyes closed, head thrown back, she savored the incredible sensations he awakened inside her abused body.

Positioning his arms on both sides of her to support his weight, Remi lowered his body to cover hers. His head dipped, and he captured a nipple in his mouth, roughly lashing his tongue against it. At the same time his hips rolled against hers.

Muscles throbbing with tremors of pleasure, Kendra surged up into him and tried to take him even deeper. Her vaginal muscles tightened around his cock, determined to seize every last inch of him. They were coming together, the completion of a destiny both had been waiting for but yet were unaware of.

Remi pulled back until he was almost completely out of her before ramming back in and holding himself there. His chest rose and fell deeply, and veins bulged throughout his neck and powerful arms.

Kendra screamed, raking her nails down his back as her body trembled. Just as she started to relax, Remi thrust again. Their bodies lunged and pounded into each other. She gasped for air just as Remi captured her lips with his, devouring her cries of pleasure with savage demand.

Her inner muscles tight, she arched her hips and then sank back. Gripping his hips with her thighs, she silently urged him to slow down, keeping his pace steady as she watched his eyes glaze, savored the rough sounds he made, heard the body-shuddering slap of his hips driving upward.

"Mmmm, don't ever stop." She whimpered, faltered and then lost control of the pace—shock and then pleasure turned her moans into primeval, guttural cries. Exquisite tension coiled around her clit.

Remi drove his cock into her a couple more times and then came hard, his body jerking against hers as he found his release.

Responding to his orgasm, Kendra let go of her control, letting the wave of pleasure wash her over the abyss. White-hot pleasure imploded in her belly, running like a river of molten lava. Her brain overloaded. Shorted out. She shook violently. A sob broke from her throat—a cry of delight wrenched from somewhere deep inside her.

Still deep inside her, Remi collapsed on top of her, trailing wet kisses along her neck as he tried to catch his breath. Willpower alone slowed his breathing.

Kendra tightened her grip on his body. "I can't believe you're here with me," she whispered in his ear. "It's just a dream, I know, but I don't want to wake up."

Remi lifted himself up, looking into her eyes. He placed a single finger against her lips. "It's not a dream. It's as real as you want it to be."

"How?"

A gentle smile turned his lips. "You've been searching for your place. It's only now that you have found where you belong."

She laughed low in her throat. "Lost doesn't begin to describe it."

"You're not alone anymore, Kendra."

Probing inside, she found an ache beneath her breastbone. She focused on it, searching. In a stunning moment, she realized that Remi completed her, made her a whole woman.

I can't lose him. . . . But she didn't want to think of that.

Kendra's desperate gaze searched his face. "You won't leave me again?"

Remi shook his head. His eyes held naked honesty. "I won't

leave you. We can have eternity together." Without saying another word, he reached out, and his open palms met hers.

They laced fingers, and he squeezed. In the brief silence, no promises were made, but Kendra sensed something had changed. It was as if he had touched something inside her, reigniting a burnt-out ember into a shining flame.

"Eternity sounds good to me."

His gaze darkened, turning serious. "When I take control of your body, the entry will not be pleasant."

Kendra shook her head. "I don't care." She tried to smile but couldn't quite manage. "Do what you have to."

Remi stroked her face. "I will try not to hurt you too badly."

Her throat tightened, but only for a moment. "I can take it," she said, letting out a shuddery breath.

Remi's head dipped. His mouth covered hers. Like a starving woman, Kendra greedily accepted his kiss and gloried in the fierce desire with which he claimed her body, mind and spirit.

Remi's body began to fade, gradually taking on the form of a vaporlike mist laced through with a strange greenish luminance. Circling her body, it spread out over her, clinging to every inch from head to toe.

Wrapped around her like a velvet cloak, the mist began to sink in, disappearing beneath the surface of her skin. His invasion was as intimate as his lovemaking, claiming every inch as two separate beings came together as one.

Aware that Remi's essence was pouring into her, Kendra released a shrill scream. An unseen hand clamped over her mouth, silencing her. She felt her insides spasm as a coldness much like death washed through her. Her heart stopped. The blood in her veins came to a halt. Only the electrical charges in her brain remained intact.

Moments later, she felt buoyant, as if floating toward an endless void of stars, suspended between life and death. A series of symbols began to rise beneath her skin, searing and branding themselves into naked, vulnerable flesh.

Animation gradually returned. Her heart thumped, raced and then resumed its normal rhythm. She again felt her blood flow. The coldness ebbed more quickly with each passing second.

Her position slowly shifted; horizontal becoming vertical.

Kendra's eyes shot open. She was upright now, her feet hovering just inches above the floor. The mirror over the vanity reflected a new and terrible being. Her short black shag had taken on electric proportions, shooting out wildly at all angles. Eyes as red and hot as coals blazed out of a face as pale as a corpse. Her skin, still terribly scarred, had been etched anew with the marks of the beast.

A power spawned of hell itself pulsed through her, and she experienced a form of elation that was almost frightening. Closing her eyes, she felt Remi's awesome power solidify inside her. She was invincible. Unstoppable.

She was possessed.

Stepping down onto the floor, a grin split Kendra's lips.

Time to play a little catch-up.

28

Gerald Carter stood over his deceased wife's body. His cell phone pressed against his ear, his voice was laced with enough hysteria appropriate for a 911 emergency. "M—my wife's dead," he stammered through a sob heart-wrenching enough to win an Academy Award. "My sister killed her—she's locked in the bathroom now—she's out of her mind, saying she'll kill herself—I'm trying to get to her now. Yes . . . please send help. . . ."

Flicking his phone shut, he shoved it into his pocket. His lips twisting into a sneer, he knelt beside Jocelyn's corpse. After checking the pulse at her wrist, he lifted her hand and then let it drop.

Jocelyn's limp hand struck the carpet with a sickening *thunk*. A pool of blood haloed her head. The iron poker lay nearby, ready to be taken into evidence.

Gerald smiled with satisfaction. "Better than divorce," he breathed. "No settlement, no alimony. Perfect."

He rose. Turned. Stopped dead in his tracks. Shock clearly rippled through him at the sight of her.

Kendra grinned. "Surprise."

His eyes bulging, a strangled cry escaped him. "My God—" He got no further than those two words.

Her jaw taut with tension, Kendra cackled. "God has nothing to do with me. Nothing at all."

As though disbelieving his eyes, Gerald shook his head. "You can't be alive," he rasped, drawing in a reedy breath. "There's no way." His gaze dropped to her wrists, his expression a combination of disgust and stark disbelief. "Not with those cuts."

Kendra followed his gaze, lifting her arms to expose the flesh of her mutilated inner wrists. But the open wounds Gerald had inflicted were no longer present—the scars were purple and swollen, closed into thick red welts.

With a tentative finger, she reached out to trace one of the welts. "Oh, those could have been fatal." Clenching her fist, she met his gaze. "Good thing I'm not human anymore."

Not human. . . .

Dawning horror crossed his features. "You used the book . . . ."

Kendra thought she saw a flash of fear in his eyes. "And I've got my very own little demon." Her hand lifted toward the space between neck and breasts. Her fingers clenched, tearing into her skin. "It's here. Inside me." A strange cackle rolled out of her throat, empty and soulless.

Gerald released a feral snarl. "Oh, I can take care of that." He turned away, blindly seeking the exit. Dashing out the side door of the den, he disappeared down a short hallway.

A voice whispered in Kendra's mind. *The library.*

Putting the demon's power to work, she dematerialized.

A few seconds later she reappeared in the library, just in time to see Gerald smash his fist through the glass surrounding the fragile tome. The panes exploded under the pressure, shattering into a thousand pieces.

Kendra watched him with detached amusement. "It's no use," she snarled fiercely. "You can't get rid of it."

Looking wildly around, Gerald ground his teeth. "If the book's destroyed, the demon will go." Ignoring the shards tearing at his hands, he ripped the cover open. His fingers clawed at the fragile pages, pulling them out and shredding the parchment. "I deny thee!" he bellowed at the top of his lungs. "You don't exist here!"

Kendra smiled and raised her arms. "Behold my power." Clenching her hands, she concentrated on bringing the power boiling beneath her skin to the surface.

A swirling fog manifested and circled the library, moving faster and faster, forming a wall against outside intrusion. Without warning, it formed into a cyclone, swooping toward the lectern. Sucking up the torn parchment, it began to reform the pages, returning each to its place. Its task completed, the fog died, fizzling away as suddenly as it had arrived.

The *Delomelanicon* was pristine. Untouched and undamaged.

Gerald stumbled away from the lectern, tripping and sprawling flat on his ass. Shock gleamed bright and hot in his eyes. "Impossible," he said between clenched teeth.

Aware his heart was pounding hard against his ribs, Kendra grinned. "The woman who sold you the book obviously didn't bother to impart its secrets, dear brother. Its pages are infested with demons, all kinds just waiting to latch on to someone vulnerable, someone confused. Someone like me. And when they manifest, they wreak hell and havoc in your life."

Gerald's face was grotesquely darkened and ravaged with hatred. Snatching up a shard of glass, he hurled it at her face. "They don't exist if you don't believe," he snarled.

Her hand shooting up, Kendra plucked the shard out of the air. Her fingers closed around its sharp edges. She squeezed tight, crushing it to dust beneath her grip. "I think you're wrong about that." Opening her hand, she let the pulverized shards scatter like petals in the wind.

Staggering away from the lectern, Gerald stared at her in disbelief. His pupils were dilated, as wide and black as bullet holes. When he came to the far wall, he slid down to the floor. "This can't be happening."

Kendra's gaze narrowed on his cowering figure. "Oh, it's only just beginning."

Closing the distance between them, she reached out. Her fingers curled around the lapels of his jacket, tearing through the expensive material.

Gerald's arms slashed out. "Get away from me, you crazy bitch!" he shrieked.

Kendra ignored him. "I think it's time for a little payback, brother." She used the advantage of her standing position to throw her weight behind lifting him and then smashing his head back against the wall.

A gush of air ejected past Gerald's lips. "You're possessed," he said. "The Devil walks inside you."

His words brought a dangerous rush of anger, and Kendra cut him off with brutal precision. "Oh, you're about to find out how much I am possessed." Reveling in her newfound strength, she slammed her stepbrother against the wall again. "The thing about the book is that it can't be destroyed. You can't tear it up, burn it up. Hell, you can't even blow it up. It always comes back together."

Gerald released garbled sounds. "There has to be some way to make it stop," he breathed more to himself than to her. Even in his disbelief his mind was still ticking, plotting his own escape.

Kendra let him drop. "The only way to get rid of the demons is to send the book on to the next victim." When he attempted to rise to his feet, she sidestepped and rammed a knee into his side, toppling him over. "And that book's not going anywhere, dear brother. Not for a very long time."

Groaning, Gerald scrambled to his hands and knees, attempting to scramble past her.

Anger storming through her, Kendra shot out her hand. One hand gripped the thick hair at the back of Gerald's head. Clutching the strands with all her strength, she drove his head into the floor.

Gerald's brow cracked against hard tile. A stream of curses frothed from his mouth. "Demons can be exorcised!" he snarled. Raw fury propelled him upward. Coming back up at her with a fresh burst of strength, he swung his fist with surprising force.

Caught squarely in the face, Kendra lost her balance and crashed onto her side. Blood poured from her nose and split lip. She spat it away, brushing her free hand across her mouth and sparing a brief glance at the blood coloring her fingers.

Shaking hard, Gerald climbed to his feet. His eyes narrowed, and a half smile appeared on his lips. "I'm going to enjoy beating the hell out of you."

Kendra bared bloody teeth. "Not if I kick the shit out of you first."

Sitting up, she slid across the slick marble floor and caught Gerald behind the left knee with one of her heels. The leg buckled beneath him. As he went down, he attempted to right himself by pitching forward. The momentum carried him headfirst through the glass wall guarding his display of ceremonial blades.

Tumbling gracelessly, he barely managed to twist his body before landing sprawled on his back. The violence of the impact stunned him. Glass shards rained down around him.

Climbing to her feet, Kendra stared down at him. Her chest rose and fell on heaving breaths. Gerald's face was a mass of bloody cuts.

Just like hers had been after the accident.

A wicked thought crept into her skull. *He hasn't suffered enough.*

Kendra's eyes rose to the display. A multitude of blades, all shapes and all sizes, filled the wall.

A grin split her lips.

One hand rose, her fingers flexing in a familiar motion. A beautifully etched dagger lifted from its place. A moment later, its hilt connected squarely with the palm of her hand. Lifting the blade in front of her face, she regarded her distorted reflection. Raw energy coursed through her. Her red eyes gleamed with unnatural sparks, the undulating luster of hellish power twisting in their depths.

Inclining her head, she looked down at Gerald's prone figure. "I think it's time to make a little sacrifice to our dark lord," she hissed.

Blade in hand, she took a step toward Gerald. She fully intended to kill the bastard. Cut out his evil heart. "Vengeance is mine." Her voice was strange and harsh in her own ears. Kendra didn't care. Only when she had Gerald's heart in her hand would she feel a grievous wrong had been righted.

She took a second step, but not a third. Some inner force took command, locking her limbs into place.

Remi stepped out, abandoning his host. He stood in front of her, a magnificent being cloaked in shimmering illumination. Like her, he was naked. Exposed. The symbols marking her naked skin faded away, vanishing entirely.

For an indefinite amount of time, Kendra stared at his motionless form. It took more than a few seconds for her mind to process what she'd witnessed. She gulped, forcing her frozen vocal cords to work. "Remi?"

He was smiling down at her. The affection in his eyes warmed and. "Yes, you are free of me."

She suppressed a shudder. "Why did you leave?"

His gentle smile softened his strong, masculine features. "You were starting to slip into the dark side, embrace the evil all men have inside them."

Conscience nudged. "I wanted him dead," she confessed. "At any cost."

"I know." Remi stared at her. "It is why I left you before you sacrificed your soul beyond all redemption. Even now I see in your eyes a decaying of your very sanity. You must step away, renounce the darkness. Renounce me."

His words sent a chill through her. "I can't."

"Do you believe in good and evil?"

The question made her ill at ease. Her heart raced with her pulse. "I'm not sure anymore."

He cut her a hard look. "Shall I tell you where evil truly lurks?"

She shifted uncomfortably. Her nerves curled tighter. A vague sense of uneasiness rippled through her. "I don't think I want to know."

Hand lifting to her face, Remi tipped her chin up, searching her face. "It is not wise to give your heart or your trust to the damned," he whispered. "Don't seek out the darkness. Please, don't give up your soul for me."

His touch heated Kendra's skin yet hurt her deep inside. For the first time the layers of his inhumanity fell away, and she saw the raw pain beneath. His concern for her was very real. A sob broke from her lips, coming from somewhere deep inside. "I would have," she replied softly. "To keep you with me."

His head dipping, Remi's warm lips brushed hers. "As much as I wish I could," he whispered against her mouth, "I can not stay with you." Heat mingled with desperation, fusing into something volatile and unstable.

As he spoke, thunder rumbled loudly above their heads. Three-pronged lightning descended from the ceiling, striking the nearby lectern. A ball of white light temporarily blinded.

When the light vanished, in place of the lectern was an eerie mist. Swirling with dizzying speed, it grew wider and wider until it seemed to enclose the library on all sides. The mist pulsed with life, changing from white to gray to black before going white again in mere seconds.

Remi stiffened as the mist closed around them both, tomb-like, desolate and threatening. The library was a billion miles away now. Thunder boomed, and lightning cracked with ferocity across the canopy of the otherworldly sky. "The gate of hell itself," he murmured.

Kendra was awestruck by the vision and dazzled by the sheer force of power she had somehow unleashed. Finally, the murky fog thinned enough to award glimpses into the heart of the underworld. Through the mist she saw lands mantled in pools of ice dotted by mountainous stretches of fire. It was so barren and vast they gave one a false sense of infinity.

Past the ice and fire was something even more terrible. Souls. The damned. Bubbling in molten lava. Entombed—awake and aware—in ice.

A chill shimmied down Kendra's spine. An odor not unlike rotting corpses assailed her nostrils. Her scalp crawled. Nausea rising, she shivered. "My God."

Remi, too, stared into the endless murk. The mist snaked around his legs as though urging his return. But still he lingered, his chest rising and falling on heaving breaths. "I cannot go back."

Kendra's throat tightened. The ache in her chest was exquisite. Fear and desire and a thousand other emotions pounded through her. "Then stay with me."

Remorse twisting his features, Remi slowly shook his head. "Long ago I fell from glorious heaven, cast into the dark and devouring place that is hell. The Lord I serve is neither kind nor forgiving. Nor does he let us go easily." His hand lifted, palm cupping her face. "Hell is truly having the emotions of a human and the duties of a demon. If I do not take a soul back for sacrifice, I will be punished. Eternally and forever."

Trembling inside as they stood face to face, Kendra stared into his eyes. The fathomless suffering she read in those eyes was nearly her undoing. Tears welled up. Each breath hitched in her throat. "I'll go with you," she whispered. "My life is nothing without you."

Remi lowered his gaze to the dagger she still clutched. His hand circled hers, guiding the blade toward his chest. "Don't try to hold on to me." He pressed its tip into his skin. "Your blade is consecrated, strengthened with the blessing of holy rite." His voice was slow, thoughtful. "Driven right, it could pierce the heart of a demon."

Remi's insinuation froze her blood. The pain in his gaze found an echo in her soul. Blinking to clear her mind of the unexpected turmoil, she tried to speak, but her words came out a harsh croak. "You can't do this." With fear and frustration a hard knot in her guts, she tried to turn away, intending to fling the wretched blade far from his grip.

Remi was faster. Stronger. Realizing her intent, his hand tightened around hers. "Grant me this one mercy. Please." Using the leverage of her weight, he drove the serrated blade hard. And deep.

Kendra blinked down stupidly. The dagger was buried to the hilt in the demon's chest. The flare of panic flashed again. Cold terror simmered, chilling the blood in her veins. "Remi, no!" A scream gurgled out of her throat.

Remi staggered back, mortally wounded. Gasping, he toppled, striking the ground on his back. Limp fingers fell away from the bejeweled hilt. A laugh burbled past his lips. "For the first time, I can finally feel something. . . ." He shivered. "Death is . . . cold. . . ."

Blinking back tears, Kendra hurried to his side. She ignored the fiery fragments of glass slicing into her bare skin when she dropped to her knees and she stared at him, a slow, shaking hand covering her mouth. "You can't leave me, damnit." Somehow she would save him. Fight for him with every ounce of strength she had. She wanted him so badly.

Remi stared up. Not directly at her, but past her, gazing off into a distance only he could see. "I know what happens when an angel falls," he gasped, a pinkish froth bubbling at his lips.

Hysteria crept in. "Don't do this to me!" Kendra cried, realizing that she was pleading, that her voice was shaking. It felt as if he'd shoved the blade through *her* ribs. The pain was so sharp, so devastating she couldn't take a breath.

Remi's gaze finally focused. He stared at her for an interminable minute. "Now I shall find out what happens when a demon falls. . . ." His voice trailing off, his gaze dimmed as his eyes lost focus. His head tipping sideways, a thin string of blood oozed from his mouth.

Silence.

Cold. Dark. Terrible.

Without warning, everything shifted focus. Kendra felt dizzy, disoriented, as if she'd stepped onto one of those spinning carnival rides. A new sound filtered into her ears—the blare of sirens blasting in the distance. The mist obscuring her reality began to disperse, seeping away. The real world was creeping back in.

No time to waste. If she waited another minute, Remi would be lost to her. Forever.

The thought was simply too much to humanly bear.

Feeling more helpless than she'd ever felt in her life, Kendra's despair darkened. Exhaustion swept through her in shimmering waves. Somehow she would save him. Fight for him with every ounce of strength she had.

A sob wrenched from her. Damn her foolish heart, but she'd fallen in love with him.

I'll sacrifice my soul to have him.

Kendra wrapped her fingers around the hilt. Grimacing, she pulled. The dagger slid out from between the bones of his rib cage. She angled the dagger toward her own body. Its silver blade was still stained with Remi's blood. Soon to be joined with hers.

Drawing a breath, she closed her eyes. Desperation slashed at her nerves. Oh, how she needed this to be real.

"Let's make a deal. . . ."

EPILOGUE

Kendra Carter walked down the long, white hallway. Smartly turned out in the latest Donatella Versace, the heels of her Manolos clicked sharply on the white linoleum tile floor. She carried a bouquet of flowers, a fresh spring arrangement that would add just the right touch.

Pushing open a door, she entered a private room. A bed, bureau, desk and a table with two chairs were arranged to give the room an illusion of spaciousness it did not really possess. Textured walls, painted eggshell white, were complemented by inexpensive reproductions of classical artists. The room was pristine, perfectly kept.

Every item present was serviceable, well used by occupants who'd lived there before. The room, with its adjoining bathroom, might have been one of hundreds in any moderately priced hotel—except that its single window was barred and screened, allowing no covert exits.

Far from being part of a hotel, the room was part of a hospital—Philadelphia's Spring Grove Hospital Center, to be exact. Once admitted through its doors, a person could not get out without a physician's release.

Stopping at the bureau, Kendra dumped out a vase full of withered flowers. She replaced them with those from the fresh bouquet, arranging the mixture of purple, white and yellow blooms. As she worked, the sleeve of her coat dress snuck up her wrist.

Frowning, Kendra tugged the sleeve back into place, covering the ugly vertical scar.

No reason to be showing those around, she thought.

Satisfied with her work, she turned toward the room's sole occupant. "How are we doing today, darling?"

Gerald Carter lay stretched out on the bed. Hands and feet restrained, he stared straight ahead. From the look of him, he'd aged at least ten years since his hospitalization. His face was badly mutilated, ravaged by scars. His eyes were glassy, glazed. His hair, once a perfect shade of golden blond, had gone white. Dead white. All former traces of beauty and youth had been wiped away by a brutal hand.

Kendra shook her head. "How sad," she murmured. Gerald had remained unmoving and unresponsive to any human voice since entering the facility.

The door opened again. A familiar figure in a white coat stepped into the room. Reaching for the chart hung at the end of the bed, he flipped through its pages. Judging from the frown marring his face, he wasn't happy.

Kendra drew a breath. "Any change, Dr. Somerville?"

The psychiatrist shook his head. "I'm afraid not. This is one of the worst cases of catatonic schizophrenia I've ever encountered."

The words chilled her, but Kendra didn't let herself react. "Is there any hope he will come out of it?"

Somerville made a few notes on Gerald's chart. "At this point, we just don't know. Your brother has been here two months, and his condition is literally unchanged. He's not responding to medication or any type of therapy."

Kendra shook her head sympathetically. "Gerald went mad the night Jocelyn threatened to leave him. Said he'd kill her before he let her go." She lifted a hand to her face, barely able to suppress her sob. "Oh, it was terrible, horrible to witness." The night flashed horribly across her mind, the images hitting her the same way bombs would strike the ground. Some days she could still feel the hot burn of the demon's power pulsing through her veins.

Somerville shook his head sadly. "I'm afraid he'll never be in any shape to stand trial for her murder. Even if he snaps out of it, the best he can hope for is a lifetime of hospitalization. He's probably going to need around-the-clock care for the rest of his life."

Kendra's hand came down. She offered a wan smile. "It's so terrible," she murmured. "Gerald was always the one with his head on straight, always doing his best to please Daddy."

"No one knows when a human's mind is going to go over the edge and snap."

Kendra barely repressed a shiver. "No," she echoed. "I suppose you don't."

Tapping Gerald's chart, Somerville cleared his throat. "I've been meaning to talk to you about electroconvulsive therapy."

Kendra's brows rose in surprise. "You mean, shock him?"

The psychiatrist hastened to reassure her. "It's not as brutal as people think."

Considering the option, she nodded. "It sounds like it might be the perfect course of treatment for my brother," she allowed. "You have my permission to do what's necessary to get Gerald back on his feet." She cast a fond glance at her brother. "After all, he did help me, and I want to return the favor."

In the back of her mind, a little being wielding a sharp pitchfork nudged. *Tenfold.*

Somerville made some more notes on Gerald's chart. "Good. I'll make the arrangements right away."

At that moment a tall man stepped into the room. Dressed in gray slacks and a white shirt open one button at the neck, his long blond hair was casually tied back. A day's worth of sexy stubble covered his face. His skin lightly tanned, a pair of designer sunglasses perched on top of his head.

Slipping an arm around Kendra's waist, the newcomer pecked a quick kiss on her cheek. "Is everything all right here, honey?"

Gerald instantly reacted to the newcomer. Fighting against the restraints holding him, he violently shifted back and forth to free himself. His face twisting with terror, his mouth flew open.

"Demon!" he shrieked at the top of his lungs. Filled with soul-searing emotion, his outburst struck like a breath-stealing punch. A series of loud, ear-splitting, hysterical screams boiled up from his throat.

Acting quickly, Somerville punched a button on the intercom by the bed. A few minutes later an aide hurried in with a syringe. An injection was quickly and efficiently delivered.

Still screeching like a madman and fighting his restraints, Gerald gradually sank back onto the bed. "The bitch is possessed by him," he muttered. Arms and legs going limp, he slipped away into a mercifully unconscious state. A sigh of exhaustion shuttered past his slack lips.

Kendra jolted at the sounds of his accusation. Far from forgetting, Gerald clearly recalled every detail of his fall into insanity. She sensed his emotions unraveling and felt a corresponding quiver of uneasiness in her gut.

Clearly puzzled, Somerville scrubbed a hand over his jaw. "This is quite shocking," the startled psychiatrist said. "I've never seen him do that before. It's the first reaction to anyone he's had in weeks."

All too aware of the male body pressed against her, Kendra

settled her hand on her fiancé's chest. Solid, tangible flesh pulsed beneath her palm. His scent filled her lungs. Knowledge of the physical ecstasy they'd shared barely an hour ago heated her cheeks. "I don't know what's gotten into my brother." One side of her mouth curved upward. "He's met Remi before."

She glanced up at the man standing beside her. All human. All hers.

Her pulse spiked. Every nerve in her body vibrated with pleasure. She'd paid the ultimate price to have him. And now that he belonged to her, she didn't intend to let him go.

Ever.

Turn the page for a preview
of Kate Douglas's novella,
"Chanku Challenge,"
from SEXY BEAST VII!

On sale now!

1

His thick paws made barely a sound as Nick Barden trotted along beside his mate. He and Beth followed three of their packmates along the service road running near the large wild wolf compounds at the sanctuary run by Chanku shapeshifters Ulrich Mason and Millie West.

At some level, Nick realized he should be loving every second of this chance to run free in the beautiful northern Colorado mountains—here he could take this form without fear of discovery or attack, without the stink of the city burning his sensitive nostrils.

Instead, he hardly noticed the myriad scents and sounds teasing his wolven senses—not the fresh mountain air or even the altogether unique freedom of running as a wolf through dark, pristine forest. No, he was much too aware of the female beside him to appreciate any of it.

Too aware of her displeasure and her silent disapproval to notice the scent of fresh game or even his own unique abilities in this powerful body.

Nothing he did seemed to please her. Not anymore.

His ass still hurt from Ulrich's screwing the other night, but when he looked back at the way he'd been acting for the past week, he figured he'd deserved what he got and then some. The power play Beth had talked him into had backfired—more literally than he'd expected.

Couldn't she see that Ulrich Mason wasn't the problem? He'd never done anything to Beth that wasn't perfectly kind and accepting. Beth's misplaced animosity was totally unfair, all part of her own convoluted baggage. Baggage she needed to deal with now if she and Nick wanted to remain part of this close-knit pack.

If he didn't love her so much, Nick never would have gone along with her stupid wishes.

There was no denying the fact he'd eventually enjoyed Ulrich's powerful response to his stupid challenge. Sex with a dominant male was worth the pain, worth the pure sense of humiliation Nick had suffered.

It had raised his level of arousal even higher.

He wished Beth would lay off. She'd focused her anger on him now, instead of on Ulrich, and it was so thick he could practically see it vibrating in the air between them. In fact, her anger was just about the only thing they had between them anymore. She'd shut him out ever since he'd blocked her constant bitching that night, even though Nick was the one who had ended up paying for the failure of Beth's stupid plan. When he chose to follow Ulrich's lead rather than hers, it meant getting his ass reamed out in a reactive display of dominance by the old guy.

Okay. So he got the message, along with some really great sex. Now why couldn't Beth figure it out? There was no point in challenging Ulrich. Nick didn't want to fight him. For one thing, he really liked and admired the man.

For another, he'd lose.

Ulrich was smart, he was cunning, and he was strong. He

had age and experience on his side, and he was a born leader whether he was in his wolf form, snarling with teeth bared and hackles raised, or staring a man down from his impressive height on two legs. No matter, it was something Nick knew he'd never be able to pull off in any form.

Why couldn't Beth accept him for what he was? In this society, this world of Chanku, he was just a pup. Barely twenty-four years old, he'd been nothing but a loser on the streets of San Francisco. Why did Beth seem to think his ability to shift would make him anything different?

Was it the fact he'd killed that guy to protect Tala? Was that why Beth expected him to be more aggressive? If that was the case, she was dead wrong. He'd killed without thinking, shifting before he even knew he had the ability.

And he'd bonded with a woman he loved before either of them really thought about the permanence of their act.

He watched Daci, Deacon, and Matt trotting together up ahead. The three of them had slipped into an amazing union, and they weren't even mated. He and Beth were mates, yet they hardly spoke to each other. He missed the easygoing relationship he'd had with Matt and Deacon, missed the freedom and the fun they'd all had together, but he missed Beth most of all. Missed the beautiful, shy young woman he'd fallen in love with.

He glanced at Beth and realized she watched him. Was she reading his thoughts? He'd been blocking . . . or at least he thought he was.

She veered off the road and trotted down a narrow trail that led deeper into the woods. Nick hesitated then decided to follow her. She stopped after a short distance and turned to face him, standing in a brilliant ray of late afternoon sunlight, dead center in the middle of a small meadow.

He halted a few feet away, ears flat, tail down. It was easier this way, acting the submissive role with Beth. It seemed to make her happy, though at this point he hardly cared.

She shifted. He faced her for a moment, still the wolf. She stared at him, her dark brows crinkled in that way she had, her arms folded over her bare chest like a disapproving teacher. He held her gaze for a moment longer. She didn't move. Didn't say a word.

Oh, hell. If he wanted to see what she wanted . . . Nick shifted and stood on two feet, wary and uncertain.

Beth raised her chin and stared at him. Sunlight poured across her beautiful olive skin and raised red highlights in her long, dark hair. Her amber-eyed gaze, so much like his own, bored into him. He held her stare.

"It's not working," she said, clasping her hands over her smooth belly. In control, as always. Naked, beautiful, standing there with a sense of entitlement, of power, like an Egyptian goddess here in the midst of the Colorado forest.

"We never should have bonded. I want out."

Her words, a statement, not a request, came as a relief. At least he wasn't the only one who felt that way.

Unfortunately, it wasn't an option.

He actually smiled when he answered her. "Great. So do I, but it's a little late for that, Beth. You heard what Tala said. A pair bond is forever. You wanted me, you've got me."

She jerked back as if he'd slapped her. "You don't want me?"

Not at all surprised by her contrary question, Nick shook his head. "You're supposed to be the one who can tell when a guy's lying or telling the truth. You tell me."

She shook her head as if some of the fight had gone out of her. "I can't tell anymore, Nick. Not with you. It doesn't work with you."

"Does it matter? You just said you want out. You've shut me out for days. We don't have sex with each other, even after a run. It's pretty obvious you don't love me anymore." He was standing up straighter, feeling taller than he had since they'd first linked, even though every word he spoke chipped away more of their bond. "So, I guess my answer's no, Beth. I don't want you. Not anymore. Not the way you are now." He shook his head, no longer smiling.

"I loved a girl who was sweet and kind, who cared about me, about the future we planned together. All you care about now is power. You're twenty-one years old, Beth. You're a baby in this pack, just like me. You have no power. Not over me, not over yourself, and definitely not over any of the others. Get used to it."

He stared at her for a long moment, holding her gaze until she finally looked away. Obviously, this conversation was over.

He shifted. *I'm going back to the others. You can come if you want to. Or not.* Nick glanced over his shoulder and watched her face. She looked brittle, like she might shatter as easily as glass. He felt bad about that, about hurting her, but he didn't trust her. Not anymore.

He still loved her, though. Goddess help him, he loved her.

With one last look, Nick whirled around and raced back along the trail. Dry grass crackled beneath his feet. A gentle wind blew and leaves dropped all around, but he focused on the trail ahead. He didn't want to think of the young woman he'd left behind.

He left her standing in the meadow, looking stunned and alone. At least she wasn't angry at him now, but he didn't feel like he'd won a victory. No, he just felt empty.

Empty and very much alone.

It was the ear-splitting *rat-a-tat-tat* of a woodpecker working away on a thick branch overhead that finally jerked Beth out of the fog Nick had left her in. She sat down hard on the rough ground and dropped her forehead to her knees.

Well, what the hell did you expect? That he'd beg for forgiveness? That he'd say everything was just hunky-dory?

No, in all honesty, she had to admit he'd behaved much

more admirably than she had. First sign of trouble, and all she'd wanted was out.

Of course, the trouble was all of her own making.

It wasn't easy to run away from yourself. Beth lay back in the dried grass and scratchy pine needles and stared at the tiny bits of blue sky visible between the canopy of leaves. The woodpecker stopped its pecking and flew away. She heard the sharp buzz of a bee searching for one last flower before winter and felt the cool brush of air across her naked thighs and belly.

Her nipples tightened from the chill, and she thought of that first time with Nick, when he'd drawn her nipple between his lips, pressed it with his tongue, and held it against the roof of his mouth.

She'd never felt anything so sweet, never known love like that in her life. When he'd filled her, when he'd stretched her with his length and width and pressed deep inside, she'd expected pain, a repeat of the violation that was all she'd ever known.

She'd felt only pleasure.

He'd chased away the memories. The nightmares, actually. Nightmares she'd lived with ever since she'd been a sixteen-year-old virgin and her stepfather had raped her. That one brutal, agonizing act on the eve of her mother's funeral had taken more from her than any girl should have to give.

No one man should have the power to defile a person's entire life, but her stepfather had managed. He'd taken what should have been hers to give, and he'd ruined it forever.

Then she'd met Nick. Gentle and kind, he'd offered her friendship, and then he'd offered love. They'd chosen together to cement their relationship with the mating bond. Beth hadn't had any doubts then. She'd thought Nick was the one who would keep her safe, the one to take the darkness that covered her soul and strip it away—and for a special but much too brief time, he had.

If only she hadn't joined Tala that night when they had sex with Ulrich. It wasn't Ulrich's fault he was older, that his age and even his general appearance reminded her of her stepfather. He hadn't hurt her. Anything but . . . in fact, Ulrich had given her pleasure.

Maybe that was the problem—the fact she'd had a wonderful sexual experience with a man similar enough in looks to her stepfather to totally reawaken the memories.

Without realizing it, Ulrich had brought back all her ghosts.

His had become the face in her nightmares.

It wasn't fair to Ulrich, but it wasn't fair to her, either. She'd thought those nightmares were a thing of the past.

Now they were back, worse than ever. Nick could have been the answer. He could have fought her demons if he'd been man enough, but he wasn't willing to challenge someone he saw as a mentor. He'd chased away the nightmares once. For some convoluted reason, she was certain that if he challenged Ulrich and won, they'd be gone forever.

Or would they?

Now she'd never know. Nick had looked totally disgusted with her, and she really couldn't blame him. It wasn't fair to ask something of a guy that just wasn't part of his nature. Why couldn't Nick, the Nick she'd fallen in love with, have been enough? Why did she need to make him into something he wasn't?

It wasn't fair to him. Not to her, either. Like an absolute idiot, she'd managed to chase away the best thing that had ever happened to her.

The sun disappeared behind the hills while Beth lay there on the hard ground. Pebbles dug into her butt and pine needles poked her thighs and back, but she couldn't find the energy to move.

Where would she go? Nick wouldn't want her back. Not after what she'd said to him today. He'd barely tolerated her since that fiasco the other night when he'd ended up getting royally fucked in the ass.

She wasn't sure if he'd actually liked it or not. In some perverse way, Beth had. She must be totally sick to have gotten so turned on watching Ulrich slam into her mate the way he had. The sex had started out so brutal, so typically male, but Nick hadn't fought. He'd merely bowed his head and accepted Ulrich's pounding violation—accepted it and eventually climaxed from it.

In fact, all of them—Ulrich, Matt, Nick, Millie, and even Beth—had achieved something amazing with their simultaneous orgasm, but it hadn't really mattered. Nick had blocked her long before his climax, just as she'd blocked him. That night, aroused, angry, frustrated with each other, they'd essentially severed the special link that bound them together.

Neither of them had attempted to reconnect since. It was like cutting off part of her body, going through the motions each day without Nick's thoughts in her head.

He'd slept in Matt's old room that first night, and the next couple nights since, sharing the cabin but not her bed. She missed sleeping beside him. Hated running beside him and not connecting. She felt the pain in every part of her body, but the place it hurt most remained the hardest to touch.

Her heart actually ached. What had she expected? That he would promise to challenge Ulrich? Even if he won, what would that solve?

Beth opened her eyes. A narrow sliver of moon was rising. It was almost entirely dark, and still she lay shivering on the hard ground. She thought of shifting, of just staying the night in the woods as a wolf, but somehow that didn't seem right. Not with the convoluted thoughts swirling darkly in her mind.

Instead, she folded her hands over her waist and closed her eyes against the moonlight. Naked, vulnerable, her body cold and aching with the night's chill.

Alone, with nowhere to go.